Jenna Burtenshaw has been writing regularly since she was nine years old. She grew up reading stories by Roald Dahl, but it was her morning walk to school through a graveyard that first interested her in gothic writing and the supernatural. She is a vegetarian and is very passionate about animal welfare – she once ran a shelter for sick and unwanted guinea pigs, which often had more than fifty residents at one time.

By Jenna Burtenshaw

Wintercraft
Wintercraft: Blackwatch

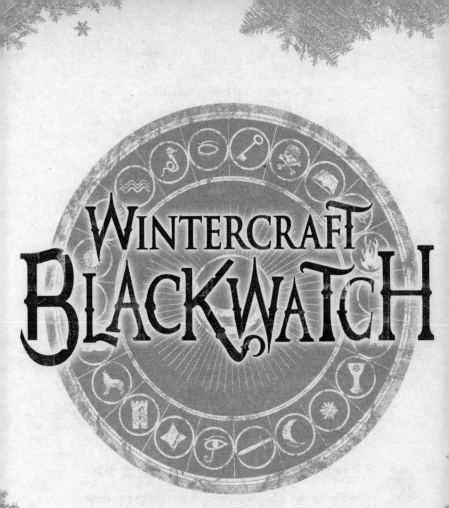

WINTERCRAFT
BLACKWATCH

JENNA
BURTENSHAW

headline

First published in Great Britain in 2011 by
HEADLINE PUBLISHING GROUP

1

Cataloguing in Publication Data is available from the British Library

ISBN 978 0 7553 7122 8

Typeset in Berling by Avon DataSet Ltd,
Bidford-on-Avon, Warwickshire

Printed in the UK by CPI Mackays, Chatham, ME5 8TD

Headline's policy is to use papers that are natural, renewable
and recyclable products and made from wood grown in sustainable
forests. The logging and manufacturing processes are expected to
conform to the environmental regulations of the country of origin.

HEADLINE PUBLISHING GROUP
An Hachette UK Company
338 Euston Road
London NW1 3BH

www.headline.co.uk
www.hachette.co.uk

For Adam,
my wonderful brother.
With love.

Contents

1

Hunted

A month had passed since the Night of Souls; the night Silas Dane had left the city of Fume as a traitor and begun his new life as a fugitive. He had murdered a council-woman, slain many of her wardens and threatened the lives of the council's twelve remaining members. In that one night he had gone from being one of the High Council's most trusted men to being an outlaw, no better than any of the smugglers and thieves he had brought to justice in his time. Word of his treachery had spread to every town in Albion. The High Council wanted him caught, but despite everything the memory of that night still made Silas smile.

Heavy mists spread across the open wilds of Albion as the darkest weeks of winter closed in. Bitter winds blasted in from the north and every morning a new layer of frost clung to the trees. Silas's crow soared high overhead as Silas rode deep into the wild counties, making his way between the small settlements that peppered the landscape. For the first time in twelve years his life was his own and he found himself enjoying his freedom upon Albion's open roads. For now, that freedom was enough.

The settlements were lawless places, beyond the reach of the High Council's rule: roughly built clusters of houses, trading posts and inns whose residents made anyone feel welcome so long as they brought silver or goods to barter with. Disguised in a travelling robe taken from the body of an unlucky thief who had challenged him upon the open road, Silas blended in among other nameless strangers, hiding his grey eyes beneath a hood during the day and conducting his business at night. Wherever ale flowed, people talked.

As snowstorms moved in steadily from the frozen north, Silas was forced to stop camping in the open each night and began renting rooms within the settlements instead. His most recent shelter was a run-down inn clinging to the edge of one of the larger eastern villages. He had heard that whisperers – information sellers – often visited there and hoped to overhear news of the search that had been mounted against him. During his second night spent hunched in its darkest corner listening to whispers shared over flagons of cheap ale, he was not disappointed.

Just before midnight, a tall man entered the inn with a thick scarf wrapped round his neck. He walked like a soldier and swept his eyes over each face in the room, scrutinising every one. Silas lowered his eyes and turned away. After weeks spent in the company of strangers, he had just spotted a familiar face. He tried not to look interested as the man nodded in greeting to a hooded stranger sitting three tables away and went to join him.

'There's been no word from any scouts on the rivers or at the coast,' he heard the newcomer say. 'None of the dockworkers have seen or heard anything of Silas Dane along the eastern or southern coasts. Either your information was wrong, or he has paid them well for their silence.'

'He will head to the Continent eventually. Keep searching. I want to know the moment he is seen.'

'Have you considered that he may not even be heading for the sea? He might not even have heard of this woman.'

The hooded man shook his head slowly. 'The council have known about her long enough,' he said. 'It will not be long before Silas hears about her too.'

Silas leaned further over his ale glass, trying to identify the speaker. He was dressed like any other common man, but beneath his plain brown coat Silas caught a glimpse of a bright red boot, polished and pristine. Those boots belonged to a councilman. If there was a councilman in that inn, a consignment of wardens would not be far away.

Silas scanned the room and identified two men he had not seen the night before. If they were wardens, they had not recognised him so far.

'Dalliah Grey is an enemy to our country,' continued the councilman. 'We have reason to believe that she will try to contact Dane when she discovers he has turned against us. Dane may have murdered a councilwoman, but Dalliah Grey committed far worse crimes before she was driven out of our lands. If the two of them join forces against us the consequences could be disastrous.'

A burst of laughter broke from a group of smugglers close by and Silas made use of the distraction. He stood up, walked straight past the two men and pulled open the inn door, stepping out into the snow-filled night. A black carriage stood waiting to his left with two wardens on board, their shoulders hunched against the falling snow. Neither of them looked his way as he headed right, slipping into the dark. If an attack was planned, the wardens' training would force them to do it now, while their target was in the open, out of sight of any witnesses.

No one came.

The inn door creaked open five times to disgorge various drunks out into the street until, on the sixth, the councilman stepped into the open with the man he had been speaking to close behind him.

'The longer Dane remains at large the less generous I shall be,' said the councilman. 'Find him. You have had long enough.'

The man nodded. 'As soon as I hear anything, you'll be the first to know.'

Silas's hand stood ready upon his blade as the hooded man walked to the carriage and the driver cracked a whip to drive the horses on. The other man stayed by the inn door, counting money out of a small coin purse into his pockets. Silas moved silently up behind him.

'How have you been, Derval?'

The man reached for his dagger in surprise.

'There will be no need for that,' said Silas, pulling his hood back a little to expose his full face.

'Silas?' The man relaxed at once. 'You have the luck of a demon, my friend,' he said. 'Do you know how many wardens were just here?'

Silas led him back into the shadows where they could talk unseen. 'What are you doing here, Derval? I hear you have been hunting me. And not very successfully.'

'I have far better things to do than hunt you down,' said Derval. 'I like living too much, but the High Council don't need to know that, do they? Where there's fear, there's coin, and you have got them all quivering in their boots since the Night of Souls. Twenty wardens killed, half the city swearing they saw spirits of the dead, and a councilwoman finally getting what she deserved.'

Silas nodded slowly. 'How is the hunt progressing?'

'It's not,' said Derval. 'The council don't know where you are, and if anyone else does, they're not talking.'

'So the councilmen have decided to head out into the wilds themselves?'

'This was an arranged meeting,' said Derval. 'He chooses the location. I spin him a lie or two and I get paid. It works for me.'

'I don't believe in coincidences,' said Silas, keeping a close eye on the street, still primed for an attack. 'Since you are here, I need something from you.'

'What kind of thing?' asked Derval, suddenly suspicious. 'I'm not giving you my horse. Not after what happened last time.'

Silas smiled. 'I need information,' he said. 'This woman the council are worried about. I want you to tell me everything you know about Dalliah Grey.'

'From the sound of it, she's as bad as you. Trouble,' said Derval. 'Word is she caused Albion a lot of trouble a few hundred years ago. Got on the wrong side of the council, killed a few of them, messed with things she shouldn't.'

'A few hundred years ago? Why are the council worried about her now?'

'Because, according to our councilman friend, the old girl *isn't dead*,' said Derval. 'Now, I have an open mind, you know that, but even I think the High Council have got it wrong with this one. Five hundred years later and they're convinced this woman is still going strong, with a grudge against Albion even longer than yours, I'd bet. All that business in the city square a few weeks ago jogged a few memories within the council. I wish I'd been there to see their faces when the veil opened like that. Some of them think Dalliah Grey was involved and it's got them worried. Let's face it, if there was a five-hundred-year-old woman out there with a grudge against me, I'd be worried too.'

'And the council believe she is still alive?' asked Silas.

'They sound convinced,' said Derval. 'Something to do with the veil, so I've heard. The old councils tried everything they could to kill her off when she was in Albion last, but nothing touches her. She bleeds, she heals. Just like you.'

'Where is she now?'

'On the Continent somewhere. All I know is the council don't want you crossing the sea to find out. But if they're worried about this woman, she can't be all that bad. She sounds like an interesting one, if you ask me.'

Silas emptied his pocket and pressed a coin pouch of his own into Derval's hand. 'This is for your silence,' he said. 'If I find out you have told the wardens about me, I will hunt you down, slit your throat and watch your blood drain out of your lifeless body drop by drop. Do you understand me?'

'As always,' said Derval. 'You keep the money coming and I keep my mouth shut. It is always a pleasure dealing with you, my friend. I hope we meet again soon.'

Silas nodded and a slight smile flickered across his eyes. 'With luck, we will.'

The two men clasped hands in farewell and Silas skulked away from the inn as quietly as he had arrived. His horse was stabled in the blacksmith's yard, right where he had left it. He unhitched the stall gate, saddled the restless beast, and rode out of the village without looking back.

Silas spent the whole of the next day on the move, staying away from the main trails. He rode his horse over snow-covered hills, through frosted fields and alongside frozen rivers. The presence of a councilman in the wilds and the council's fear of the woman called Dalliah Grey had helped him to make a decision.

It took two days to find a hidden dock where smuggling ships set sail for the Continent. Once there, he convinced a captain to allow him passage on the next vessel to leave that night by offering his horse in trade. If what Derval had said about Dalliah was true, Silas had to meet her. Given enough time he could hunt down anything, and his reputation as the High Council's most capable collector was known as far as his name had travelled. If he could find her, one of the council's oldest enemies could well become his greatest ally.

The ship set sail just before sunset on to a calm ocean, and as soon as he was at sea, watching his homeland drift out of sight, Silas knew he was doing the right thing.

The journey to the Continent would have taken only a few hours in fine conditions, but the northern countries were in the middle of a freezing winter. Ocean currents were carrying sheets of ice southwards down the Taegar Sea, forcing ships to push their way through and making the crossing a slow and treacherous one.

Silas spent most of the journey out in the open on deck, but as the hours passed and the evening slipped into the dead of night he crouched in the centre of the cargo hold, cleared a space in the dirt on the floor with his hands and pulled open the neck of a black drawstring pouch. Rows of fat leather sacks swung from bars lined up above him, each one swaying gently, following the slow motion of the ship as it cut through the icy waves. He could hear chunks of ice grinding against the hull, scraping at the wood like a thousand fingernails as he emptied the pouch's contents out on to the floor.

A handful of coins rattled out first, then a silver ring and three rolled notes. Two of the notes were sealed with buttons of wax, but the third had cracked open and was busy unfurling itself slowly across the floor. Silas pocketed the coins and the ring and picked up the open note. The seal was dark green and stamped with a rolled scroll: the mark of Albion's High Council. He struck a match and held the flame close to the paper to read its words.

Order is Hereby Given for the Capture of
Silas Dane.
Traitor, Thief & Murderer.
Collectors May Claim a Substantial Reward of
Gold and Land
upon Presentation of this **Dangerous Criminal** to
the Warden of the Watch.
North Tower, High Council Chambers, Fume.

Silas looked over at the dead man who had owned the pouch. His body was still warm, his neck twisted awkwardly against the floor. Collectors were resourceful and persistent, but he had not expected one to find him on the open sea.

'Good work,' he said, nodding towards the man's lifeless eyes. 'You came closer than most.' He rubbed a streak of blood from his cheek with the back of his hand. A shallow cut burned there for a second or two before the skin sealed itself perfectly, healing in moments, leaving no sign that there had ever been an injury. The collector's attack had taken Silas by surprise. It would not happen again.

He allowed the match flame to catch upon the corner of the page, consuming it in a burst of heat and embers. 'The council does not give gold to dead men,' he said. 'You should have known better.'

Silas stood up, grabbed the collector's wrists and dragged him roughly across the floor. Then he unhooked an empty leather sack from its hanging place, wrestled the body into it and hooked it heavily back into place. No one would find it until they arrived at port, and by then he would already have left the ship behind.

Silas left the sack swinging with the rest and made his way to the front of the hold, where a trapdoor led up on to the main deck. He climbed a short ladder, grabbed the door's handle and pushed it open, letting moonlight spread across his face. The deck was rough and untidy, tracked with deep scratches and stained with everything from wine to animal dung. The smugglers did not care what they carried, so long as it brought them a profit at the end of the journey. There had been eight men on the ship when it left the dock, including Silas and the captain, whose clothes bristled with hidden weapons since he trusted his own crew as little as he trusted the strangers who had paid their way on board.

Silas carried a weapon of his own: a sword forged of blue-black metal that was still sheathed beneath his stolen robe. He stood out in the open, listened carefully and made a note of every man's position on the ship. The captain was pacing in his cabin; he could hear his boot-steps scraping on the floorboards. The helmsman was at the wheel and two young men were climbing among the rigging, bundled in thick clothes and arguing loudly with each other. The fifth man was in the galley cooking potatoes and old beef, another was snoring in his sleep, and the last would give him no more trouble: the dead collector, swinging gently in the hold.

He checked the position of the stars. The night was clear and moonlight shone upon the floating ice, making the frosty surfaces shine like ghostly lights as the ship travelled north-east. Silas knew the journey well. They were following the wide sea channel that spread like a scar between Albion and the Continent, heading for the northern Continental town of Grale. He had made that journey many times during his time in Albion's army, and so far it seemed the captain was keeping his word. The ship was set to reach Grale within the hour. They were right where they were meant to be.

As the moon moved steadily across the sky, the ship's heaving sails caught a favourable wind and sliced more swiftly through the frosty waters. None of the crew questioned the whereabouts of the missing passenger – he could have fallen overboard and no one would have cared

– so while the smugglers ate their midnight meal Silas patrolled the ship instead, looking for anything else that was out of place.

If one collector could follow his trail on to that ship, a second could have found it just as easily. He stood at the back of the ship, behind the helmsman's tied-off wheel, and looked back towards Albion. His homeland's dark cliffs had long since retreated over the horizon, but between the ship and the distant coast Silas spotted something moving in the water. It was a low black shape, far enough away to be indistinct, even to his sharp eyes. Something was following the ship. Silas made sure he was out of sight, and watched.

It could have been a whale. Small whales often travelled along the Taegar Sea in winter. But as the shape drew closer a square of black cloth flapped silently above the waves and Silas spotted two shadows crouched beneath it, struggling to keep a small sailing boat on course. The ice had been enough to slow the large ship down, but its hull left clear waters behind it and the little boat was manoeuvrable enough to nip safely between any chunks that passed its way.

Silas walked through the shadows and stepped up on to the ship's guard rail. He balanced there perfectly, pulled off the stolen robe and let the icy wind rip through the long leather coat he was wearing underneath. He looked down at the churning ocean. The water sliced and foamed beneath him, black and fast. He waited until the two shadows were looking away, then stepped casually off the rail, plunging feet first through the air and down into the freezing ocean.

The water swamped over his head and the ship's

powerful wake captured him and pulled him down into the depths. He opened his eyes, waited for the current to release him, and remained underwater, reorienting himself in the direction of the little boat's hull. The weight of his sword pulled downwards and the ocean blurred his vision, but he did not need clear sight for what he was about to do. His sharp ears lifted tiny sounds from the water, listening for the creak of ropes or the echo of the men's feet shuffling across the boat's oiled wood. Dull thuds carried towards him, and Silas's heartbeat throbbed glacially slow as he stretched out his arms and swam silently towards his enemy.

No breath left his lungs as he reached the boat and hung beneath it, keeping one hand pressed against the wood, feeling for the movements of the people above as vibrations against his fingertips. One man was talking loudly enough for Silas to hear, and he concentrated until the words became clear.

'. . . enough to bring down a walrus, that one. Don't think I'll need it, though. Good old-fashioned cunning . . . that's what'll finish him in the end. I'll bet he hasn't seen the likes of me in his lifetime, no matter how tough they say he is. Hey! You even listening?'

Silas felt a hard jolt reverberate through the boat. The other passenger yelped but did not answer.

'Ignorant rat! I never shoulda brought ya along. You're as useless as a pig at a rabbit shoot. Maybe I should throw ya over the side right now and test those weedy little arms of yours. What do you say to that?'

Silas placed his other hand on the hull and pulled his knees up into a crouch. The hull was slippery, but he held on and moved along it in a silent crawl until he was as far from its occupants as it was possible to be. His grey eyes broke the surface of the water and he pulled himself up, making the boat rock and shift as he climbed aboard. Two pairs of terrified eyes glared at him in the dark.

'It can't be!'

The collector reached for his blade, but Silas was faster. He took five steps across the boat, sent the sword spinning into the sea, then wrenched the man's arm behind his back before throwing him casually over the side.

'Hey! S-stop!' the man yelled as the boat left him behind. 'C-come b-b-back!' Silas ignored him. In water that cold the fool would be dead within minutes, so he turned his attention to the second passenger, who was now cowering beneath a blanket, a useless sword quivering in his hand. Any apprentice who gave up a fight so easily deserved to be run through by his prey.

Silas drew his own sword and wrenched the blanket away in his fist. A young boy looked up in terror, dropped his weapon and held his grubby hands up to protect his face. Silas glared down at him and dragged him to his feet. This was definitely not an apprentice. He was scrawny and weak; a servant boy brought along to do whatever the collector did not want to do himself.

The boy looked down at his feet as his master's pathetic shouts faded into the distance. Silas studied him carefully. The smugglers' ship was moving away and the little boat was starting to drift off course.

'Can you sail?' he demanded.

The boy nodded quickly.

'And do you know how to reach Grale?'

He nodded again.

'Then get to work. Give me any trouble, and I'll put

13

you over the side just like your master. Understand?'

Silas released the boy, who set to work immediately, checking a compass that was sewn into his left sleeve and adjusting the sails to carry them steadily across the waves.

'Keep the sail up,' ordered Silas, wringing the sea water from his clothes and drying his skin as best he could on an old blanket. 'Follow the ship until you see land, then turn in towards the cliffs. I do not want to be seen.'

Under the boy's guidance, the little boat cut swiftly through the waves while Silas stood at the bow, looking out over the ocean to where the distant shores of the Continent would soon be moving into sight. A single lantern slung from the great ship's bow glinted ahead of them as the boat kept pace. Silas whistled once – a long piercing call – and was answered by a deep cackle from somewhere amongst the huge sails.

A small shadow dropped towards the sea and a bedraggled crow skimmed the surface of the water and flapped up to land upon Silas's shoulder. Its feathers were scruffier than usual and a white line of feathers upon its chest was dull and dirty. It did not like being on open water and it huddled close to Silas's neck, fluffing itself stubbornly against the freezing wind as distant lights gradually sparkled into life on the horizon.

While many of Albion's main towns clustered along the central spine of the country, most Continental towns clung to the coast, as if trying to escape from the sprawling forests, mountains and lakes that dominated the territory further inland. Every western town had guards posted along its beaches in case of an attack from Albion, but Grale's guards were far less particular about whom they allowed in their waters compared to those posted in the larger towns further south. Grale was too far from anything to be a useful landing point for an invading army, and anyone who risked travelling there found nothing but the pungent smell of fish and smoke to welcome them. War or not, there was still silver to be made and Grale was still open for illegal trade.

At night the town looked shabby and bleak. The glowing lights came from lanterns slung along wires above Grale's empty streets that hummed like strings of bees whenever the wind blew through them. The rough faces of Grale's once white buildings had been stripped back by centuries of powerful sea winds and the people who lived in them were as cold as the streets they walked during the few sunlit hours of their darkened days. The town stood humbly at the mercy of the elements and its residents were opportunists, every one of them devious and unpredictable. Silas had endured dealings with them before.

'Pull in the sail,' he ordered. 'Now.'

The boy obeyed. They were too close to the coast to risk being seen, and before Silas could even demand it the boy had a pair of oars at the ready, preparing to row them to the shore himself.

'No,' said Silas, noticing that the oars were the same thickness as the boy's scrawny arms. 'I plan upon arriving sometime before next week. Give them to me. You keep watch for lens lights.'

Grale had been a traders' port before the Continent's war with Albion had begun, and its inhabitants could still be persuaded to barter with smugglers who did not plan to stay too long. The smugglers' ship's arrival would already be expected. Special provision would have been made for it at the docks at a designated time, but Silas would be given no such privilege. If just one man saw the boat out there on the waves, the rest of them would know about it in moments and decide what to do about it.

Silas rowed swiftly. The sooner he was out of sight, the better.

The land rose into looming cliffs on either side of the wind-lashed town, each mass topped by a stone watch-tower. The boy shivered in silence as they crept inshore. Silas was concentrating on avoiding the clutches of rocks that rose stealthily out of the rising waves when something glimmered up ahead, a flicker of light where a light should not have been.

Halfway up the cliff face, a shadow moved. Silas kept rowing. Another stroke of the oars . . . two . . . three, carrying the boat closer to the shore. The hairs on his neck began to bristle. He looked up – saw nothing – and then a sound high above him left no room for doubt. There was the thinnest rattle, a scrape of metal against stone, and a gentle hiss as something fell out of the sky.

Silas was already on his feet. He grabbed the boy's arm and pulled him over the side of the boat. The crow fluttered up into the darkness and Silas hit the water on his back as a weighted net swamped down on to the boat. The ropes caught upon the mast and tented across it like a dead jellyfish. The air filled with arrows. Silas released the boy and plunged underwater.

More arrows ripped past him, but his attackers were shooting blind. They had expected him to strike out for the shore and were misjudging his position by a good few feet. He treaded water to stay close to the surface and a squeal of fear sounded nearby as the boy slapped the water uselessly with open palms, battling to stay afloat.

The frequency of the arrow strikes allowed Silas to calculate how many enemies there were as he swam back towards the frightened boy. A black-shafted arrow stabbed into his arm and he pulled it out without flinching, filling the water with a swirl of blood. He grabbed the boy's ankle and pulled him down under the water. The sea foamed with air as the lad flailed and fought against him, but Silas kept hold of his foot and dragged him along, heading for the rocky shore.

The arrows stopped. Silas swam faster. Whoever was up there would be making their way down to the waterline. At last his hand came up against a cold mass of cliff shale. To his right was a huge expanse of rock, solid and black; to his left was a path leading up into the town.

The sea rose and fell against the coast, pulling the two swimmers away and forcing them back again. Above them four shadows ran along the sheer side of the cliff, suspended by ropes that let them swing between two distant ledges with ease. Silas knew that technique. He had seen it before, which meant that those men were not just ordinary guards. They were something far worse.

'Blackwatch,' he breathed.

The Blackwatch were elite soldiers of the Continental army, every one of them highly trained in stealth, infiltration and assassination. Silas had encountered many of their agents in the past but he had not expected to see them there. If the Blackwatch were in Grale, his search for Dalliah Grey was going to be more difficult than he had anticipated.

Soon the men moved out of sight and Silas pulled himself out of the sea, dragging himself up on to the rocks at the base of the cliff. The boy was right behind him, and the moment he slithered up on to solid ground Silas grabbed him by the scruff of the neck and hauled him to his feet.

'They *knew*,' he said coldly. 'They knew I was coming. How did they know?'

The boy did not answer.

'What is this?' Silas dragged on a leather cord hung round the boy's neck and found a glass lens hanging there.

The boy cried out as loud as his pitiful lungs would let him. 'Here! He's here!'

Silas grabbed him by the neck and loomed over him. 'You have chosen the wrong side, boy,' he said. 'Pray that you never see me again.'

The lad's eyes widened in fear, but he was not looking at Silas; he was looking behind him. Silas saw a shadow move in the reflection within the boy's eye. He watched it carefully, saw the gleam of a blade shining in the moonlight, and dodged smoothly as it stabbed towards his back. The man wielding it stumbled, the boy ran and Silas killed his attacker instantly with a swift snap of the neck.

Silas reached for the rock face and pulled himself up the cliff, hand over hand, making for a ledge a few feet above him. The rocks were slippery and smooth, but he reached the ledge, got to his feet and drew his sword ready to defend himself. The ledge was part of a curved pathway sliced into the cliff rock and Silas followed it upwards to gain the advantage of higher ground as the rest of the Blackwatch closed in.

The sea roared against the cliffs as he climbed higher. His crow screeched a warning and he stopped, spotting a bowman posted up ahead, watching the waves. Silas moved along the rock face, staying out of sight, and took the bowman by surprise. The man loosed an arrow, missed his target, and was dead before the arrowhead found its way into the sea.

More Blackwatch moved in, flanking Silas on both sides. There was nowhere to go. Arrows flew, but Silas was fast on his feet, dodging every one until a second net edged with weighted blades launched towards him from the dark. The net tangled around him, capturing him beneath it. Silas fought to free himself but the rope had a metal core that could not be cut. He stopped struggling as his enemies gathered around him. He waited, choosing his moment.

'Secure him.'

Silas did not see who had given the order, but he had no intention of letting anyone see it through. Only six men were left, five with bows or swords raised, and one – the leader – standing behind them, silhouetted in the moonlight. Silas waited until they had crept close enough and then stood up quickly, making the net lift with him. The Blackwatch scrambled to secure the edges and Silas lashed the ropes, using the weighting blades as weapons against them. Two men died when their throats were slashed and a third fell to a thrust of Silas's sword. He wrenched the net up over his shoulders and threw a fourth man into the sea, leaving only the leader and his last man standing close by.

'Silas Dane,' said the leader. 'Welcome back.'

Silas knew that voice, thick with the deep tones of the Continental north. The voice of an enemy. It had been twelve years since he had heard it last.

'Bandermain,' he said. 'I should have known.'

Silas's fingers flexed around the hilt of his sword, eager

to fight, but this was no time for bloody reunions. The Blackwatch never worked alone. For every group Silas had encountered in the past another had always been posted nearby, and he did not have time to fight them all. He had been betrayed by a child, and the enemy had found him before he had even set foot on land. His arrival on the Continent was not going to plan.

The last Blackwatch agent raised his bow ready to let loose an arrow. Silas looked out across the ocean, and as the bow snapped he bolted straight for the edge of the path. The arrow snicked behind him, dangerously close to his neck. The bowman quickly readied another and Silas's feet left the ground as he leapt from the cliff, launching himself far out into the air. The north wind streamed against his face and the sea beneath him bristled with rocks as he brought his arms up into a deathly dive and plummeted down into the waves.

He plunged hard into the shallow water, buffeted by the tide, which sent him slamming back into the cliff. The rocks sliced his arms and the force of the ocean raked his body hard against the coast.

The remaining Blackwatch looked down from the path, not daring to follow their target into the sea, but there was no sign of life in the water.

Silas was gone.

2

Judgement

Kate Winters sat at the back of the empty meeting hall, staring at a pair of slim wooden boxes that stood side by side on a small semicircular stage at the front of the room. One was painted white, the other black, with a wire basket hooked on to either side, each box standing half as tall as a man.

'There they are,' she said quietly. 'Those boxes are going to decide everything.'

Edgar sat down, passed Kate half a sandwich and propped his feet on the arm of the chair beside her.

'They're just boxes,' he said. 'It's the people who use them you've got to watch out for.'

Kate looked back at the main door. The meeting hall was the largest chamber in the sanctuary of the Skilled's underground cavern, and one of the oldest. Like most of the structures there most of it was built into the cavern wall, but the stone outer walls were curved slightly, making it look different from the rest. It was a communal space set aside for important meetings and events, and was left standing empty most of the time.

Edgar leaned back and stared up at the vaulted ceiling, where paintings of all the Skilled who had lived and died there in the last twenty years were pinned into place. 'I don't know who thought that was a good idea,' he said between bites. 'This place gives me the creeps.'

Kate did not look up. She could sense the pale ghosts of the people those faces had belonged to, caught within the veil between life and death, unable or unwilling to leave the living world behind. She tried to ignore them, but since the Night of Souls it had become difficult to block them out.

'When do you think they'll start to arrive?' she asked.

'We've got plenty of time,' said Edgar. 'You'd think they'd at least let you sit in on the decision. It's your life. If anyone deserves to hear the verdict, it's you.'

'I don't think we should have come here.'

'Why? No one's going to see us.'

'No, I mean *here*. To this cavern. The Skilled don't want me here. None of them do.'

'They're just nervous,' said Edgar. 'They'll do what's right in the end.'

'I hope so,' said Kate.

Asking the Skilled for help had been more difficult than Kate had expected. From the moment she entered their cavern on the Night of Souls she had feared she was making a big mistake. Silas was right. The Skilled did not understand her, and they definitely did not want her among them.

Kate had spent her first day in the cavern being

questioned about the murder of Mina, the Skilled's leader, who had died while Kate was in her care. They took her uncle Artemis away and would not let her speak to Edgar or his brother Tom for three days. No one believed that Silas Dane was the one who had killed Mina. They thought that Kate was behind it and it had taken a long time for Edgar and Artemis to convince them not to keep her locked away.

During the past few weeks they had agreed to hold an informal trial, which seemed to consist of everyone except Kate giving their opinions of what had happened. They consulted the veil and argued with each other over the best course of action to take against her, but no one was interested in what she had to say. For the last few weeks Kate had been free to move about the Skilleds' underground street, but she was not allowed to leave. The vast tunnels of the City Below were off limits to her, it had been a whole month since she had seen the sun, and she was forbidden from using her abilities to enter the veil at any time.

What the Skilled did not know was that she was a Walker, and the world between life and death was open to her all the time. Walkers did not simply look into the veil as the Skilled could, they *entered* it, sending their spirits deep into the half-life – the realm between life and death. For the Skilled, dealing with the veil was like looking through a window that kept them safe and separate from what was going on around them. Walkers were different. When they connected with the half-life, frost spread across their skin and their consciousness separated from the living world, throwing their spirits completely into the unknown.

None of the Skilled was willing to teach Kate more about her connection with the veil. They had not even questioned why her silver-sheened eyes looked different from theirs. They had simply cut her off, refusing to do anything except ignore her. Edgar and Tom were the only people who really spoke to her. Even Artemis – who rarely bothered to hide his dislike of the Skilled – was strangely distant, and seemed to spend more time with them than with her.

'What do you think the verdict will be?' she asked.

'They'll have to admit you didn't do it,' said Edgar. 'This is all just for show. You've lived with them for a whole month now and you haven't had the urge to go around stabbing anyone, have you?' He lowered his voice and raised his eyebrows deviously. 'There are a few of them *I* wouldn't mind seeing off if the opportunity presented itself. I think spending all that time with Silas has rubbed off on me.'

'I'm serious,' said Kate. 'This isn't a joke.'

Edgar shrugged. 'Don't let them get to you,' he said. 'It has to go your way. You'll see. Where are you supposed to be while the meeting's on?'

'Someone's meant to be watching me. I heard a couple of women arguing over whose turn it is tonight. I don't think either of them wanted to be left alone with me.'

Kate's eyes flashed with silver as she looked down and Edgar stared at her secretly. He still wasn't used to seeing her eyes do that, and it usually meant trouble.

'It's happening again, isn't it?' he said.

'It's not too bad.' Kate glanced at the ceiling. 'It's those pictures. They attract the shades sometimes. It makes it harder to shut everything out, but it's OK.'

'The Skilled should be helping you with this stuff,' said Edgar. 'Not treating you like a criminal.'

'They think I was working for Silas,' said Kate. 'I don't think anything's going to make them change their minds now.'

A door creaked open at the side of the stage, on which three chairs had been set facing out towards the rest.

'Watch out!' whispered Edgar.

The two of them slid off their chairs and on to their knees as a man's voice carried across the hall.

'. . . it is not only a matter of our laws, of course. It is the message it would be sending. On that we must be perfectly clear . . .'

'Quick!' said Edgar. 'Head left!'

Kate crawled between the chair legs as quietly as she could and Edgar scrambled after her, heading towards an antechamber with an old stone tomb sitting in the centre of it, separated from the main hall by an open door.

'I do not have to tell you how dangerous this situation is,' continued the man, as Kate ducked round the door and Edgar pressed in against the other wall, crouching out of sight. 'From what I have heard, the great majority of votes are going to lean the same way. If today goes the way I expect, you may find that it is time for you to make a hard decision.'

Kate looked out through the gap between the door's hinges. The speaker was Baltin, one of the most respected members of the Skilled. The man standing next to him had his back to Kate, but she recognised him at once.

'Is that Artemis?' whispered Edgar, looking round the door frame. 'What's he doing here?'

'Are you ready?' Baltin placed a hand on Artemis's shoulder.

Artemis looked out across the hall. 'Yes,' he said quietly. 'Bring them in.'

Baltin nodded to the open stage door, and someone behind it began ringing the low bell, announcing that a meeting was about to begin.

'What now?' said Edgar. 'We can't stay here. Someone will see us.'

'Shh.'

Two minutes passed before the hall's main doors swung open and people began filing in one by one. Kate recognised each of them from her time in the cavern. She knew every face, where they lived and exactly what they all thought about her. A few of them were polite enough whenever she was nearby, but not one of them had ever taken the time to speak to her. She was an enemy living within their walls. Edgar might be confident that they would find her innocent, but Kate was not so sure.

Of the eighty-eight people who lived in that cavern, just over half regularly chose to attend meetings in the hall, but this time it looked as if every one of them had shown up. Not all the Skilled wanted take an active role in Skilled business. Many just wanted a safe place to live away from the wardens. As those who were interested in Kate's trial took their seats, quiet chatter filled the room. Kate waited for Artemis to step down from the stage, but Baltin gestured for him to sit in one of the seats upon it instead.

'They're letting him stay,' whispered Edgar. 'That might be a good thing.'

Kate wasn't listening. The Skilled hardly ever let

ordinary people sit in on their meetings, and to let one take pride of place on the stage was unheard of. A shocked whisper spread through the gathering as Artemis sat down and a small woman claimed the other chair, leaving the central one free for Baltin.

To Kate, that woman was the most dangerous person present. She was the magistrate, there to record everything that was said in that room and make sure that whatever was decided was carried out quickly and completely. Kate had long given up hoping that things were going to go her way. Whatever punishment she was going to face, the magistrate would be the one to see it through.

The woman eyed the crowd carefully and Kate stepped back. She had questioned Kate many times, but it did not seem to matter how honest Kate was or how often she protested her innocence; she would not listen.

Baltin raised his hands for silence, and as the crowd quietened down a sense of anticipation settled over the hall. 'I am sure we all know why we are here,' he said. 'Just over four weeks ago, three of our old friends came to us for protection: Edgar Rill, whom many of us know and trust like a son; Tom Rill, whom we have known and trusted equally long; and Artemis Winters, our reluctant friend from the north, who has done us great service in the past despite his long-held suspicions of our people. For that, we welcome him here among us today and honour him as we would a brother.'

Gentle applause rippled across the hall. Artemis looked down at his feet and did not even raise his head to acknowledge their respect.

'Now,' continued Baltin. 'To business.'

The magistrate attracted his attention with a rap of her ink pen on the arm of her chair.

'Yes, Greta?'

'Where,' she asked slowly, 'is the girl?'

Baltin smiled at the crowd before turning to her. 'She is safe in a guardian's care,' he said. 'Once she is . . .' He stopped and corrected himself. '*If* she is charged, she will be taken swiftly to the lockhouse where she will be passed over to you. Until then she remains under careful watch. You have my word on that.'

Kate and Edgar looked at each other. The magistrate recorded Baltin's answer on her page and then gazed round the room.

'I never liked her,' whispered Edgar.

Kate did not say anything, but the magistrate definitely made her feel uneasy.

Baltin turned back to his audience. 'To resume,' he said, 'there was indeed a fourth visitor to our home. One who is, perhaps, a little less welcome than our three friends.'

'*She is a murderer.*'

Baltin squinted down at a man in the first row. 'Excuse me?'

'We all know what she did. There's no point in dressing it up. She killed Mina, and Seth too! Or have we all forgotten what happened to him for trying to bring her to justice?'

Kate's heart sank. Silas had claimed a second victim in that cavern on the day he had taken Mina's life. Kate had not known his name.

'I don't like where this is going,' muttered Edgar.

Baltin raised his hand for quiet.

'That is a separate matter altogether,' he said. 'It is not why we are here today.'

'We all know she did it,' said the man at the front.

'Perhaps,' said Baltin. 'But, for now, we are here to vote upon her guilt or innocence of the crime against Mina Green. Nothing more or less. Those of you whose votes may be tainted by any other concerns should leave this hall now. No one here shall think the less of you. Indeed, you shall be respected for your honesty.'

No one moved.

'Very well,' he said. 'As a people, we have always striven to act fairly towards our own. Today, I trust, will be no different. We have all had time to reach our decision over recent weeks. Now we shall pass judgement on what we have heard during that time. Do you all have your stones?'

A murmur of agreement went up around him.

'Then let the votes be cast. Innocence.' He placed his hand upon the white box. 'Or guilt.' He placed his hand upon the black. 'With order, please. Begin.'

Everyone in the hall stood up as one, except for the oldest invitees who stood up more slowly and shuffled up the stage steps to cast the first votes, forcing everyone else to snake back in a respectful line behind them. One by one they approached the two boxes, each of them carrying a small cloth pouch in their hands. Inside the pouches were two ordinary grey stones, one of which had been left plain, the other carved and burned with a thick black line. Each person had to approach the boxes with a stone in each hand and drop them, palms down, one into each box, so no one knew which choice they had made. The number of marked stones in each box would be counted separately, and if the total matched the number of voters the count would be deemed fair and the verdict given.

Kate heard the dull clunk of stones being dropped two by two, and forced herself to watch. The man who had spoken up made no secret about which box he was dropping his marked stone into, and strode proudly off the stage as soon as his vote was cast.

'What do I do if the verdict is against me?' Kate whispered when half the people had returned to their seats. She had never dared to think about what might happen next. How did the Skilled treat people who were found guilty of murder?

'Let's see what happens,' said Edgar, squeezing her hand gently. 'Not everyone's an idiot like him. The Skilled are good people. I still think they'll cast their stones the right way.'

Artemis, Baltin and Greta the magistrate were not allowed to participate in the vote, but once the final two stones had been cast Baltin was responsible for conducting the count. Kate heard a rattling surge of stones as he opened the boxes' side hatches and the baskets filled one by one. The people waited in silence. All anyone heard was the dull tap and scrape of the stones scratching against each other as Baltin took the count from the white box.

Kate found herself squeezing Edgar's hand even tighter. She held her breath. Maybe this was why people weren't invited to their own judgements. The waiting . . . not knowing . . . it seemed endless. She wanted to shout at Baltin to hurry up, just to get it over with, but Baltin was a careful man. He had a job to do, and he would do it right. An eternity later, he moved on to the black box.

Kate tried to read his expression, but all she saw was calm determination.

'Not long now,' said Edgar.

At last Baltin straightened and slowly went to stand behind the box. He paused for two breaths until, finally, he opened his mouth to speak.

'The count is fair,' he said. 'You have all honoured yourselves with your honesty. For that, you have my thanks.' He turned to Artemis, who was staring at him, his eyes filled with silent desperation, but could not meet his gaze. 'The verdict is given,' he said. 'With a count of sixty-eight stones to twenty, Kate Winters, by order of this gathering, has been marked guilty of murder.'

'What?' Edgar shouted out, forgetting that he was meant to be hiding, but his yell was drowned out by the cheers that filled the hall. He tried to stand up, but Kate held him back. 'They can't do that!' he said. 'This isn't right!'

'It doesn't matter now.' Kate tried to calm him down. 'Leave it. I don't want you getting into more trouble because of me.'

'You can forget that.' Edgar tried to squirm out of her hands, but she held on tight.

'You're not going to change their minds.'

'No! I brought you here. I told you we would be safe. This wasn't supposed to happen!'

Baltin's voice cut through the noise of the gathered crowd. 'The magistrate will now verify the count, and I would like to thank you all for your judgement on this day. Be assured, the prisoner shall be brought to justice swiftly, and in a manner befitting the nature of her terrible crime.'

'What does that mean?' asked Kate.

'I don't know,' said Edgar, but Kate knew he was lying.

'Edgar, what does it mean?'

Kate forced him to look at her, and she saw terror in his eyes.

3
Enemies

Silas heaved himself out of the ocean and limped on to the coastal path. Two small firelights illuminated the cliff face as the Blackwatch lit torches and headed down to continue their search, but Silas did not look back. The path led him straight into the heart of Grale and a soaking wet stranger on the streets at night was not going to go unnoticed for long. He moved through the dark, leaving a trail of seawater squelching behind him, and passed underneath a series of narrow arches cut into the long terraced buildings whose dirty walls swallowed the moonlight.

Six such arches passed over his head and at the seventh he saw a man crouching in a doorway. Silas kept walking. The man shifted position, as if to make sure he would be noticed. Silas recognised a Blackwatch tactic when he saw one. That man was a decoy, posted there to make him turn and choose another route, guiding him into an ambush. If the Blackwatch thought he was going to play their games they were very wrong.

In one smooth move, Silas kicked a loose rock up from the ground, caught it, and hurled it at the waiting man, striking him hard on the temple and sending him slumping to the ground. He approached cautiously. The fallen man was unconscious, but still breathing. Then came a signal from the dark – the flash of a tiny lens light from the furthest end of the arches. Another member of the Blackwatch was checking in.

Silas checked the man's pockets and found the leather pouch that held his lens. An ordinary guard's lens would have been a small circle made from cut glass with a dull metal frame, but the Blackwatch were not ordinary guards. Their lenses were convex discs of shaved crystal, faceted round the edge and mounted in a thin twist of silver. With no moonlight to reflect back beneath the arches, Silas slid a match from a slot in the lens pouch, lit it and raised the lens to his chest, flickering a signal to the waiting man. He knew a few of the Blackwatch lens codes, but had no way of knowing if the one he had used was still active. There was no reply. The code must have been old. He had given his location away.

Silas dropped the match, pocketed the lens and looked up. He was standing in a narrow space between two rows of back-to-back buildings. The sky was a sharp black slit between them and the gap between the stones was barely three feet wide. He heard footsteps advancing towards him, so he edged further down the pathway, grabbed hold of a stone protruding slightly from the wall and pulled himself up. He clung to the wall like a bat, creeping upwards and pressing his heel against the wall behind him to gain more height wherever the stones were too smooth to climb. Then he stayed still, clinging on by his fingertips and the toes of his boots as a Blackwatch agent approached.

When the officer discovered the injured man, he readied a crossbow and searched the alleyway for any sign of life. His target was gone. Silas watched him take two paces into the darkness. He saw and heard the flare and fizz of a match, then, *flick-flick-flick*, a lens light signal cut through the dark.

Silas smiled. They had lost him.

Four more Blackwatch officers gathered between the arches as Silas continued his climb towards the rooftops. His fingers ached as he clung to the wall. His muscles were tiring. Something had changed. He had to get out of sight.

He reached the neat black tiles, squeezed up between two matching chimneystacks and stepped on to the sloping roof. Once there, he checked his position. Grale was a small town and he was close to its centre. The moon cast long shadows from the forests that wrapped around Grale like a horseshoe on three sides, and the ocean was silvery black. Silas could see the covered dock where the smugglers' ship would be spending the rest of the night. He turned away from it and followed the rooftops for as long as they lasted, then threw himself at a post holding up one of the lantern strings, grabbed it with both hands and slid silently to the ground. He tried to shift his thoughts into the veil as he ran, using it to sense his pursuers' presence before they got too close, but the veil was not there. He could not sense anything.

Silas stopped running.

The veil had been a part of his life every day for the past twelve years. For it to suddenly be gone . . . it was impossible. Unthinkable. He searched for the familiar silhouette of his crow against the sky, but he could not pick the bird out against the background of shifting clouds.

The street opened on to the bank of Grale's only river, a wide, fast-flowing waterway crossed by three old bridges linking one side of the town to the other. Silas followed the bank to the nearest bridge, a stone-built pathway barely a carriage-width wide. Crossing it would leave him too exposed and he was about to return to the cover of the streets when Blackwatch agents emptied out of the alleyways up ahead. There was no time to reach the buildings so Silas slithered down the bank instead, ducking out of sight beneath the bridge.

The old structure was weak and unstable, with large gaps in its sides where high waters had washed chunks of it away. Years of river debris strangled the stone pillars holding it in place and old tree trunks had been sunk into the river bed to support its weakest points. Silt and soil settled around Silas's feet as he waited ankle-deep on an underwater ledge, his black coat camouflaging him in the shadows. The Blackwatch signalled to each other, but instead of searching for him along the riverbank they backed away and retreated into the side streets. Silas heard them leave and peered out of his hiding place. A typical Continental welcome, he thought. Nothing had changed.

A scrabbling sound scratched close by, and his crow scuttled through the shadows, head down, like a rat in the dark. He bent down to pick up the bird, which snapped its beak, agitated, as footsteps echoed overhead. Silas stood still, sword at the ready. A wet rope glinted in the moonlight on the river. One end of it was wrapped round a rotting tree trunk, the other trailing across the water. Two men ducked back under the surface when Silas looked their way. How could he have missed them? The Blackwatch had not lost him. They had surrounded him.

The sound of straining horses carried from the riverbank. The rope tightened. Too late, Silas realised what was happening. He tried to run, but the rope was already doing its work. The rotten tree trunk was starting to give, lean and split. The weight of the bridge was not enough to stop the timber from shifting and the first stones began to fall; stones that became an avalanche, collapsing into the river and crashing down on to Silas's ledge.

The crow launched itself through the destruction as a chunk of rock slammed into Silas's shoulder, punching him to the ground. He tried to get up, but there was no time. He threw his arm over his head to protect himself as the bridge fell in, burying him beneath a hail of rubble and sealing him in the dark.

Kate looked out into the meeting hall at the people she had once trusted; people who believed she was capable of murder. Many of them were nodding their agreement with Baltin's words, and some were even applauding the decision, as if some great criminal was about to get the justice she deserved. The sight of so many enemies made Kate feel cold. Artemis had tried to keep her away from the Skilled. He had tried to protect her from their world all her life. Now she knew why.

She looked for her uncle up on the stage. He was just

sitting there, silent. 'I don't believe this is happening,' she said.

'Someone has to do something,' said Edgar. 'We need to get you out of here.' He left the safety of the ante-room and stepped straight out into the meeting hall, drawing angry looks and shouts of surprise from people sitting close by.

'Wait,' whispered Kate. 'What are you doing?'

Edgar hesitated for a moment, not sure what to say, until one of the Skilled spoke out.

'You are not meant to be in here,' she said. 'What's going on?'

Baltin spoke loudly from the stage at the front of the hall, 'Is something wrong?'

'Edgar has been hiding in here, listening to us,' said the woman, as the whole hall turned to look at the intruder. 'He's not supposed to be here, Baltin.'

'Why not?' demanded Edgar. 'I care about what happens to Kate, and I know that she deserves a lot better than this. Being turned upon by people who should be her friends.'

'That murderer is no friend of ours,' said the man sitting at the front. 'We have no argument with you or your brother, but that girl has brought death to this cavern. She is a threat to us all.'

Edgar walked up to the stage. 'Artemis, tell them they're wrong about Kate. Tell them they mustn't do this.'

Artemis hung his head, tapping his fingertips together nervously. 'I . . . I can't,' he said.

'Why not?'

'I can't keep her safe any more. Not on my own,' he

said. 'This place . . . these people. They understand what Kate is going through. They can help her.'

'Help her? They think she's a murderer!'

'I know that. But up there, on the surface, the wardens are still looking for her. I can't let the council find her again.'

Artemis handed Edgar a folded piece of paper. Edgar opened it and read it quickly. It was a wanted poster, showing Kate's face and her name written in thick black letters. Edgar scrunched it up in his fist.

'That doesn't mean anything,' he said.

'You told me we could trust the Skilled,' said Artemis. 'You were the one who said to bring Kate here.'

'We didn't have any choice!'

'And I don't have any choice now,' said Artemis. 'Baltin has given me his word that no harm will come to her. I don't want to do this, Edgar, but it is the only way I can see to keep her safe.'

'So you're just going to let them lock her away?' said Edgar. 'Just shut her up and forget about her, is that it? Do you really want that to happen?'

'At least she will be safe,' said Artemis. 'That's all I can hope for her now.'

Baltin pressed a reassuring hand on Artemis's shoulder. 'The girl's guardian has made no objection,' he said. 'Kate will be collected and taken to the lockhouse. We will decide her punishment in due course.'

The gathered people all stood up at once and Edgar climbed on to the stage, unable to believe they were all calmly making their way back out into their lives.

'You can't do this!' he shouted. 'I told her you would help her, but you're just as bad as the council! You're treating her the way they have treated you for centuries, all because you're afraid of what you don't understand.'

No one responded. Many of the Skilled looked back at him as they left, their dark eyes flashing with anger. The door of Kate's hiding place moved and Edgar saw her looking straight out at Artemis. As far as she could tell, he had not even tried to convince them that she couldn't have killed Mina, that she would never kill anyone. Artemis saw her and turned away.

'At least you're ashamed of what you're doing,' said Edgar.

Artemis stood up. His clothes were scruffier than usual and he looked as though he had not slept for days. 'Baltin,' he said, 'there is no need to send your people after Kate.'

'The decision has been made, Artemis. I warned you this could happen. You agreed that it was right.'

Artemis wrung his hands, struggling with what he was about to say. Kate waited for him to speak up for her, to try to put right what the Skilled had got terribly wrong, and then he raised his hand and pointed directly at her hiding place. 'She is there,' he said.

Kate could not believe what she was seeing. Artemis could have distracted Baltin, or at least said nothing. He could have given her a chance to explain herself and maybe make some kind of difference to the judgement passed against her. Instead he just pointed at her, handing her over as if he too was convinced of her guilt.

Edgar jumped off the edge of the stage and bolted between the rows of seats towards her. 'Kate!' he shouted. 'We have to go!'

But Kate was not ready to leave.

The air in the meeting hall was changing. Something

was shifting within the veil. Kate heard a sound like roaring thunder, the spirits around the paintings in the ceiling looked suddenly clearer, and she felt the veil tugging at her thoughts, fighting for her attention against what was happening in the room. Dizziness overwhelmed her. The ceilling pressed down towards her and the walls leaned in. She backed slowly into the anteroom, pressing her back against the tomb in the centre of the floor. It was hard to breathe. The sound of rushing water echoed around her, her body would not move, and she heard the screech of a bird from somewhere nearby.

Kate slid down the side of the tomb and sat on the floor. Images flickered in front of her eyes: water, feathers and stone. She could smell the tang of blood and feel the rough touch of stone crushing her fingertips. None of it made any sense. She couldn't stop it. All she could do was let it happen. She wanted to scream but her lungs would not work. Then Edgar was in front of her. He took hold of her hand and the veil pulled back. The images faded. Her body came back under her control and tears were streaming down her cheeks.

'Come on,' said Edgar, gently pulling her to her feet. 'We'll get out of here.'

'No,' said Kate. 'Something's wrong.'

'A lot of things are wrong right now. We have to go.'

'I think it's Silas,' said Kate. 'Something has happened. I could *feel* him.' She looked down at her hands, remembering the pressure of the stone pressing on them. 'He's hurt.'

'We can talk about that later,' said Edgar. 'There's nothing we can do about it now. Are you coming?'

Kate nodded. She let Edgar pull her into the meeting

41

hall and they slammed out of the front door side by side.

The Skilled's cavern was dimly lit to simulate the night that hung over the City Above. The lantern light gave a warm glow to the curved ceiling of red bricks and illuminated the two long rows of houses where the Skilled lived. They had been too slow. Greta the magistrate was already standing in the street, flanked by two of Baltin's strongest guards, waiting for her.

'Great,' said Edgar, keeping tight hold of Kate's hand.

'The judgement has been passed,' said Greta. 'The verdict was fair.'

'It is more than she deserves,' said one of the men. 'We should hand her over to the wardens for what she has done.'

Edgar whispered to Kate without moving his lips. 'If we're going, we have to go now. Follow my lead.'

The two guards flinched when it looked as if Edgar was going to move. Greta took a step closer.

'The cavern is sealed,' she said. 'There is no way out.'

More of the Skilled were gathering around them, their dark eyes fixed intently upon Kate. Her hands felt icy cold, and beads of water dripped to the ground as the heat of Edgar's grip melted the frost that gathered on them as the veil closed in.

'What are they doing?' asked Edgar, refusing to let go.

'It's not them,' said Kate. 'It's the vell. Something is different about it.'

'Miss Winters?' Baltin's voice spoke behind her. 'It is time to answer for what you have done. Come with us now. You can do yourself no good out here. Let the boy go.'

Kate realised that she was holding Edgar's hand so

tightly that his fingers were turning white, and she let go of him at once.

'That's right,' said Baltin, signalling the two men to walk slowly towards her. 'Edgar, stand aside, if you please.'

'No. You can't just take her!'

'Don't you see what is happening?' said Baltin. 'She does not have full control of her link to the veil, and that makes her dangerous. She may not even remember killing Mina. Do you want the same thing to happen to you?'

Kate's pupils sheened with silver as they reflected the lamplight.

'This girl has already gone too deep into things which are none of her concern,' said Baltin. 'The Night of Souls was . . . there is no other word for it, it was an abomination. The effects of the damage Kate did in that circle are still being felt across the veil. She is dangerous and always will be dangerous. We cannot allow her to make the same mistakes again.'

'She used a listening circle,' said Edgar. 'It's hardly a crime.'

'In our world, it should be,' said Baltin. 'She opened a listening circle, exposed a crowd of innocent people to the dangers of the half-life and interfered with the fates of thousands of tormented souls. If sheer luck had not allowed her to contain the shades in that circle the consequences would have been unimaginable.'

'But she *did* contain them,' said Edgar. 'She didn't open the circle. Da'ru did. If Kate hadn't taken control of it who knows what would have happened. She helped people that night, something the Skilled haven't done for a very long time.'

'As I said. Luck,' said Baltin. 'It could have all ended very differently. Do not forget the blood that was shed because of her. Wardens and a councilwoman all slain within an active circle. Do you have any idea what could have happened if Kate had lost control?'

'Those deaths weren't Kate's fault!'

'Perhaps not, but it doesn't change the fact that those circles are instruments of great unknown power. Even the Skilled do not yet know the extent of their influence upon the living world. Kate's actions were reckless, and we may only now be beginning to see the consequences. She tore a gateway between the worlds of the living and the dead; one larger than any that has been seen within living memory. An act like that has far-reaching effects. Who knows how many are yet to suffer for what she has done?'

'Rubbish!' said Edgar. 'Kate didn't harm anything or anyone and you're all crazy to think that she ever would.'

'That's enough,' Baltin said sternly. 'You are a guest in this cavern, Mr Rill. Remember that.'

Edgar was about to argue, but a flicker of doubt crossed Kate's mind. What if Baltin was right? What if she had done something wrong? What if she was dangerous? Kate knew too well how close the hundreds of people in the city square had come to death on the Night of Souls. She had seen the current of death with her own eyes, she had watched it claim the life of the councilwoman Da'ru and she had helped do its work. Baltin was right: if anything had happened to the gathered people that night she would have been responsible. She could not risk anything like that happening again.

Kate stepped forward and turned to Edgar. 'I'm going

with them,' she said. 'It'll be all right.'

'No, it won't. They won't let you out again. They'll keep you down here. Kate!' But Baltin's men were already surrounding her.

Two of them held Edgar back as Kate followed Baltin down the cavern's main street, heading towards a small building that was off limits to anyone except the one who held the key. The locks on the door were stiff from disuse. Baltin swung open the door and stepped inside the candlelit darkness, signalling for Kate to follow.

Inside was a single room that the Skilled used as a lockhouse. Someone had been in recently and prepared it for her arrival. There was a bed next to the door, a long table stacked with old books that looked as if they had come from someone's dusty attic, and a row of shelves that ran all the way round the circular wall, holding four lit candles, already burned halfway down.

'For your own sake, I suggest you get used to this place,' said Baltin, his voice echoing dully round the room. 'You can do no harm in here, and you shall remain here until we decide upon a more permanent solution.'

'I haven't hurt anybody,' said Kate, as Baltin positioned himself between her and the door. 'I didn't kill Mina.'

'This is not just about that,' said Baltin. 'We all knew what you were, even before you did. You may think you have not hurt anyone, but the veil does not lie to us. It warned us about you four years ago and it says that, given time, you will. I have people to take care of here. They trust me to do what is right, and this is right. Do you really think Mina would not have done the same once she had learned everything she could from you?'

'Mina welcomed me into her home,' said Kate. 'She

trusted me, just as she trusted my parents. They gave their lives to help the Skilled. Do *you* really think I would break that trust?'

'Children are not their parents,' said Baltin. 'You may be right about Mina, but look what happened to her. The veil warned us about your . . . unique capabilities. I respect your family, I always have, but I would be a fool to ignore that warning now. I cannot afford to trust you, Kate, and since you agreed to be brought here, I do not think you even trust yourself. You will have regular meals, but no visitors until we decide what to do with you. Beyond that, I can promise nothing.'

Baltin left the room, leaving Kate standing there alone. He turned the locks tight and rattled the door after each one to make sure it was sealed. The moment the last lock slid into place, he and his men walked away and silence fell hauntingly in the room – the kind of silence that suggested that someone was standing close by, trying not to breathe.

Kate picked up the nearest candle and held it up. She felt as if someone was watching her. Her skin prickled, and it was only then that she noticed the trails of frost veining her arms. The veil was closer than usual in that place and it made her uneasy. 'This is it,' she told herself aloud, sitting down on the bed. 'This is what you have to look forward to for who knows how long.'

A deep whisper circled round the room in answer to her words, and Kate shivered. She dared to reach into the veil a little and saw the shadowy forms of shades standing against the walls like statues carved into the stone. Seeing them so clearly no longer scared her, and their presence gave her some small comfort as she sat there on her own. If Baltin wanted her to stay out of the veil, locking her away was not going to do any good. He had to have known that. Sitting there in the silence, Kate could not help thinking about what kind of permanent solution he and the magistrate had in mind.

4

Bandermain

'Wake him up.'

A voice trailed sluggishly through Silas's mind as he tried to piece together what was happening to him. Rope bit into his blood-soaked wrists, and the smell of damp earth was overwhelming. He was in a cellar, tied to a chair and unable to move. That was all he could be sure of without opening his eyes. His mind, taking that as a command, tried to lift his eyelids. One of his eyes was badly swollen and the lid would not budge. The other was sticky with blood, but as his eyelashes pulled apart he took in all the details of his surroundings in a single blink.

A candle flame was burning just inches from the tip of his nose. Behind the flame was a face, watching him, and beyond that were at least three other men, each one armed and staring blankly at the wall behind him. Silas tried to move as his senses gradually returned, and pain flashed down his leg. The bone felt as raw as a rod of red-hot iron.

Tiny movements allowed him to test his limbs one by one. One of his shoulders was dislocated, making his left arm feel detached and heavy, and every movement sent pain searing through his body. Instinct forced him to stay as still as possible. Most of his finger joints felt cricked and twisted, one of his ankles was broken and his right arm was cracked in at least two places. He tested his lungs. A crackle of broken ribs rippled in his chest and he knew not to breathe deeply again. It felt as if every part of him was bruised, broken or bleeding. This shouldn't have been happening. He should have been healing.

'You should be dead.' The face behind the flame stood up, taking the candle with it. 'Why aren't you dead?'

The question was not meant for him. The gravelly voice was talking to itself, studying Silas carefully. Silas did not like to be studied.

The shadow of the man caught in the candlelight dominated the entire room. His shoulders were wide and powerful, his strong arms well used to wielding a sword. His face bore the thin scars of many battles and his pale lips were curled up into a look that was half curiosity and half grudging admiration. When Silas had seen him last, this man had carried a two-handed sword upon his back, and whilst the rest of the Blackwatch wore daggers in their belts, he still bore the same weapon that had claimed many Albion soldiers' lives. Its hilt rose from its place against his right shoulder, the pommel wrapped in black leather banded with well-worn gold.

'Started travelling with a pack, have you, Bandermain? You must be getting old.'

Celador Bandermain was taller and older than Silas, and had often proven himself to be a master strategist with the strength and stamina of a bull. The last time Silas had seen him, he had commanded more than half the Continental army. He was an accomplished fighter and his strength had matched Silas's own whenever they had met in battle. But that was in another life, before Silas's spirit had been torn away. A lot had changed since that day.

'I always knew I would be the one to bring you down,' said Bandermain. 'I was right.'

Light flooded his face, casting thick shadows across deeply set eyes which gave away nothing of the thoughts that lay behind them. He was wearing the long red coat of a high-ranking member of the Blackwatch, and many strangers might have thought him handsome at first glance, but there was an edge of danger to his appearance – an edge worn only by people who had killed and loved to kill. It was a trace of darkness that could only be sensed by another killer, or by his victims in the fatal moment when they realised they had become his prey.

'I thought you would be long dead by now,' said Silas, using his lungs as little as possible. 'Isn't that what normally happens to officers who let the enemy walk free from their lands?'

'That was a long time ago,' said Bandermain. 'I have learned from my mistakes. I have regained the trust of my leaders many times over, while you, so I hear, have recently lost the trust of yours. Treachery. I never would have expected that from you.'

Silas kept his eyes upon Bandermain, but said nothing.

'I have heard many rumours about you since you were last here,' said Bandermain. 'Now I can see that at least some of them are true. Bridges fall. People beneath them die. Every one of them. Every one . . . except for you.'

'Strong bones,' said Silas. 'Hard head.'

'I do not think so. We are not as ignorant as your people like to think we are on this side of the sea,' said Bandermain. 'We know about the veil, and we know what your High Council plans to do with it.' He signalled to one of his men, who stepped forward and unrolled one of Albion's newsposters for Silas to read. It was a recent copy, less than a week old, but the main story was one that had been repeated over and over again for many years. 'What do you have to tell me about this?'

War To End
New Strategies Set Into Place.
Continent To Feel Might Of Scientific Advances.
Albion On The Attack!

Silas coughed a mocking laugh. 'You believe that?' he said. 'How many of those have you intercepted? One? Maybe two? *This* is what you are afraid of? I used to look forward to facing you in battle, Celador. Now . . . I just pity you.'

Bandermain's fingers twitched, but Silas knew he would not attack a prisoner, not one who could be useful to him. Despite the company he kept these days, Bandermain was no fool.

On any other night not even the Blackwatch would have stood a chance against Silas, but something had changed, and Bandermain was being far too confident considering the bloodied state Silas had left him in the last time they had met. A pale scar was still clearly visible along Bandermain's jaw, one that had been given to him by Silas's blade. Silas had shown him mercy that day. He did not intend to do so again.

'I know what you have become,' said Bandermain. 'I ordered my men to prepare for a long hunt. Capturing you was meant to be a challenge for them. Yet here you sit, proving yourself to be no more of a threat to us than a fish in a net. I find that interesting, if not a little disappointing.'

'You know nothing about me.'

'I know that you can heal without medicine. Fight and not tire. And tonight I saw you stay underwater longer than any man alive.'

'That would be a very interesting trick,' said Silas. 'But as you can see, you cannot believe everything you hear from across the water.'

'You do not sound like a man who is in pain.'

'I have had practice.'

'I am sure that is true,' said Bandermain. 'There are people who would be very interested in acquiring you. You are a legend, my friend. Children talk about you in the streets. They play games and take turns to be the one who vanquishes Silas Dane, the "mighty soldier from the west".'

'I have no interest in your country's young,' said Silas. 'Is that where the Blackwatch gather their information these days? From children in the streets?'

'You would be surprised just how far my spies have reached,' said Bandermain. 'As things stand, it would be seen as a service to both our countries if I were to kill you right here in this room, but after tonight I think we both know that is not as easy as it appears to be.'

Silas felt his broken fingers begin to crack and click back into place. The bones racked with pain as they re-joined, but he tried not to draw attention to his returning strength. 'The boy in the boat,' he asked. 'Was he one of yours?'

'No,' said Bandermain. 'He knows as little about lens lights as you do, but his clumsy signal was enough to attract our attention. He thought that turning you over to us might earn him mercy. That choice was all that saved his life. You should have kept a closer eye on your shipmates, Silas. The captain in particular. We all knew you would leave Albion eventually, and my men were ready to find you when you did. I have had people watching you for a lot longer than you think.'

'I'm sure you have,' said Silas. 'I, however, have had no one watching you. You are not that interesting. In fact, my men and I haven't given you a thought for years. We have had far more important things to do.'

Bandermain stood tall, failing to hide the anger simmering behind his eyes. 'Important things like treachery? Murder? Betrayal?' he said. 'My contacts tell me you have had dealings with witches. You have protected them, given up your good name to help them. What did they give you in return?'

'I have protected no one,' said Silas.

'Yet on the Night of Souls, "Silas Dane, grand champion of Albion's warden army" turned on his own. The city square of your capital ran red with blood. Isn't that how your council's historians are telling it? There was a time when I would not have believed such stories. You betrayed your High Council, killed your own men and murdered the woman you had sworn to protect, all to save one Skilled girl you had been sent out to hunt. That is not the Silas Dane I remember. The enemy I knew valued honour above all else. He would not have turned against his oath without good reason. If his council had asked it of him, he would have slit that girl's throat and let her veins bleed dry. Instead, you chose a different path. It was fine work, I'll admit, but you left yourself open, Silas. It got my attention.' Bandermain stepped back and nodded to the guard holding the newsposter. 'Show him.'

The guard rolled up the first poster and unfurled a second smaller page. Silas knew what it was right away. The paper was rough and yellow, cheaply made. Servants would have sat in their dozens making copy after copy and distributing them across Albion for as many people as possible to see. It was a wanted poster. He knew it even before he saw the ink, but when the guard turned it his way he was surprised by the face drawn upon it. A young girl with long black hair and cat-like eyes. Unmistakable.

'I see that you know her,' said Bandermain. 'She is the girl you were protecting. Isn't she?'

Silas said nothing.

'Miss Kate Winters. Daughter of Jonathan and Anna Winters. Last Skilled member of the Winters bloodline. This girl was your ally. You killed for her and committed treachery for her. Which leaves us with the question . . . why did you leave her in Fume to die?'

Silas looked directly into Bandermain's eyes, letting the deadness of his soul connect with the fire in the heart of his enemy. 'I did nothing for the girl,' he said. 'She is of no interest to me.'

'Yet she interests so many others. You knew that when you left her behind. Did you warn her before you turned and ran?' Bandermain placed his hands on either side of Silas's chair, close enough for Silas to smell the scent of meat upon his breath. 'Did you tell her that she would be hunted down like an animal in the street? Because I would very much like to make that promise a reality. I know that she has something to do with you and your . . . condition. I know she is hidden somewhere within Fume, but she will be of no use to me dead.'

'I do not care what you want,' Silas said coolly. 'The girl seems very much alive to me.'

'Your little trick in the city square as good as painted a target upon her back,' said Bandermain. 'My men are closing in upon her as we speak. They will find her.'

It was no surprise to Silas that Bandermain had risen so quickly through the ranks of the Blackwatch. He was by far the Continent's most adept and devious liar, but there, in that room, he was not adept enough. 'You don't know where she is,' said Silas.

'Then why don't you save us the time of a prolonged hunt and enlighten us? A lot less blood will be spilt that way. I do not want Blackwatch swords tainted by Albion blood any more than necessary.'

'Why are you asking me?' said Silas. ' "The echo of every word spoken leads to the ears of the Watch." Isn't that what your people believe? You have ears everywhere. Hear everything. Or are you saying they are wrong? Have things changed since you were put in charge? Your men should have the ear of the highest leaders in your land. Instead they lurk around smugglers' holes, threatening slave boys and getting themselves killed by enemies they really shouldn't have challenged in the first place.'

Bandermain leaned closer, his face red with anger, and Silas took his chance. He twisted his right arm free from the ropes and grabbed his enemy's throat, squeezing it tight. Bandermain did not react, but the Blackwatch fell upon Silas at once, and even though his strength had not fully returned it still took four men to free his hand and tie his arm back to the chair. Bandermain stood his ground as Silas was restrained again, a wide bruise blossoming across his neck. He did not seem surprised. Instead, he looked down at Silas with a sinister expression of victory.

'Good,' he said, rubbing his throat. 'Very good. And here I was beginning to think you were going to disappoint me.'

Silas's injured shoulder felt as if spikes were being driven deep into the muscle with every movement, but he smiled menacingly, daring Bandermain to come close again.

'We are finished here,' said Bandermain. He turned his back and walked to the door with his men following after him.

'You won't find her,' said Silas.

Bandermain stopped on the threshold and looked back. 'We will,' he said. 'If the fools you have left her with do not kill her first.'

The Blackwatch filed out and Bandermain's sharp coughs echoed from the walls as they walked away. The lock clicked behind them and Silas was left alone.

Kate did not bother trying to sleep. Once Baltin had gone she slid a small package out of a special pocket she had sewn inside her coat, and unfolding a neatly arranged wrap of black cloth she uncovered a book bound in old purple leather. If Baltin knew she had that book he would have taken it away from her at once. It was as thick as her fist, and her fingertips tingled with cold as she touched the silver lettering on its cover.

Wintercraft

Wintercraft was one of the rarest and most dangerous books in Albion. Within its pages was the life's work of a group of Walkers who had lived centuries before Kate was born – people who could enter the veil, just like her – along with the many experiments they had conducted into what they found on the other side. The Skilled did not like the practice of Wintercraft. They saw the veil as something to be studied, not entered and experimented upon, and Kate had witnessed the damage that the knowledge within this book could do for herself. It had almost cost Kate her life on the Night of Souls, and it had endangered the lives of hundreds of people who had seen it put to work within the city square, but *Wintercraft* was a part of her. She had to protect it.

Many of its pages had been written by Kate's own ancestors, and her parents had died trying to protect it from the High Council when she was just five years old. The book held answers that the Skilled were unable to give her about what it meant to be a Walker, and even though parts of it were difficult to understand it had become a comfort to her. Only Edgar knew that she still had it. With nothing else to do in that place, she wrapped herself in the bed blanket and began to read.

The hours snailed by, and Kate found herself dozing over the open pages, dreaming of shades, listening circles and wardens. Her mind wandered back to the time she had spent with Silas, to the faces of the people he had killed and the souls of the people he had helped her to set free, and the memory of it jolted her awake. She scrambled out of her blankets, reached for the security of her candle and lit a second one from a box on the room's curving shelf, just in case the first flame went out. The shades had gone and she had already put out the other lights, not liking the shapes they cast up the walls. A scar on her left arm stung a little; a thin line left from a cut made weeks ago when Silas had stolen her blood. 'Silas,' she whispered to herself.

Then the scratching sounds started. *Krrrr . . . krrrr . . . krrrr . . .* It sounded as if something was trying to claw its way into the room.

Suddenly two candles were nowhere near enough. Kate dragged the candle box from the shelf and held handfuls of them against the open flames, dripping a trail of wax on to the floor beside her bed and standing the candles up in it one by one. She held one in front of her, trying to pinpoint the sound, but it seemed to be coming from everywhere at once. Then she pressed her hand against the door and tiny vibrations thrummed against her fingers. Someone was outside, trying to scrape their way in.

The scratching stopped and she crouched in front of the door, peering out through the middle keyhole. She heard something snap and something metallic rang out against the lock and skidded off across the cavern floor. Someone swore under their breath and Kate pulled back as a metal wire stabbed through the keyhole, dangerously close to her eye. 'Who's out there?' she asked, but no one answered. She moved to the upper lock, hoping to get a look at her visitor's face, but all she could see was a mess of black hair bent forward as its owner concentrated on his work.

Kate tugged her sleeve down over her right hand and waited by the middle lock for her moment to strike. When the wire poked through again, she snatched at the hooked end and pulled hard. The wire threaded straight through the door and when Kate looked through the keyhole, Edgar's eye was looking back.

'What are you doing?' he demanded.

'What are *you* doing?'

'Getting you out of there.'

'It sounds as if you're trying to wake the whole cavern,' said Kate. 'Just leave me alone. I'm fine where I am.'

'Leave you alone? In there? Of course. Why didn't I think of that? I'm sure you're having a great time sitting in the dark.'

'I was asleep actually,' she lied.

'Glad you're having fun.'

'Go away. Before someone sees you.'

'Give back my wire.'

'No.'

'Kate, come on. I'm trying to help.'

'I don't need your help.'

Edgar fell quiet. 'I've got it all planned out,' he said at last. 'We can get out of here. Find our way to the surface. I've even got supplies.'

'No.'

'Just think about this for a second.'

'I have thought about it,' said Kate. 'Baltin was right. I don't trust myself. Weird things keep happening around me, and I don't want you to be caught up in it again. Maybe I am better off in here. Go and find your brother. Take him up to the surface if you want to. I'm staying here.'

'No you're not,' said Edgar, walking away a few steps before coming back. 'You think I need lockpicks to get you out? Well, I don't. Baltin has the keys. Maybe I'll just borrow them for a while.'

'You can't do that. You'll get caught.'

'And what? End up in there with you? It sounds like it's all honey and roses from what you're saying. Why should I be bothered about that? I'm getting that key and then I'm coming right back here, whether you want to be let out or not.'

'Edgar, don't. Edgar!'

Edgar bolted across the cavern. The lights were still dimmed and the only people about were the two watchmen posted at the cavern's only two ways out. He crept along the street, glanced over at the main door and saw a guard sitting with his back to the wall, eating sandwiches and reading newsposters smuggled down from the City Above. Just one minute and he could be in and out of Baltin's house, keys in hand. No one would be any the wiser until it was too late. He and Kate would be long gone. He thought about his brother Tom. Tom had fitted in well with the Skilled. He had even shown some small ability to see into the veil. They were pleased with him, and he liked living there. Tom might miss Edgar for a while, but he was in the safest place he could be. Kate, however, was not.

Edgar made his decision. He crossed the main street, found one of Baltin's windows unlocked, and slithered his way in.

5

Crossed Daggers

Kate paced around her room, waiting for Edgar to return.

At last a key scratched in the first door lock. One by one the locks turned and Kate stood in front of the door with her arms folded as it was pushed open. But the person on the other side was not Edgar. It was Baltin, wearing red pyjamas and a dressing gown and holding on to the doorframe for support. He looked tired. His face was an odd sickly green.

'Baltin?'

Edgar was there, holding a lantern a few steps away, and he shrugged his shoulders apologetically.

'Miss Winters.' Baltin bowed his head slightly and strode into the room. The bed sagged as he sat down on it. 'Close the door,' he ordered as Edgar followed him inside. 'Close it, boy!'

The door could not be locked from the inside, so Edgar stood with his back pressed against it instead.

'What's happening?' asked Kate.

Baltin shifted his weight on the edge of the bed, and sat there with his head in his hands.

'I found him tied up in his house,' said Edgar. 'He won't say who did it. He told me to bring him straight here. He didn't even call the guards.'

'Because the *guards* will be of no use to us,' snapped Baltin. 'An enemy is loose in this cavern, and I think Kate knows who it is.'

Kate thought at once of Silas, but that was impossible. There was no way he would risk coming back to Fume with the wardens out looking for him.

'The veil has pulled away from us,' said Baltin. 'I can't see into it any more. Can you?'

Kate could sense the veil all around her, waiting just beyond the reach of her ordinary senses. Nothing had changed so far as she could tell, but if Baltin thought there was something wrong it was best for her to play along. She shook her head.

'This is worse than I thought,' said Baltin. 'You have to talk to him, Kate. You have to stop him. Whatever he's doing. He has to stop.'

'Who?'

'Silas Dane.'

'You saw Silas?' Kate asked. 'Here?'

'Who else could have attacked me?'

'Silas wouldn't do this,' said Kate. 'Not here. He wouldn't risk being seen.'

'He's done a lot worse,' said Edgar.

'But why Baltin? And why bother tying him up? Silas wouldn't do that. It wouldn't serve any purpose. It can't be him.'

'No one else knows how to find this cavern. He's the only one who . . .' Baltin's voice tailed off, and he looked anxiously around the shadowed room. 'He's already in here, isn't he?'

'You have the only key to that door,' said Kate. 'There's no one else in here.'

'You're lying,' said Baltin. 'You're protecting him. Why is he here? What does he want?'

Kate grabbed a lit candle and circuited the room, lighting up every space the flame could reach. 'See?' she said. 'No one's here.'

'Then he is still outside. You brought him here. I have to warn people. Get out of my way!' Baltin pushed Edgar aside and peered out of the top keyhole. 'It's too late,' he whispered.

Kate stepped forward and looked out for herself. From the lowest keyhole she could see right down to the illuminated archway of the meeting hall. There was no one out there. Everything was quiet. But when she looked out of the one Baltin had used, it was blocked and black.

'He's right outside,' whispered Baltin.

'No one is out there,' said Kate. 'There's something stuck on the door, that's all.' She did not stop to think about what that something might be as she opened the door, ignoring Baltin's protests, and peered round it. A large piece of black-edged paper had been pinned over the lock, and she noticed at least a dozen others spread around the cavern. Most of them were scattered loose on the floor, but a handful had been pinned to a few doors. She pulled the paper down as Edgar joined her outside.

'What is it?' he asked. 'What does it say?'

Kate looked at the blood-red letters scrawled thickly on the page.

You have our demands.
Deliver what we require.

There was a mark printed at the top of the page – a pair of crossed daggers with two letters underneath. *BW*.

'It has to be the wardens,' said Kate. 'What does BW mean?'

But Edgar was already gone. He was back inside the lockhouse, stopping Baltin from leaving the room. 'The person who attacked you,' he said. 'Did he say anything?'

'Move aside, boy.'

'Did he give any names? Anything?'

'The veil has drawn back,' said Baltin, looking at Edgar as if he was losing his mind. 'Silas Dane is responsible for this, and he will be stopped. Nothing else matters now.'

'No. This is nothing to do with Silas,' said Edgar.

'And how do you know that?'

'Because of this.' Edgar stabbed a finger into the mark on the poster. 'Haven't you heard of the Blackwatch before?'

'I don't have time to listen to this,' said Baltin. 'We all know what is going on here.'

'You have to listen! When I worked for the High Council people would find posters like these outside the council chambers every few months. The Blackwatch are part of the Continental army. The person who attacked you tonight was probably a runner. The Blackwatch send them to Albion now and again to remind the High Council that they can send assassins to their door at any time and to let them know that the Continent is not just going to go away. Sometimes they bring demands, other times they just spread their posters and go. The wardens used to do a good job of covering it up whenever there was a runner in town, but I've never heard of one being sent into the City Below before.'

Baltin pointed to the poster in Kate's hands. 'So the man who left this . . .'

'Was just the messenger,' said Edgar. 'You don't want to be on the wrong side of these people. If you think the wardens are bad, trust me, the Blackwatch are worse.'

'But how did the runner get in here?' asked Kate.

'Probably broke his way in. His orders will be to spread the same message all around the City Below,' said Edgar. 'I'll bet he doesn't even know that the Skilled live in this cavern. If he did, I don't think he would have just upped and left so easily.'

Baltin pushed past Edgar and snatched the poster from Kate. 'That makes no sense,' he said. 'If these "Blackwatch" are looking for something, why leave this? Why not just sneak in and take whatever they want? Or just let the runner do it?'

'Because they're looking for something in particular and they don't know where it is,' said Edgar. 'They want to scare people into finding what they want for them and flushing it out into the open. Fume is much larger than most Continental cities. It would take forever to find something here. Add the City Below to that and you have months of searching on your hands. The Blackwatch want whatever it is quickly. They won't want to risk the wardens finding them before they have it.'

'But what do they want?' asked Baltin. 'They didn't

make any demands. They didn't ask me for anything.'

Edgar snatched another loose poster up off the cavern floor and pushed it into Baltin's hands. It was written in the same red ink as the first.

Deliver Kate Winters and be spared.

'It's you, Kate,' said Edgar, turning to her. 'They're coming for you.'

Kate should have been surprised, or at least a little worried. Instead she just shrugged her shoulders. 'Them and everyone else,' she said.

Baltin read the poster again. 'That's settled, then,' he said.

'What is?' asked Edgar.

'There have been arguments about how best to deal with Kate's unique position amongst us,' said Baltin. 'This just proves that she is even more of a threat than we first thought. Come back inside, both of you.'

Edgar stepped forward, but Kate held him back. 'No,' she said. 'We're not going in there with you. If the Blackwatch are looking for me, I'm not going to just sit in that room and wait for them to figure out where I am.'

'What I have to say cannot be heard by just anyone,' said Baltin. 'If more people knew what I know, they would not be so friendly towards you here.'

'Friendly? Every one of them hates me!'

'They do not know everything,' said Baltin. 'Come inside.'

'No.' Kate backed away and Baltin's face grew serious, any pretence of friendship fading at once. Kate felt the veil descending again and ghostly shapes moved behind

Baltin. She tried to ignore them, but seeing them there sent a familiar chill through her bones.

'Your uncle knew the dangers you might face if he brought you here,' said Baltin. 'But the consequences of leaving you out in the world, unwatched and untrained would have been far worse. He knew what had to be done, and I thought you were sensible enough to see it too.'

'I want to understand what's going on as much as anyone,' said Kate. 'I want to help.'

'You gave up your right to a free life the moment you started dabbling in things that were none of your concern,' said Baltin. 'You allied yourself with Silas Dane and you still expected to find friendship amongst us? The only reason you were not thrown out of this cavern the night you arrived was because of threats like *this*.' Baltin crumpled the Blackwatch poster in his fist. 'You are a threat to everything we have tried to protect for hundreds of years. The veil responds more to you than it does to any of us, and it is clear we are not the only ones who have recognised it. This is not just about you any more. Do you know what could happen if the Continental leaders got their hands on you? I would hand you over to the High Council myself before I would live to see that day.'

'Hold on,' said Edgar. 'That's a bit steep, isn't it?'

'If we had recognised Kate's ability when she was younger, things might have been different. As it is, her mind has been opened to the veil without proper training or care. With ancestry like hers that is disastrous. When we thought Kate had not interited her parents' Skill, we were relieved. The Winters family's abilities are legendary.

As Walkers, their spirits can enter the veil directly, but their link can become so strong that they do not just step into it, they *attract* it. If their spirit is powerful enough, the veil can become unstable around them, and bleed freely into the living world. When that happens, just being close to them can send the souls of people around them into death.'

'You think Kate can kill people, just by standing next to them?'

'Given the right conditions, yes,' said Baltin. 'It has happened before. The Skilled have tried to prevent the Winters blood from being passed on for generations. Now Kate is the only Skilled Winters left. Exposing her mind to the veil unprotected was like pouring oil on a flame. Silas Dane ignited something inside Kate that will never stop burning. If she is not controlled, she could well be the death of us all.' Baltine turned to Kate. 'Why do you think Artemis never told you the truth about your family? He knew this could happen. Silas Dane ruined you, Kate. He made you dangerous and uncontrollable, just like him. It amazes me that you do not see that.'

'I know what I can see,' said Edgar, trying his best not to look as unnerved as he felt. 'You're scared.'

'Of course I'm scared. I'm scared for all of us,' said Baltin. 'You might not have seen what Kate really is, but we are not fools. We know the signs. The silver in her eyes, the way the veil changes when she is nearby. We know what she is. Kate's kind can be dangerous as much for what they don't know as for what they do. All it takes is one mistake and people will die, just like Mina.'

'Mina was stabbed,' said Edgar. 'The veil had nothing to do with it.'

'If Kate were allowed to explore her abilities and develop them, she would eventually *use* them,' said Baltin. 'That must not happen. If she is kept in the dark there is at least a chance that the veil will draw back from her permanently. Her link with it may simply . . . wear off.'

'Wear off?' said Kate. 'That is what you're all hoping for?'

'If it doesn't, people like these Blackwatch will keep hunting you,' said Baltin. 'They will force you to influence the veil in the way they want and that will put us all in danger. You could be a brutal weapon. We cannot let that happen.'

'So, I'm meant to stay down here in that room until I'm "cured". That's what you're saying?'

'I wish it was,' said Baltin. 'This attack changes things. We do not have time to wait any more.'

He moved before Kate realised what was happening. Ducking behind her, he pressed a short blade up against her throat.

'What are you doing?' Edgar demanded.

'Making sure I have your attention. I never wanted it to come to this, but I have a responsibility. I have to do what's right. Now, step inside.'

Edgar did not move. Baltin's hand was shaking, the blade brushing against Kate's skin. He did not look like the kind of man who had hurt anyone before, but he was nervous enough to make a mistake and cut her without meaning to if things got out of hand.

'All right,' said Edgar. 'Let her go.'

'Get inside!'

Edgar raised his hands and started to walk. 'What are you going to do?' he asked.

'What someone should have done weeks ago.'

'Does Artemis know about this?'

'Move!'

'He doesn't, does he?'

'I said move!' Baltin pointed the dagger at Edgar in anger, and Kate got away from him as soon as the weapon left her skin.

Baltin faltered, not knowing what to do, or whom to threaten next. Edgar threw himself at him and tackled him to the floor, pinning him on his side and forcing him to stay still as Kate prised the dagger from his fingers.

'*Guar*—' Baltin tried to shout for help, but the struggle had stirred dirt up from the floor and he choked on it, his shout becoming a hacking cough.

'Is he all right?' asked Kate.

'He's fine. Help me put him in the room.'

'Wait,' Baltin wheezed as the two of them took an arm each and dragged him along. 'Think about what you're doing.'

'I've thought about it,' said Edgar, lifting a bunch of keys from the pocket of Baltin's dressing gown. 'You attacked us. We defended ourselves. Sounds fair enough to me.'

'Kate can't leave this cavern. She can't!'

Edgar closed the door, sealing Baltin inside.

'You don't understand!' Baltin's fist hammered on the other side of the door and Edgar left the key hanging in the middle lock.

Kate looked in through the upper keyhole. 'You turned Artemis against me,' she said. 'What did you say to him?'

Baltin's eye appeared at the lock. 'I told him the truth,' he said. 'He did not believe it at first until we showed him what we knew. But Artemis is a logical man. He could not deny what he had seen with his own eyes.'

'What did you show him?' asked Kate.

'We showed him the veil,' said Baltin. 'We gave him proof. He knows that you are not a simple girl any longer. He know how dangerous you will become.'

'Why didn't you show me this?'

'Because the veil would never show you what we can see,' said Baltin. 'You cannot witness your own future, Kate. We can.'

'Don't listen to him,' said Edgar. 'We can go, right now, before anyone realises he is gone.'

'What did you see?' asked Kate.

'We know you can never leave this cavern,' said Baltin. 'We cannot protect you if you do. We gave you a chance, Kate. If you run now, we will have no choice but to hunt you down, for your own safety and to protect the future of Albion.'

'Why?'

'I cannot tell you that.'

'You were going to kill me.'

'I was willing to do what must be done.'

'I will never trust any of the Skilled again,' said Kate. 'I don't know what you saw in my future, but I know I won't be spending it here, however long it lasts. Goodbye, Baltin. Tell Artemis he'll never have to worry about "protecting" me again.'

'Wait!' Baltin shouted as Kate turned away from the lockhouse. 'Guards!'

Kate kept her eyes straight ahead, walking along a street she had once thought was safe, not wanting Edgar to see the tears on her face. 'There is no place for me here,' she

71

said. 'They can keep the veil and Artemis to themselves. I don't want anything to do with them any more.'

She could hear the dull thuds of Baltin's fists hammering on the inside of the lockhouse door as she and Edgar hurried away. It wouldn't be long before one of the guards heard him, and when they found him locked inside and their only prisoner missing there would be no convincing them that she was not a threat. Any safety that had existed in that place was gone now.

'Are you serious about leaving Artemis behind?' asked Edgar, following Kate along a path between two houses and emerging in a small rock garden on the other side.

'He'll turn me over to them the moment he sees me,' said Kate. 'And you can't come either. What about Tom?'

'He likes it here,' said Edgar. 'He'll be safe enough. And I'm not letting you go out there alone.'

Kate did not say anything. No words would be enough to say how grateful she was to have at least one person left whom she could trust. Edgar hoisted his bag on to his shoulder and Kate hurried along with her head down as the guards' warning bell sounded behind them.

'They've found him,' said Edgar. 'Let's go.'

6

Allegiance

When the Blackwatch had gone Silas tried to free himself from his chair, but his body had other ideas. Going for Bandermain's throat had hurt him more than he wanted to admit. His muscles screamed out whenever he tried to move them and his broken bones grated together, forcing him to stay still. He should have been able to loosen his ropes and break his way out of that place easily. Instead he was stuck to the chair like an animal caught in a trap.

The room he was in was an ordinary cellar. The floor was thick with decades' worth of coal dust and dirt but there were clear spaces round the edge of the floor where boxes or old pieces of furniture had been sitting until recently. Bandermain's men must have emptied it in a hurry, and it was clearly not meant for holding someone securely.

For years, the worst fate for any soldier of the Albion army was thought to be finding themselves in the hands of the Blackwatch. He had heard stories about the mistreatment of prisoners under Blackwatch guard during past campaigns into Continental territory, and had known dozens of men who had been taken by their agents. Only two of them ever found their way back, carrying gruesome stories that helped to make the Blackwatch legendary among those who were sent out to face them.

Silas was not worried for himself – the Blackwatch were no threat to him – but he was concerned about what they planned to do with Kate. If the Continental leaders finally got their hands on a powerful member of the Skilled it could turn the tide of the war spectacularly against Albion. They knew Kate's name. They wanted mastery of the veil and now they knew exactly whom to hunt to get it. What greater prize could Bandermain present to his masters than a girl able to demonstrate the power of the veil and a traitor to Albion who could not die? The Blackwatch would not stop until they had what they set out to collect. Trouble was heading into the heart of Albion, and Kate was going to be right in the middle of it.

Silas tried to reach out for the veil, but again he felt nothing. Kate was a weapon just waiting to be found and he could not do anything to help Albion so long as he was tied up in someone's worthless cellar.

Blackwatch voices filtered down from the room above. A door slammed shut and Silas could hear harsh coughs and a conversation unfolding through the floorboards overhead. Bandermain and his men were close by. He stayed still and listened.

'Send in more men,' said Bandermain. 'Call them back from border patrols. Use the ship and tell them not to return until they have the girl in custody. We are close enough to the attack to risk a few lives. Concentrate our efforts upon the capital, but do not neglect the northern cities. Send men everywhere we have the manpower to reach and make sure all agents are aware of their responsibilities well ahead of time.'

'They have already been informed,' said another voice.

'Have they found their way into Fume's understreets?'

'All entrances to the City Below are being monitored, sir. Runners have been sent down into the tunnels, but our agents are holding back until the posters are distributed, as ordered. If our intelligence is correct, we should have control of the main gathering points by dusk tomorrow.'

' "Should" is not good enough,' said Bandermain. 'Those people live underground like ants. They will put up no significant resistance. I want to know the moment we have those gathering points.'

'Yes, sir. There are birds in flight as we speak. We are expecting fresh reports very soon.'

'Good work,' said Bandermain. 'Keep me informed.'

The situation was worse than Silas had realised. The Blackwatch were not just interested in acquiring Kate. Her capture was simply the first stage of a much larger plan. An invasion. He had to act. If he could do nothing else, he could at least try to slow them down.

'You. Outside,' he said loudly.

The cellar door opened and two Blackwatch officers who had been standing guard came in.

'Bring Bandermain in here,' he said. 'Tell him I am ready to talk.'

Bandermain took his time answering the summons and when he finally returned he came alone. 'I am here,' he said. 'So talk.'

'How does it feel?' asked Silas. 'To be the one who captured me? Think of the glory that will be yours when you present me to your leaders.'

A flicker of pride crossed Bandermain's face. There it was, thought Silas. There was the adversary he knew so well.

'You and I both know that our leaders are more concerned with outdoing one another than with bringing an end to this war,' said Bandermain. 'I have no interest in earning the praise of fools any longer. There are greater battles to fight, and you are far more valuable to me than you could ever be to them. They would parade you through our towns in an iron cage and invite children to spit at you through the bars. You would be the freak of Albion, captured and weak. I have more respect for you than that.'

'I can see that,' said Silas. 'Not many people have enough respect to crush me with a bridge. Perhaps I will return that "respect" to you one day.'

Bandermain smiled. 'In normal circumstances, I doubt even a bridge would have been enough to stop you,' he said. 'I have learned that you are unusually weakened here. The veil does not favour my country as powerfully as it does your own. While you are here, you are disconnected from it, and whatever abilities you have acquired clearly rely upon the veil for their strength. You have left your home at a dangerous time, Silas. Albion's connection to the veil is not what it once was. The veil is falling. The link your country has enjoyed for so long is decaying as we speak. You may not be able to hear your little spirit voices here, on my land, but imagine what will happen when the whole of Albion is plunged into the half-life. Your people will no longer be able to tell the difference between the living and the dead. Spirits will walk the land for every living soul to see. There will be chaos. Your people will fall into madness and turn upon each other. Albion will die, and the Blackwatch will be there watching while your country's arrogance brings about its destruction.'

'You know nothing about the half-life,' said Silas.

'You would be surprised,' said Bandermain. 'It is interesting what you learn when you have the right friends. If you have knowledge that can be of use to me, I suggest you share it with me now, while my patience lasts.'

Silas considered his options. Bandermain had always been sceptical of the veil. He had called those who believed in it 'fools' and 'witches', but now he was talking about the veil's falling as some kind of inevitable event rather than an irrational fear or a fantasy. He had to know more. He had to earn Bandermain's trust, and to do that he had to give him what he wanted. He had to make a sacrifice. 'I know where Kate Winters is,' he said.

'Where?'

'Somewhere your men will never find her. At least not on their own. If you want her, you will tell me exactly what is going on here. No lies.' Silas sat back in his chair, sending a stab of pain needling along his spine. 'Now, are we going to talk?'

'You are in no position to make demands.'

'I think I am in an excellent position,' said Silas. 'I have information you need. Tell me why you want her, and she is yours.'

Silas's face was unreadable, and as his demeanour changed so did the atmosphere in the room. He did not need the veil to affect the environment he was in, and the threat from his words spread around the room like smoke, making it feel small and airless, as cold as a place cut deep underground. Bandermain reacted to the change at once. His eyes narrowed briefly. Fear, Silas knew, was a powerful weapon. 'I did not need the veil to incapacitate your men,' he said. 'I did not need it to lead them across Grale on a chase through the night, and I will not need it to put an end to your life when the time comes.'

'You cannot even stand up on your own,' said Bandermain. 'And even if you could, killing me would not help the girl.'

'I do not doubt that,' said Silas. 'You are not that important, Celador. Your men are sworn to obey the orders of the Continental leaders, but I doubt even they would waste so many of you scouting along the coast just in case one enemy were to swim ashore. You have already admitted that your goals are no longer the same as theirs, and you are not known for your ability to think for yourself. You are the sword, not the hand that wields it. You are a man who takes orders, which means that someone else sent you here. Who was it?'

'Where is the girl?'

'I think I am not the only traitor in this room,' said Silas. 'Your men will see it too before long.'

'My men know exactly why we are here,' said Bandermain. 'They are loyal men. Loyal to me, and to our country. We know what we must do, even if our leaders do not.'

'Kidnapping a young girl,' said Silas. 'Since when have the Blackwatch begun hunting the innocent?'

'She is not innocent. The Skilled are no more than a valuable resource to be found and exploited. They are

78

secretive and underhand and she is the only one left alive who has dared to show her face in public long enough to let her identity become known. She is wanted by your High Council yet she has no interest in helping them. She is affiliated to no one, and that makes her useful.'

'Useful to whom, exactly?'

Bandermain clenched his fists, and when he opened them again Silas caught a glimpse of his open palms. His left hand had a deep cut sliced across it, one that could only have been made by the slow cut of a sharp blade. The skin was healing slowly and someone had stitched it together neatly with thin black thread.

'What happened to your hand?'

'War is bloody. Or have you hidden away from it for so long you have forgotten?'

'That is not a war wound.' Silas opened his own hand, revealing an old white scar that matched Bandermain's cut exactly. 'Who gave you that cut? Who are you working for, Celador?'

'Someone who hates Albion as much as I do,' said Bandermain. 'Someone who has a deep interest in you and your life, pitiful as it has become. You may enjoy living in the gutter like vermin while your country falls apart, but I still have a hand in influencing the direction of this war. Albion will die much sooner than you think, and my men and I shall be the ones to strike the final blow. I serve my country in my own way. *That* is honour. Perhaps you will recognise that before the end.'

Bandermain walked to the door and faltered in the doorway. One of his knees gave way and an officer stepped forward to support him, but he leaned against the doorframe and waved the man away.

'What's wrong with you?' asked Silas as a bone in his own neck snapped back into place. 'Old wounds giving you trouble?'

Bandermain ignored him and gave an order to his men. 'Have the carriage prepared,' he said. 'We are leaving now.'

'Yes, sir.'

'I have been told that your injuries are likely to heal within a matter of hours,' he said, turning to Silas. 'You will tell me what I need to know long before then.'

'You still have not told me why you want the girl,' said Silas. 'It is a simple enough question.'

'You will find out once we have her,' said Bandermain. 'In the meantime, there is someone who is very interested in meeting you. Where we are going, you will be made to talk. You are going to help us win this battle, Silas. Your time is over. Albion will fall and you will watch it burn. You can be sure of that.'

Bandermain left the room, and the moment the lock clicked into place Silas fought against his bonds and studied his surroundings again, determined to find a way out. Three of the walls were plain slabs of solid brick, but the fourth had a patch halfway between the floor and ceiling that was partly boarded with wooden slats. Now the sun was rising higher he could see tiny flecks of light seeping from the other side, cutting through the dark. He cursed out loud as his broken ankle realigned with a sickening crack. He tested it carefully. The bone was still knitting together, but it was strong enough to stand on. One of his arms was still useless, and his right leg was still heavily bruised, not nearly ready to mount an escape. One arm and one leg would have to be enough to get him over to those boards.

Silas twisted his wrist out of its bonds and freed his left hand, delicately sliding the useless arm between the buttons of his coat to keep it still. He wrenched the ropes round his ankles loose and pushed himself up, forcing his crushed thigh muscles to work. There were times when he had cursed the veil and hated it for healing his body and prolonging his life; now it was all but gone he found himself willing it back. The last thing he wanted was for his knees to give way and to have Bandermain find him crawling around on the floor.

Silas turned the chair and used the back of it to help him limp over to the boards. Every step was an effort, but he could smell fresh air on the other side. He pulled one of the boards away and looked into a narrow space that slanted upwards towards strips of sunlight caught behind what looked like a small wooden hatch. He pulled more boards from their nails until the entire opening was exposed and looked up along an old coal shaft.

The building was silent. There was no sign of any Blackwatch close by, but there was no way he could climb that shaft with a damaged shoulder. At least that was something he could fix for himself. He slid his left arm gently from its support, gritted his teeth and slammed his shoulder hard into the wall. The bone jolted back into its socket with a sickening thud, his shoulder muscles exploded and he growled with pain, grinding his healed fist into the stones as he waited for it to subside.

The coal shaft was cluttered with dead leaves and litter that had blown through the cracks in its upper hatch over many years. As soon as he was able, Silas squeezed into the shaft, sliding along on his side and pushing with his good leg until he was clear of the cellar. The walls and floor were filthy, but he had enough of a grip to make it all the way to the top, only to find that the wooden hatch was locked and its catch was rusted shut. He held on to the wall, twisted himself round and raised his good knee, aiming straight for the lock. One kick and the door shattered outwards, exploding into the cold light of mid-morning. No guards came running, so Silas dragged himself out, legs first, into the middle of a quiet alleyway. His crow was waiting for him, looking down from the windowsill of a building close by. 'Making yourself useful, I see,' said Silas.

The crow flew down but he batted it away. 'Keep watch,' he said. 'Stay high. Do not let anybody see you.'

The crow obeyed and soared up high above the roof-tops. There was no sign of the Blackwatch, so Silas used the wall to support himself as he made his way slowly down the alley. Every step was a torture, but he kept going. He needed somewhere to rest and heal. Four streets away he found it.

The Blackwatch's house was built in a quiet part of Grale, and Silas found it easy enough to stay out of sight whenever someone threatened to walk his way. The crow stood out against the grey clouds, circling high above a fenced-in patch of frozen grass. Iron gates hung ajar within the tall black fence, and beyond the gate Silas saw the pale grey shapes of headstones set into the ground. He pushed through into the silence of a large cemetery, left the overgrown path and headed straight across the graves towards a circle of old crypts gathered round a central point where four paths met.

None of the crypts was locked, since no one on the Continent would dare desecrate the resting places of the dead, but the door he chose was stiff and the hinges screeched as he scraped it aside, revealing a small flight of steps leading down into an airless space thick with the smell of forgotten years. Silas summoned his crow down from the sky with a low whistle, scraped the door shut behind them and followed the steps down into the dark.

Sunlight streamed in through cracks in the forgotten roof and old stone coffins with heavy lids were lined up along the walls of the small cavern below. Spiders clung to every corner in webs that were old and thick, and the walls ran so far back into the earth that he could not see the end of them in the dim light. The crypt was quiet and peaceful. He sat down on the cold stone floor and his crow hopped down beside him. Even without the veil he could feel the eerie stillness of the place and it reminded him of home. 'Just a few hours,' he said, cracking his damaged elbow joint and pulling his sleeve up to inspect a vicious bruise that was blossoming all the way along his arm. He propped himself against one of the coffin platforms and sat facing the door, listening for any sign of the Blackwatch outside.

Slowly, the day darkened into a shivering evening. His injuries and his escape had drained him of what little energy he had left and, by the time the moon began to rise, Silas had fallen asleep, safe in the company of the dead.

7

Ashes & Stone

Kate and Edgar headed for the cavern's outer wall and followed it until they spotted a narrow door cut into the stone. The cavern's only clock chimed out the quarter-hour above the meeting hall and when it fell quiet Baltin's angry shouts echoed from the walls. People would start waking up soon, and Kate and Edgar did not want to be there when they did.

The cavern's rear door was rarely guarded. It led into an old section of the City Below that the Skilled did not often use, but it was always kept bolted and locked.

'My lockpick,' said Edgar, holding his hand out. 'Quick!'

'What? You mean this tatty bit of wire?' Kate dragged the wire she had taken from the lockhouse door out of her pocket and passed it to him. 'Can you open it with that?'

'Just stand back and watch a master at work.'

Edgar dug the wire into the keyhole as Kate slid back

the bolts. The mechanism inside was old and stiff, but the lock soon clicked and he swung the door open with a grin of pride. 'It's a lot easier when someone isn't dragging at it from the other side,' he said.

Lanterns emerged from the houses behind them. More shouts went up and Baltin's voice carried above the rest. 'Sound the alarm!' he ordered. 'Find her!' Glancing back, Kate spotted him striding down the middle of the street, still in his dressing gown, with two of his men behind him.

'Kate,' said Edgar, already inside the tunnel. A row of dead lanterns were hooked on the wall and he lifted one down, struggling to open the glass case. 'Are you coming?'

Kate followed him into the blackness of the tunnel, but a handful of people were already heading their way. Kate closed the cavern door, leaving Edgar struggling to light matches in the dark. He held the lantern under his arm until at last one of them sparked and flared and he managed to light the stubby candle inside, flooding the space with light.

'Goodbye, Artemis,' Kate whispered to the door, before she turned her back on it and walked out into the dark.

Kate did not like the tunnels that made up the labyrinth that was the City Below. The last time she had walked through them she had been on her way to meet the Skilled, knowing that they would blame her for their leader's death. Turning to them had been her only option at the time. It was the only way to keep the people around her safe. Now she was heading into the tunnels with no idea where she was going or what she was going to do next.

The lantern cast shifting shadows on the walls and Kate tried to ignore the gentle whispers that travelled along the paths. If there were shades down here, they would be attracted to her presence. Without the protection of the Skilled's cavern, her spirit would shine like a beacon to the dead wandering these passageways and there was no way she could block them out.

Most of the tunnels were narrow and grim with only a rare light to break the suffocating stillness. Some were recently made, a hundred years ago or less, but most were ancient and a few of them had become unstable, their ceilings held up by wooden scaffolds that she and Edgar had to duck under as they went.

'So far, so good,' he said, choosing a direction with confidence whenever they came to a junction in the path, until they reached a point where five tunnels radiated out like a star, where he hesitated. 'I think . . . it's this way.'

'I thought you knew your way around,' said Kate.

'I used to,' said Edgar. 'The upper tunnels at least, but things have changed a bit since I was last down here. It's harder to know which way to go.'

'What about that one?' Kate pointed to a tunnel that was narrower than the rest. There were no old buildings sunk into its walls to suggest it had once been used as a street. The mouth of the tunnel was framed by a wooden doorframe and the floor was scattered with crunchy grit and earth, as if it had just been opened up recently.

'Why that way?' Something scratched behind them and Edgar spun, holding the lantern high. 'What was that?'

'Keep the light low,' said Kate, pulling his arm down.

'They're coming,' whispered Edgar.

Kate crept into the tunnel and felt her way along the walls. Edgar was not far behind her and his light cast her shadow along the ground ahead of her, making it difficult to see very far. After four weeks underground Kate's eyes had been given plenty of time to get used to the dark but she did not need to see the walls to know that there was something unusual about them. These stones had not always been bare. There were holes drilled into them at regular intervals. Holes that had once held something. Lantern hooks maybe?

'I don't like this,' whispered Edgar. 'This path doesn't lead up to the surface. Let's go back.'

Kate could sense the veil nearby, like a mist of energy crackling in the air. She could feel the presence of shades within the tunnel, lots of them, all reaching out to her, trying to get her attention. Their whispers spoke quietly in the walls, willing her along. She concentrated on where she was putting her feet. No matter where the tunnel led, anything had to be better than being back in the lockhouse.

'We're heading down, not up,' said Edgar.

'I know.'

'Then shouldn't we go back? Find another way?'

Kate's eyes fogged over, just for a second, and instead of blackness the tunnel suddenly appeared washed in a dull grey light. The stones glowed gently, as if they were lit from deep inside. She stopped walking. 'There's something down here,' she said.

'You saw something?'

'I'm not sure.'

'Is it something good or bad?'

'I don't know yet.'

'Is it the Skilled? Are they ahead of us?'

'I can't tell, can I, with you talking all the time?'

Edgar looked back the way they had come. There was no sign of anyone back there, and when Kate started walking without him he hurried to catch up. The movement of their bodies stirred up the stagnant air, raising thick breezes of dust from the floor.

'This is definitely not the way out,' he said.

Kate's eyes fogged over again, and this time the feeling did not lift. The link between the veil and the living world was stronger here than in other places she had been, as if something down here was attracting it. The tunnel became wider the further they went and she saw thin doors set into the sides of it, most of them cracked and hanging awkwardly from broken hinges.

Edgar shone the light into the space behind one of them. 'Someone has cleared these rooms out,' he said. 'There's nothing in there. We could hide in one.'

'No,' said Kate. 'We have to keep going.'

They kept walking, following the path to the very end where it stopped at a final dark red door. The handle had been smashed from its fixings and the door swung open easily against her hand. The two of them stepped inside and Edgar shone the lantern around an oval room with alcoves sunk into the walls at shoulder height, each one holding a small wooden box no bigger than the book Kate still had hidden in her coat.

'Funeral boxes,' she said. 'Filled with ashes of the dead.'

'Well that isn't creepy at all,' said Edgar.

The room was filled with long tables, each one covered in sackcloths that hid whatever was on it from view. It looked like someone was storing things in there. The clothes covered a collection of small shapes that were all roughly the same size, but neither Kate nor Edgar wanted to lift the sacking to look at what lay beneath.

'Maybe we can hide in here,' said Kate.

'I'm not spending more than five seconds in this place.' Edgar unclipped the lid of one of the boxes and curled his nose at the ashes he found inside. 'The boxes are full all right,' he said. 'But there's no inscription on the front of any of them. It should at least say who the ashes belong to.' He shut the box carefully. 'Does it feel a bit odd in here to you?'

Kate ignored him and walked deeper into the room. Whatever the things beneath the cloths were, she did not like the feeling she had when she walked past them. It was a pulling sensation, as if each one of them was connected to her by string. All the cloths were fresh and clean. They had not been there for very long. Then she spotted something up ahead. A collection of tools had been abandoned against a narrow door in the wall. The door was broken, and the space beyond it was filled with old spiderwebs. As she drew closer she saw that something had been partly excavated from behind a covering of old bricks halfway up the wall; something made of stone with a curved edge set with a ring of small circular tiles.

'Edgar,' she said. 'I think I've found what the person who opened this room up was looking for.'

Edgar made his way towards her, squinting in the lantern light. 'Is that . . .?'

'It's a spirit wheel,' said Kate.

Only the right hand side of the wheel had been cleared of its covering bricks. Kate could see half of the stone tiles that ran round the central palm-stone, but the main carving in the middle had been scraped away.

'I've never seen one of these before,' said Edgar, reaching out to one of the exposed tiles. 'What is that? A wolf?'

'I think so,' said Kate.

Edgar touched the tile and the wall quivered, making him snatch his hand back. 'It still works,' he said. 'Why didn't they uncover it the whole way?'

'And why did someone wall it up in the first place?' said Kate.

There was something not right about that room. Edgar shivered, and Kate felt it too.

'Maybe we should ask it something,' he said. 'We could ask it to tell us the quickest way out. Wasn't that what these things were made for? To give directions?'

'Not all spirit wheels can be trusted,' said Kate. 'This one has to have been bricked up for a reason.'

'It's got to be worth a try,' said Edgar. 'I've got enough food and water in my pack to last us a couple of days, but after that we'll need more. If this thing can help us reach the surface, I say we give it a go.'

Edgar pressed his palm against the centre of the circle. The hidden tiles rattled gently behind the wall, but other than that nothing happened. There was no movement, no illuminated symbols, or at least nothing either of them could see. 'It's broken,' he said. Then a faint glow like gentle firelight spread along his outstretched arm and one of the tiles shone with a splutter of inner light before fading again. 'Did you see it?' he asked. 'Which symbol was that?'

'It was the closed eye,' said Kate. 'That means no. The open eye means yes.'

'So that means it heard me! It's saying it's not broken, right?'

'I still don't think this is a good idea.'

'I suppose we have to stick to yes and no,' said Edgar. 'Unless you know how to read the rest of these things.' He kept his hand on the wheel and concentrated on his question, speaking the words slowly and clearly out loud. 'Are we heading the right way to reach the surface?' He waited a few seconds and looked at Kate expectantly. 'Anything?'

'Nothing.'

The wall shuddered. Edgar snatched his hand away and the circle of tiles began grating slowly round in a clockwise direction. A handful of them sank back and rotated as they passed the cleared space in the wall, but they kept moving steadily, refusing to settle.

'It's not meant to work without someone's hand on it,' said Kate. 'Why is it moving?'

'*I* don't know,' said Edgar. 'What do we do now?'

Old mortar sprinkled down from the spaces between the bricks as they rattled against the force of the vibration behind them. Kate and Edgar stepped back to a safe distance, knocking against one of the tables and sending one of the covered shapes rolling out from beneath the cloth and cracking on to the hard floor. It was a soft crack, as if whatever it was had offered little resistance, smashing instantly. Kate looked down. Beside her feet was an upturned skull, its empty eye sockets staring up at her.

Edgar raised his lantern as the spirit wheel kept turning, and the light cast soft shadows from all of the cloth-covered shapes in the room. 'They're all skulls,' he whispered. 'Someone is collecting skulls down here!'

Then the wheel stopped, Kate and Edgar looked back at the wall, and a dull light glowed behind the covering of bricks. Edgar walked up to it and pressed his cheek up against the tiles, trying to see where the light was coming from.

'How do I read it?' he asked.

'The important symbols glow,' said Kate. 'What can you see?'

'There's only one,' said Edgar. 'It looks like . . . a snowflake, I think.'

That got Kate's attention. 'Ask it something else.'

'All right.' Edgar pressed his palm against the wheel again and spoke out loud. 'Where can we go where no one will find us? Where will we be safe?'

The stones tiles trembled a little and then the wheel ground into action. The tiles turned heavily round their clockwise path, and the snowflake carving settled at the three o'clock position where Kate could see it clearly. All other movement stopped at once, and the fiery glow brought the symbol to life even more brightly than before.

'Still the snowflake,' said Edgar. 'This is a waste of time.'

'It's my name,' said Kate. 'It means Winters.'

'Does that mean it wants to speak to you?'

The open eye tile flickered weakly.

'Ask it something,' said Edgar.

'No. I'm not touching it.' Kate had used spirit wheels before, but this one was different. Just by being near it she could tell that it was older. Darker. A feeling of sadness spread from it and filled the room. She could feel it clinging to her soul. The whispers in the walls returned, and Kate could hear the spirit in the wheel speaking to her in a voice that was distant and strange, but the words made no sense to her.

'All right then,' said Edgar, who could hear nothing. 'Let's leave this creepy room of death behind. We'll find our way up on our own.'

The whispers in the room grew gradually louder. Kate's eyes were drawn back to the wheel, and to the illuminated snowflake that burned brighter as she concentrated upon it. Then the tiles began to spin.

'Is that meant to happen?' asked Edgar. 'Why is it moving like that when no one's near it?'

The tiles quickly gathered speed, then one . . . two . . . three of them settled together where the snowflake had just been. A bird, a dagger, and a pointed mask. Each symbol burned fiercely in the dark, but for Kate, looking at that spirit wheel was like staring into a void. The symbols appeared to float upon a black mist. Her mind emptied of every thought and darkness spread round the edges of her vision, leaving nothing but the image of the wheel. Her body slipped into a dead calm as a half-heard voice whispered through her mind. The wheel wanted her to listen. It wanted her to touch it. To connect with it.

Bird. Dagger. Mask.

She stepped forward, barely aware of what she was doing, and pressed her hand into the centre.

The moment her palm made contact with the stone the three symbols' images focused powerfully in her thoughts, overlapping with a burst of memories that flooded past her eyes faster than she could acknowledge them. She tried to focus. She tried to understand what the wheel was trying to say. The less she resisted it the clearer the images became.

*

The symbol of the bird flickered over memories Kate had of Silas and his crow, and she knew at once that he was what it was meant to represent.

'The bird is Silas,' she said out loud.

'Silas? What's he got to do with anything?' asked Edgar, as Kate gripped his hand tight, using it to anchor herself to the living world.

The dagger dripped blood, and Kate saw it gripped in the hand of a dangerous man dressed in red with a long scar trailing across his jaw. She did not recognise his face, but she could sense that he had taken many lives before, and there was a small body, bloodied and still, curled up at his feet. She tried to see more, but the details blurred if she concentrated too hard, and she did not need to see whose body it was to get the wheel's message.

'The dagger means danger,' she said.

'Silas is in danger? Why is it telling us that?'

'I don't think it's Silas. I think it means us.'

'No surprise there then,' said Edgar. 'What about the last one?'

Only the mask was left, but the images that came when Kate focused upon it did not make any sense. She could see a town full of white buildings, a ship sitting in a covered dock and a line of black cliffs with waves crashing against the rocks. Beyond them was a wide green forest and two spires of a much older, darker building rising in the distance. It looked like two tall towers that had been built side by side and it was surrounded by a wide patch of stony ground patched with pockets of green earth.

The wheel took her closer to the spires; right up to a boarded window that had once been painted black. One of the wooden panels had fallen away and she could see into a room that looked warm and inviting. A small fire was burning in the hearth, the floor was covered in deep wool rugs and there were dozens of beautiful mirrors and old paintings leaning up against the walls. Kate looked closer at those walls and saw words carved into the bare stone. Names and dates had been etched into the spaces where the paintings had once hung.

Her senses sharpened. She could feel someone close by, watching her. She turned away from the window and found herself face to face with an older woman – maybe sixty years old – with black hair that was clipped smartly short and grey eyes that had seen more years and held more memories than Kate could imagine.

A hand squeezed Kate's shoulder and she jumped, pulling her hand away from the wheel and breaking out of the vision to find Edgar standing where the woman had been.

'Are you all right?' he asked.

Kate nodded and Edgar blew out his lantern. 'The corridor,' Edgar said quietly. 'Someone's out there. They've found us.'

8

The Secret in the Skull

Kate could not see anything in the darkness. All the symbols on the spirit wheel had stopped glowing and it had returned to its dead state. She pulled Edgar down behind one of the table as voices moved towards the door.

'There is a spirit wheel in there,' said one, as the shadows of two men filled the doorway. 'If Kate went near it, it could be dangerous.'

'I don't care! She is out here somewhere, and I can't go back without her. If there's even a chance she's in there, we have to look.'

'That's Baltin and Artemis,' Edgar whispered close to Kate's ear.

'This room is a restricted space,' said Baltin. 'I can go in, but you have to stay outside. You must stay back.'

Kate heard a whispered argument between the two men and then a lantern swung into the room. Its sudden light was blinding and Baltin squinted behind it, edging his way in.

'Kate? Edgar?'

The spirit wheel thrummed with energy as Baltin drew closer. Kate could feel it reacting to his presence, but Edgar felt nothing.

'Stay there, Artemis,' said Baltin. 'It is not safe in here. The floor is unstable. You have to know where to put your feet.'

Kate and Edgar held their breaths in the dark. Baltin was lying. The room was as safe as any other in the City Below. They ducked beneath one of the covered tables before Baltin's lantern light swept too close, and he moved down the rows oblivious of the two pairs of eyes watching his boots walk by.

Baltin stopped a few steps from the spirit wheel and shone his light on to the ground. He had found the fallen skull. Kate looked between two of the tables and saw him slide his fingers into the eye sockets and lift the skull unceremoniously to his face for a closer look. Fragments of bone splinted to the floor from the damage caused by the fall and he kicked them aside as if they were worth less than dust. 'I told them to clear this place up,' he muttered quietly. 'Not that this one will be any good to us now.' He dropped the skull back on to its table and left it rocking awkwardly on its side. 'Waste of time.' He moved on and ran his hand round the exposed part of the half-excavated spirit wheel.

'Anything?' Artemis's voice carried in from the corridor.

'Nothing,' said Baltin, holding his light up to the symbols. 'No one has been in here.'

Fear climbed into Kate's throat. Baltin had been in that

room before. He had noticed something that was out of place. The symbols were in a different position and from the look on his face he was quickly realising why.

'She made it work,' he whispered.

He turned quickly, scowling beneath deep eyebrows as he searched the room for signs of life, holding the lamp out in front of him. Kate and Edgar stayed still as he lifted the corners of the cloths one by one. Any sound was likely to give them away.

'How did you make it work?' he whispered. 'What did you do?' He kept moving, his light spreading dangerously close. They had to move.

Kate had only the fleeting light of Baltin's lantern to see by, but it was enough to notice a few seconds' gap between his lifting one cloth and reaching the next – not enough time for them to slither between tables, but there was another way. Kate pulled Edgar close to her and whispered in his ear. 'Follow.'

Baltin thrust his light beneath the next table, and before he could drop the cover and step towards theirs Kate crawled as fast as she could out of the back of her tablecloth with Edgar rolling out behind her. Baltin's lantern shone into the space they had left and the two of them stayed completely still until the light pulled away and he moved on to the next.

They were out in the open, exposed in the wide space between the table and a stone wall. Kate did not want to stay there, and as soon as Baltin was far enough away she tugged Edgar's arm and began crawling back towards the spirit wheel. Baltin had his back to them and Artemis was still blocking the doorway they had entered. Their only choice was the broken door.

'Baltin? What are you doing in there?' said Artemis.

'Quiet!' Baltin snapped back.

'There are other tunnels to search. We should keep moving.'

Artemis was becoming restless and he continued to question Baltin, eager to move on with the search. Kate used the distraction to get to her feet. She could move more quickly and quietly that way. The spirit wheel was right ahead. The symbols were so dark and lifeless it was easy to think she had imagined them glowing with light. She did not realise how close she was to the table beside her until her hand brushed the cloth and a rush of energy rippled against her skin.

She could feel the shape of the skull under her fingertips, but it was too late to pull her hand away. Sudden images flooded her thoughts, confused and garbled, as if the spirit the skull belonged to was trying to share everything it remembered with her at once. Baltin was just on the other side of the cavern, but frost glittered along Kate's fingers and swept past her wrist. The spirit in the skull was dragging her into the veil, and she had no choice but to let it happen. The images kept coming, faster than thoughts, as the frost reached her eyelashes and she was drawn completely in.

'The wheels are all we have left. This is the right decision. We have already waited too long.'

Kate was standing in the same oval cavern, only now it was washed with candlelight. Dozens of oozing candles burned in the alcoves cut around the room and the tables were gone, replaced by groups of wooden chairs arranged in four separate circles, their legs roped together, each circle leaving a single space leading into the centre of the room where an ornate spiral had been carved into the floor.

Most of the chairs were empty, except for the three that sat closest to the wall where the spirit wheel should have been. But instead of a circle of ancient carved stone, there was a deep hollow cut into the wall. Three men were hunched over on the chairs, drawing sharpening stones along bright silver blades and talking quietly, not wanting to be overheard. They all wore simple grey robes, each with a belt that had a book hanging from it; tiny books the width of fingers, each one perfectly bound in silver and black.

Kate looked down at the hand that had touched the skull and saw a silver blade grasped between her fingers instead. But they were not her fingers. She was looking down at a woman's hand some years older than her own, a hand that was well used to digging in the earth, with a bracelet of herbs knotted around the wrist: a talisman Kate recognised as one worn by those often dealing with the dead. The sight of the strange hand shocked Kate. This had happened to her before, but that did not make it any less terrifying. She was inside someone else's memory, witnessing an event as it had once been seen through that person's eyes; the eyes of the woman who had once owned the skull.

Kate felt the woman's heartbeat rise as she walked towards the three men and one of them looked up.

'Is he prepared?' he asked.

'There was some . . . resistance,' said the woman, her words vibrating in Kate's throat as if she were speaking them herself. 'He has been restrained.'

'Good. No one wishes to relive last night's events. It was wise to take action.'

'Are you sure he is ready?' asked the woman.

'We need the wheels,' said the tallest man. 'We have already waited too long. The city will fall in the end, but after what we have done . . . it is our duty to put it right.'

The woman bowed her head curtly, then turned to lead the three men out of the cavern. As they made their way out into the corridor a cry of anguish echoed through the tunnels nearby.

'Let us hope our friend has been restrained tightly enough,' said one of the men, and Kate was sure she heard a smile in his voice.

Once she was inside it, Kate saw the corridor as it had been in its prime. A few brass lanterns hung from hooks along the wall, but between them was gathered a collection of far more gruesome artefacts: a human hand, severed at the wrist, that looked as if it had been preserved in yellow wax; a skull with no teeth whose eye sockets had been carefully filled with mud; and a collection of perfect bones – human, Kate guessed – all of them long, stripped and polished, with initials carved neatly into the very centre of their length.

Kate tried not to notice the other dead things, but they were part of the memory and she had no choice but to see the strings of bird skeletons spread wing to wing, and the long sticks of wood pierced with rows of teeth and smeared the dull colour of old blood.

The man's shouts sounded louder now, and there was a light up ahead, leading off into a room that Kate and Edgar had not seen on their way to the spirit wheel – one that had probably been sealed up long ago in her own time. She tried to pull away from the memory, but she did not know how to break herself out of it. Without someone to help her, she was trapped.

The woman continued to walk steadily towards the room,

no matter how much Kate willed her feet to stop. She could hear the voices of the men talking behind her, but she did not know what they were talking about. The woman was as transfixed as Kate was upon the light of that doorway, and her memory did not recall what they were saying. Kate felt her footsteps slowing as they neared the threshold of the room and she dared to hope she would be spared the sight of what lay inside. Then the moment of hesitation passed and the woman stepped into the light.

What Kate saw in that room would stay with her for the rest of her life. She had seen something like it long ago, in a printed picture – she couldn't remember where – and her mind instantly registered two things: that this was a moment that meant something – one that was set to be a turning point in Albion's history; and that she knew who these people were. The bonemen. Keepers of the dead. Men and women who had once been trusted to bury and care for Albion's dead in the vast tombs beneath Fume, people who were generally seen as having done good work – not the kind of people who hung bones on their walls, carried blades and restrained people so they shouted out like that.

The picture Kate remembered was an artist's view of the bonemen's last collective deed before they disappeared from history. Their last funeral. The interment of the man thought to be their leader. No one knew his name. In the picture at least sixty bonemen were standing round a coffin in an otherwise empty room, their heads bowed to represent the ending of an age that would die with that man. It was a beautiful picture, drawn in black ink, but Kate now knew that it was a lie.

The bonemen were gathered there, surely enough, but the room was not the plain one the artist had depicted. The floor was alive with energy. Thirteen freshly carved spirit wheels were laid flat on their backs creating a stone mosaic upon the ground and soft light spread from their symbols like a blue mist floating just above the floor. It looked as if thirteen individual listening circles had been opened at once, creating thirteen separate tears between the living world and the veil.

More mud-eyed skulls watched from the walls, and in the centre of it all was not a body in a coffin, but a man who was still very much alive. He had been stripped to the waist and laid on top of one of the spirit wheels with his wrists and feet bound tightly to a plank or wood laid underneath him to keep him still. Two of the bonemen were kneeling on either side of him, painting inky symbols on his chest. His eyes were tar black, but when they moved Kate saw that they had the same sheen of silver as her own. He was a Walker, and a powerful one, just like her.

But none of that could help him there. Kate could feel the combined will of the gathered bonemen dominating the thirteen wheels. Not even a Walker could fight against a force of energy like that, but it did not stop the man from trying. Kate could feel him reaching out to the wheels one by one, his spirit searching for a way to close them but finding none. Then he shouted again, his voice black with anger.

'Dalliah!'

The bonemen with the ink finished their work, and everyone in the room turned to see a woman entering the room. She was younger than most of the people there. She wore the same grey robes as the others, but her long hair was knotted into ragged plaits and her face was drawn and thin. She did not walk forward, but looked down at the closest spirit wheel as if it were a snake ready to snap at her ankles should she take another step.

The man in the centre considered his words carefully, knowing that he had only one chance to stop what was happening. 'Dalliah,' he said, battling to keep his voice calm, 'Wintercraft caused this mistake. Wintercraft will put it right. This is not the way forward. This is not what we do.'

Dalliah drew her own silver blade and handed it to the boneman beside her. 'It is now,' she said.

The boneman crossed the spirit wheels, gripping the blade at his side.

'The veil is not meant to be used this way,' said the bound man, watching him approach. 'There is no guarantee this will even work. We do not know enough. We need more time!'

The boneman with the knife knelt down, placing his hand across the bound man's mouth, and Kate felt the energy in the room shudder as the silver blade was lifted and the point stabbed down. The man's death was swift and silent. Kate caught a glimpse of red blood pooling near the boneman's feet and watched it bleed down into the carvings of the central spirit wheel. The memory flooded with the woman's emotions: guilt, grief, fear and doubt, all wrestling for Kate's attention while she looked on in horror. Then the memory turned and focused upon Dalliah, who was watching the man's death with quiet reverence. There was no guilt or grief on her face. Her grey eyes were empty of any emotion as she began to whisper a short verse – one that Kate had read before.

'A circle made of blood and stone, to bind the words of soul and bone. A meeting place for those who seek the spirit sleeping underneath.'

Kate felt two conflicting bands of energy spilling out across the floor; one seeping from the dead man's blood, the other being spread by Dalliah herself. The two forces joined together above the dead man, and as the gentle mist of his spirit rose up to be carried into the current of death, her energy acted as a wall, forcing his spirit down. Down into the spirit wheel. Down into the stone. The blood bled deeper into the wheel, and once the spirit was trapped, the energy within it died instantly. The wheel became dull and dead, with only the faintest vibration of energy at its core suggesting that there was anything unusual about it at all.

The room fell silent then. All eyes were on the bloodstained carvings, until the man's killer stood up, his blade slick with blood, and spoke for them all.

'Did it work?'

'It worked,' said Dalliah, sweeping her eyes around the people, a dangerous smile lighting up her face. 'Now for the rest.'

'The rest?' The voice came from Kate's throat as the woman stepped forward. 'We were told one would be enough,' she said. 'We have taken one life. We are finished here.'

Dalliah met the woman's eyes, and cold fear washed through Kate's soul. Fear of what that woman was, and fear of what she could do.

'We are only finished when I say,' said Dalliah. 'Do it.'

With those words twelve more blades flashed into action. Kate saw a handful of bonemen turn suddenly upon the others, stealing lives and binding souls into the spirit wheels with more spilled blood. The walls echoed with their victims' screams and the wheels flickered out one by one as the bodies of the dead fell across them. It all happened too quickly for anyone to react, but the horror of what the woman was seeing choked through the memory as she stumbled back, turned, and stood face to face with one of the men she had brought to that room.

Kate saw the dagger and the silent apology in his eyes.

Cold silver plunged deep into her chest. Kate felt the blade grate against bone, the explosion of heat and fire as the dagger found her heart, and the shuddering pull of eternity as the final wheel claimed its soul.

Kate opened her eyes to blackness. She thought she was screaming, but the frost of the veil still had her throat and no sound came out. Her hands flew to her chest, but there was no dagger, no blood. Her heart was racing, and she did not know where she was. She was lying on her back on a cold floor with something soft underneath her head.

She sat up and felt deep grooves sliced into the floor beneath her fingers. For one terrifying moment her confused mind thought she was still inside the bonemen's room, sitting on top of a spirit wheel. Then logic took over. She was no longer inside the memory, but she was not in the skull room either. The walls of this place felt closer together and someone was crouching nearby, breathing nervously in the dark. 'Edgar?' she whispered, as soon as her voice returned.

Something shuffled beside her and she heard the scratch of a match. Light flared across Edgar's face and he held a finger to his lips to warn her to be quiet. They sat in silence while the match burned down and Edgar lit another, shielding the flame with a cupped hand.

'I think they're gone,' he whispered at last.

'Where are we?' asked Kate.

'You fell,' said Edgar. 'Something happened.'

Kate sat with her arms clutched protectively over her chest where the dagger blow had landed, her forehead throbbing with a dull ache that was gradually getting worse. Something tickled against her left eyebrow and when she rubbed her hand across it her fingers came away dark and wet.

'Don't touch it,' said Edgar. 'You hit the table pretty hard before I caught you. Here, put this against it.' He pressed something soft into her hand and her head stung as she tried to stop the trickle of blood.

'Did Baltin see us?' she asked.

'He would have,' said Edgar, 'but the spirit wheel started moving again when you fell. Baltin just stood there staring at it, as if he was obsessed by the thing. I got us out through the narrow door before Artemis came in to see what was happening. You're heavier than you look, you know.' Edgar smiled before the match flame scorched his fingers and fell to the floor, flickering out. 'Better save the rest of these,' he said, not lighting another.

'I'm sorry for what happened,' said Kate. 'I didn't even know the skull was there until I touched it. I think there was a shade in there. It showed me memories. Horrible things . . .'

'So long as you're all right, that's all that matters,' said Edgar. 'How does your head feel?'

'Sore.'

'I don't suppose it showed you anything useful, did it?' said Edgar. 'I thought the wheel was pretty useless, but if it hadn't distracted Baltin when it did he'd be marching us back to the cavern right now. At this point, I'm willing to take any help we can get.'

Kate considered telling Edgar what she had seen, but it did not feel right to talk about murders that had happened so close to the place where they were sitting, no matter how many hundreds of years ago they might have been committed. 'Nothing important,' she said, though with the possibility that shades might still be lingering close by she felt uncomfortable saying those words out loud.

'Maybe we should stay here for a while,' said Edgar. 'Get our bearings before we head out again.'

'How are we going to do that?' asked Kate. 'We're lost, aren't we?'

Edgar let the question hang in the darkness between them, which said more than any answer ever could.

After what Kate had seen she was glad to be able to stay still for a while, but the longer they sat there, the more the silence and gloom of being underground spread around them like thick fog, threatening to steal her senses one by one.

Baltin had found one of the missing spirit wheels and had been collecting skulls in that room for a long time. Bonemen skulls, including those whose spirits had long been sealed away inside Fume's spirit wheels. The thought of what the bonemen had done chilled Kate, but the idea of the Skilled digging up old bones unsettled her too. Baltin had seemed almost hysterically fearful of Kate's connection to the veil and had been willing to kill her to prevent her from using it again. Now it appeared that he was involved in something even more sinister himself.

The veil plucked at the edges of Kate's consciousness as the wheel's warning weighed heavily on her mind. And even there, sitting in the stony shadows of their tiny hiding place, she did not feel safe.

9

The Messenger

Silas woke not long after midnight to the earsplitting sound of lightning striking close by. His chest burned. His heart, usually steady and unnaturally slow, raced up to a speeding irregular beat and his skin blazed with heat. Pain spread like veins across the left side of his chest, stabbing into his heart like a core of flame. The intensity of it took him by surprise and he clutched a hand to his body, waiting for the feeling to pass. He had felt the stab of metal many times before. When he opened his shirt to inspect the skin he half expected it to be stained with blood, but his palm came away clean.

Rain streamed down in rivulets through the ruined roof and he stood up, shaking his wet hair and feeling the strength returning to his body again. He tested his arms by clenching his fists and feeling the healing muscles stretch beneath his skin. He had to move. Pure luck was all that had prevented the Blackwatch from finding him in there, and a thunderstorm was not going to stop them from continuing their search.

He climbed the stairs to the crypt door and opened it to a bitter blast of icy wind. Outside, the sun had not yet begun to rise, the rain was already freezing where it had collected on the ground, the paths were slick with fresh ice and scatterings of hailstones had blown up against the crypt walls. The ground crunched beneath his boots as he stepped out into the cemetery and heavy clouds crossed the sky like purple bruises streaked with sulphurous yellow and crackles of blue. He smelled the air. It was too late in the year for storms. The land was too cold, and yet the clouds still hung steadily within the arms of the mountains, hurling rain down on to the cold houses below.

He turned up his coat collar and his crow flew out of the crypt, huddling on to a bare tree branch and fluffing itself up for warmth. A bolt of lightning shook the ground, striking somewhere in the forest to the south. Silas walked back through the cemetery towards the iron gates, ignoring the spearing rain that needled down around him. The Blackwatch had taken his sword during his capture. They had emptied his pockets and left him with nothing. The last of his silver was gone, his hidden blades, everything that could have been of some use to him, but the short time he had spent in their custody had given him something more useful than any of those things. It had given him an idea.

With the early hour and the rain pelting down hard, Silas had the streets to himself. There was no sign of the Blackwatch anywhere on the southern side of the river and many of the lantern strings over the streets had snapped or been blown out by the wind. A few early risers were standing at their windows watching the unseasonal weather, but those who saw him backed away from the glass as he walked by.

Silas's mood matched the ferocity of the sky. He made his way towards a small row of shops, found one that specialised in trade goods and broke his way in while barely breaking stride. There was a rumble from the upper floor and a short man ran down the stairs still in his night-shirt, wielding a dagger, determined to defend his shop. He stood still the moment he saw Silas standing in the doorway. His face fell and he lowered the dagger slowly.

'There are some items I require here,' said Silas. 'You are going to get them for me, and then I will leave you in peace.'

'A-all right,' said the shop owner, backing up a few steps. 'Anything you want. Take it. It's yours.'

'I require paper, a pen, ink and string, and a container, no longer or wider than a woman's finger, with a stoppered top.'

The shop was small and well stocked. The man collected most of the things he needed from behind the counter, placed them in front of Silas and headed off in search of the container. Silas leaned on the counter to write a short letter and bit off a long length of string with his teeth while the man rummaged in a small drawer at the back of the shop.

'Will this do?' He hurried back, holding out a small glass vial between his finger and thumb. It had a small crack running down the side of it, but it would serve.

'Good enough,' said Silas. 'And I'll take that as well.' He pointed to the dagger in the shop owner's hand, and was handed it at once.

'Of course. Anything you need.'

Silas slid the dagger into his belt, picked up letter, string and vial, and walked back out into the street.

The wind tried to snatch the paper from his fingers as he pushed it into the vial, stoppered it and tied the string tightly around it in four strong loops. 'Crow,' he said. The bird flew down from the shelter of a high window on the opposite side of the street and landed on his wrist. Silas looped the string over the bird's head and tied an extra knot around its middle and across the centre of the vial to keep it tucked into place against its chest. The crow snapped its beak in complaint and shook its wings the moment he was finished, ruffling the glass amongst its chest feathers. Silas had never used his crow as a messenger before, but if the Blackwatch's tattered pigeons could make it across the sea he was certain his bird would.

'This must reach Kate,' he said. 'Do you remember her?' The crow squawked once. 'Look for her in the streets beneath Fume and stay with her until I find you again. I will come for you. Go!'

The crow took flight, cutting through the driving rain and heading out towards the sea. Another streak of lightning lit up the sky and Silas saw something standing on the other side of the street. A woman, watching him through the rain.

'You have arrived,' she said.

Silas started to cross the street towards her, but when he looked up again she was gone. He stood on the cobbles where she had been and could feel the bristle of the veil within the air. He looked along the houses but there was no sign of her anywhere.

'I told Bandermain he would not be able to keep you

against your will.' The woman's voice came from a doorway behind him. Silas turned and she held out a piece of paper for him to take. 'If you want answers, meet me there,' she said. 'I will wait for you. There are things you need to know before we begin.'

Her grey coat was hooded, but the eyes beneath it were pale and lifeless. When Silas looked into them he saw nothing. No spark of life, no glint of a soul lying behind their glassy sheen. It was like looking at his own reflection; dead and cold.

'You are Dalliah Grey,' he said.

The woman pushed the paper into his hand. Her skin was stained with old soil and her fingernails were worn back to the quick. 'The veil is falling,' she said. 'We may already be too late.'

She tried to walk away but Silas took hold of her wrist and would not let her go. Her skin was icy cool and he felt the familiar thrum of the veil playing around her like a haze of wild energy, dangerous and fascinating at the same time.

'I will answer all your questions, Silas,' she said. 'The Blackwatch do not have to be your enemy today, and neither do I.'

'What do you have to do with the Blackwatch?'

'Less than they think. The balance of power is shifting. If you trust me, you will regain everything you have lost. Read the note. Meet me there.' Dalliah's hand twisted in Silas's grip. Her thumb joint cracked and her fingers slithered free. 'I walked your path centuries ago,' she said, snapping her bone effortlessly back into place. 'You are still young, Silas. You have not yet seen the world that I know. You should be thanking me, not doubting me. The only reason you are still alive is because of me.'

'It would take more than the Blackwatch to finish me,' said Silas.

'Today, yes,' said Dalliah. 'But twelve years ago, things were very different. You were a different man.'

'What do you know about that?'

Dalliah backed away. 'Answers will come,' she said. 'For now, you should go.' She pointed past Silas along the darkened street. 'The Blackwatch are here.'

Silas turned and saw the silhouette of a horse walking across the end of the road. He slipped into the shadows, out of sight of the Blackwatch patrol, and when he looked back Dalliah was gone. He was about to set off after her when the echo of hoofbeats sounded behind the houses and a lithe grey horse raced out into the street carrying the hooded woman on its back. She snapped the reins once and headed off in the direction of the Blackwatch.

Silas unfolded the paper she had left behind and discovered a map of Grale with a route marked out, leading into the southern forest and ending at a circle marked in black ink. He had not come all this way to have the person he was looking for slip away so easily, and her worries about the veil were too interesting to ignore. It would take too long to travel her route on foot. He needed a horse.

Horses and boats were the only viable means of transport between Grale and the other towns along the Continental coast, so the western edge of Grale contained more than its share of stables. Silas moved through the streets, across a river bridge and along to the largest of the stable blocks, where a group of agitated horses were grunting and stamping, spooked by the storm. He opened the stable doors and walked between the stalls, inspecting the beasts inside. Only one of them was calmly cropping its hay, completely uninterested in what was happening outside; a brown mare with white patches between its ears and down its left flank. Silas unbolted the stall and rubbed his palm along the horse's nose. Its eyes were healthy, its ears straight and alert. 'A beast without fear,' he said. 'You will do.'

He did not waste time saddling up, but pulled off its night blanket and led it out into the open. It walked evenly and its hooves were well shod. It flicked its ears against the rain as Silas climbed on to its bare back, knotting his hands into its mane. Once up, he kicked firmly and the horse responded at once. Silas turned it towards the gate, raced it to a gallop and cleared the obstacle in one powerful jump, thumping down into the cobbled street.

The horse carried him over the river, towards the tree line that marked the southern border of the town. The flicker of a lens light shone to Silas's right up ahead, and another answered it to his left. He had been seen.

He drove the horse harder, sending it charging along the cobbles and on to a wide dirt track. He kept his eyes on the road ahead as he plunged into the mouth of the forest and hurtled between the trees. He remembered the markings on the map and shifted his weight, guiding the horse down a small side track, abandoning the course the woman had set for him and finding his own way instead. He had no reason to trust a stranger on foreign soil and could not rule out the possibility that he was being led into a trap.

Low branches whipped past his ears as he leaned in to the horse's neck, ignoring the thunderclouds overhead.

The horse ploughed through the undergrowth, slowing down as Silas took it off the track. It scrambled up the side of a muddy hill and he led it back on to an overgrown track where it stamped restlessly in a circle, unsure where to go. Silas let his instincts lead the way. He tugged the horse's mane, brought it up on its hind legs and forced it to turn. The horse whinnied, slammed its front hooves back down into the earth and kept going, head down, muscles pumping, eyes wide with the thrill of adventure. Silas looked back – there was no sign of the Blackwatch behind him – and decided to follow the track as far as it would go.

The horse ran on until its body became laced with sweat, then a glint of light caught Silas's attention in the trees. He was about to turn away from it when he realised that it was too high up to be the flicker of a Blackwatch lens light. Something was glowing at the end of a track up ahead, beyond a turning marked by a pair of old dead trees. Silas led the horse between them. The ground was scarred deeply by carriage wheels, which had left behind long frozen cuts within the earth. Those cuts ran like tiny rivers, flooded with icy rainwater, and the horse picked its way among them until it reached a clearing where a high stone wall held a pair of blue glass lanterns on either side of an open gate.

Silas brought the horse to a stop between them. It stamped and worried, not wanting to go any further, and whatever it was sensing, he could feel it too. It was like standing on the edge of an abyss, not knowing when the ground was going to fall away, yet being certain that a deadly drop lay just ahead. There was danger in that place. It had known death. The wind swirled through the trees, throwing sharp rain into Silas's face. He dismounted and left the horse loose at the gate before stepping on to the land alone.

A neatly pebbled pathway cut across a courtyard patched with ovals of frosty earth that were barely visible in the darkness. Silas followed the path, and at its end a great black building came into sight. Moonlight sparkled from the few glass windows the huge house had left; the rest were boarded, with long tendrils of old plants creeping unchecked up its walls.

The building was immense. Its central point was marked by two circular-walled towers pressed side by side and topped with spires of slate that reached up towards the sky. Everything about the building was old, worn down and yet strangely familiar. The gargoyles set high among the roof eaves were exact copies of those found upon buildings that Silas remembered in Fume. The towers were the same height and shape as some of the memorial towers in that city, and the long windows were made of the same green glass that was set within its oldest buildings. It looked as if an ancient part of Fume had been lifted up and placed there in the middle of a Continental forest.

The house was in darkness except for one firelit window on the ground floor. Silas heard the sound of horses gathering behind him. He turned and saw eight Blackwatch agents on horseback lined up at the gate. He could not see Bandermain among them and they did not draw their weapons; they seemed unwilling to step on to the land. Silas felt the welcome weight of the stolen dagger at his belt, but they all sat there, watching, as he walked steadily over the pebbles and stopped in front of the building's main door.

The woman from the town was already standing there, waiting for him. She raised a hand and the Blackwatch sank back into the forest, retreating at her command. Two of them climbed down from their horses and pulled the gates shut, closing them against the dark trees as the rain pelted down.

'As you can see, I do not like visitors,' said the woman. 'The Blackwatch know not to set foot on my land without an invitation. I asked them to follow you and make sure you arrived safely. The forest is a treacherous place.'

Silas stood tall, his loose hair slicked down by the rain. 'I do not require your protection.'

'I disagree,' said the woman. 'You need protecting from yourself and your own ignorance. You may look younger than your years, but you have still barely begun to live upon this world. It would be foolish of you to ignore me. You cannot afford to let your suspicions cloud your judgement. Especially now.'

'Then you are Dalliah Grey?' asked Silas.

The woman placed her right hand to her chest and bowed slightly in greeting. It was an old gesture, one that had not been common on the Continent for over two hundred years. 'I have had many names,' she said. 'That is one of the oldest. It is rare for me to hear it spoken out loud.'

'That is what happens when you live like a ghost,' said Silas. 'People forget.'

'Good,' said Dalliah. 'But if they had forgotten, you would not be here. My name still carries weight back home in Albion. That is good to know.' Anyone standing close to Dalliah would sense that there was something different about her; something powerful and barely

118

restrained living beneath the face of a woman who appeared to be only just reaching the brink of old age.

If she truly had known centuries of life, those years did not show upon her face. She looked strong and fit, and her hair was short and perfectly black. But her eyes were haunting, her chest did not rise and fall with regular breaths, and the air around her was thick with threat. It was the same feeling people experienced whenever they were near Silas. He had never sensed it for himself before. It was the aura of a predator.

'Please,' said Dalliah. 'Join me inside. Weather like this is no place for a conversation and I am sure you have questions.'

'Only one, for now,' said Silas, standing his ground. 'Why did you invite me here?'

Dalliah studied his face and stared into his eyes as if she could read the memories written behind them. 'Perhaps you should ask yourself why you accepted my invitation,' she said. 'I believe you are here for the same reason that I asked you to come. You can feel that something has changed. You try to deny it, but you cannot ignore what you have sensed forever.'

'And what is that?' asked Silas.

'The girl whose blood runs within your own. The girl who commands the veil more powerfully than any of her ancestors before her. You know she is in danger. You have felt her within you, even here in these empty lands.'

It was true that Kate Winters's blood had become bonded with his upon the Night of Souls, but Silas had not sensed anything of her within the veil since he had left Fume weeks before. Then he remembered the pain in his chest when he had awoken within the crypt. He had not considered that the pain could somehow have been connected to her. Now he was not so certain. 'I have felt nothing,' he lied. No matter who Dalliah was, he was not ready to trust her with talk about Kate.

'You know the truth, even if you cannot accept it,' said Dalliah. 'Together we can put right what you have broken. Kate Winters is no ordinary young woman, but she persists in entering the veil with her mind unprotected. She is endangering herself because she is ignorant, and she is feared by those who should be helping her. No good will come of this, Silas. The girl's life is in danger, and it is all because of you.'

10

The Gatekeeper

Whatever had happened in the room of skulls had tired Kate out. She lay curled up asleep on the floor of their tiny refuge and Edgar sat beside her, gently stroking her hair.

He waited for his eyes to get used to the blackness. There was no hint of light anywhere along the tunnel that ran alongside their hiding place, and any sounds made in the distance carried impossibly far, making everything sound much closer than it was. He heard what could have been footsteps, scuttlings, and whispers of wind that were like voices hissing beside him, and he shivered. He did not like the dark. It was just another place for things to go wrong. Anything could creep up on someone in the dark.

A scratching sound skittered close by and Edgar sent one of his few remaining matches flaring into life. 'Just a rat,' he whispered, as a black rodent scuttled brazenly across the floor. Edgar liked rats and was happy to leave it to its business until he spotted a second one nibbling at the corner of his backpack.

'Hey!' He snatched the bag out of reach and slapped his hand on the ground. 'Go on. Get out!' The rats just stood there watching him, so he opened his bag, broke a small piece of bread from a loaf he had hidden there and threw it towards them. The rats set upon it at once and scuttled away before Edgar's match burned out and he lit another.

He put the bag down and opened it carefully in case there was anything lurking inside. Apart from the bread everything looked untouched; there was a knife, a few apples, a length of thin rope, a chunk of cheese wrapped in cloth, a glass bottle filled with water, a bundle of spare candles and a couple of pies that were at least three days old. It wasn't much, but it had been all he could find and it was going to have to last them until they could find some more food. With the Skilled out there looking for them, that was not going to be easy.

At least he recognised a good hiding place when he found one. They were in the front room of a cavelike house that had been dug out centuries before for use by the bonemen when they had worked this far underground. There wasn't much left of it – the rest of the house was already buried – but it was enough to keep them safe. The doorway had been crushed beneath an earth fall years ago and the only way to get in or out was by slithering through the glassless window.

Edgar had left the window exposed so he could see any light spread by people searching for them. Kate lay asleep beneath it, her skin sickly and clammy to the touch.

Edgar had only seen her like this once before, in the first week after they had gone to the Skilled for help. She had gone too far into the veil too fast and had trouble separating herself from it again. He should never have suggested using that stupid spirit wheel. Things like that always caused more trouble than they were worth. Whatever Kate wanted to do next, he was going to help her.

Kate was scowling in her sleep, and when he felt her forehead he found it even colder than it had been before. He shrugged off his coat and laid it over her, shivering despite his layered jumpers, which were all holey and threadbare. We are going to get out of here, he told himself. We can do this. Just keep heading up. If a tunnel heads up, it heads out. That's all we have to—

A wash of light spread suddenly along the wall outside. Edgar stepped over Kate and leaned out of the window.

Two lamps swung in the darkness, carried by two women wearing brown dresses with hoods over their heads. They were talking to each other and had large packs slung on their backs, but they did not seem to be in any hurry to get where they were going. Their voices carried softly along the tunnel.

'Which way now?'

The lights stopped moving, and both women held their lanterns up to the wall.

'Left.'

The two women headed off round a narrow turning and the light from their lanterns disappeared.

'Traders,' whispered Edgar. 'What are they doing here?'

Making sure that Kate was still asleep, he lit a fresh candle in his lantern, stepped over her and clambered out of the little window. He crept forward, and when he reached the point where the women had been standing he looked up at the same patch of wall. There was nothing there. 'What were you looking at?' he murmured. Then he found it. Just before the turning the two women had taken, a collection of deep scratches had been cut into the wall a few inches below the ceiling.

'Path 63,' he read out loud. 'TW – E. SM – S. What is that supposed to mean?' A sound in the tunnel behind him startled him. He swung his lantern round and a face came towards him in the dark. 'Kate?'

'That light is bright enough to tell everyone where you are,' said Kate. 'What are you doing?'

'Two traders passed by here and read something on the wall,' said Edgar. 'I came to have a look. How are you feeling?'

'As good as I'm likely to feel down here,' said Kate. 'Sleep helped.'

'Did you bring the backpack?'

'Right here.' Kate turned so he could see it on her back.

'All right. Give it to me and take a look at this. What do you make of it?'

'It looks like a signpost,' said Kate, sliding the bag off her shoulders and passing it and his coat back to Edgar. 'The first two letters must stand for a place, and the last one tells you which direction it is in.'

'How do you know that?'

'What else would it be? You said yourself it's easy to get lost down here. Signposts like this must help the traders find their way around. Maybe we could follow them.'

'That sounds like a good plan to me,' said Edgar. 'Are you all right to walk?'

'I told you, I'm fine,' said Kate. 'Show me where they went, but keep your voice down.'

The wall curved round to the left and Edgar led the way. There was no sign of the traders and small paths branched away from the tunnel in so many directions it became impossible to guess which route they had taken.

'Maybe this wasn't such a great plan,' said Kate.

Edgar held his lantern high, checking the walls for more directions. The same letters kept appearing over again: SM – S.

'We're heading somewhere, at least,' said Edgar. 'There must be something down here.'

The tunnel eventually forked into a wide Y-shaped junction, and sunk into the wall joining the two paths was a large black door. It was made of old wood but it had been rehung on new metal hinges not long ago.

'Where do you think that goes?' asked Edgar.

'Up, hopefully,' said Kate. 'I can't see anything written on the wall.'

'Do you think someone lives in there?'

Kate dared to press an ear to the door. 'I can't hear anything. The floor is worn away here. Lots of people have walked this way.'

'Then either the person who lives here is very popular, or this is a public place,' said Edgar. 'Do we risk it?'

Kate was about to answer when a loud voice echoed down the tunnel to their left. She grabbed the door handle and swung the door open. 'It's our best chance,' she said.

The two of them ran inside and closed the door behind them.

'There's no lock,' said Kate, searching for a way to seal the door, and when she turned to see where they were her heart sank.

They were standing on a stone landing at the top of a circular shaft that cut deep down into the earth. A staircase curled down the walls, illuminated dimly by yellow lights far beneath them. There was no guard rail to prevent anyone from stepping over the side and the steps were ancient and uneven. Shadows danced along the staircase and musty air fogged up against their faces as Edgar's lantern bathed the walls in a flickering glow. Part of the staircase led up to their right, but the only doorway Kate could see up there had long been bricked up.

'It looks like we're already at the top,' she said. 'The only way is down.'

'Good news, as ever,' said Edgar, looking away from the dizzying drop.

The staircase was just wide enough for the two of them to run side by side. Edgar stayed close to the wall and took care where he was putting his feet, while Kate took the steps two at a time and was already two levels down when someone opened the door they had just passed through. Kate and Edgar stopped where they were and pressed their backs against the wall as a voice carried down the shaft.

'. . . no reason for them to go down there,' it said. 'They'll be heading for the surface, or hiding somewhere. Let's keep moving.' The door squealed shut.

'Who was that?' asked Kate.

'I didn't recognise the voice,' said Edgar. 'Probably one of Baltin's men.'

'It's very quiet down here. We're lucky they didn't hear us.'

'Quiet is good,' said Edgar, slapping his hand nervously against another bricked-up doorway. 'I like quiet. Doesn't look like we're getting off here, though. Let's try the next level.'

They followed the staircase deeper and deeper down but any exits they came across were blocked up, locked or, in the case of one particularly ancient door, crossed with a dozen chains with a warning painted on the wall beside it.

FELDEEP PRISON
NO ENTRY. NO ESCAPE.

'Nice,' said Edgar. 'I vote we leave this one far behind.'

The stairs spiralled on and Kate was glad when the bottom finally came into sight. There were more lights down there, a welcome sign of life, and she led Edgar towards a small wooden sign that was marked with an arrow and the letters SM. They followed the arrow into a low tunnel, which looked promising enough until a battered gate blocked their way.

The gate had been welded together using salvaged metal from at least three other gates and it leaned at an awkward angle across their path, with the twisted letters SM bent into its centre. Beside the gate, three long pull chains snaked down the wall.

'What are those for?' asked Kate.

Edgar shrugged in the dark and something creaked up ahead. A small wooden shutter was tucked in between two stones and it flapped open, chased out by a thick plume of pipe smoke. A wrinkled face appeared in the space behind it and a thick rasping voice said: 'Buy, sell or trade?'

Kate and Edgar looked at each other, neither knowing what to say.

'I don't have all day,' said the voice, dissolving into a glut of choking coughs. 'You want in, or not?'

'In where exactly?' asked Edgar.

'Stupid kids.'

The shutter slammed shut, wafting bitter smoke into Kate and Edgar's faces.

'Wait!' Kate tried to open the gate, but it was sturdier than it looked. Edgar reached up for one of the chains and pulled one at random, sending a tiny bell ringing inside the wall. The shutter opened again and the face returned.

'Trade then, eh?' he said, squinting at them with suspicion. 'Let's see what ya got.'

'Er . . .'

'No stock, no way in,' said the man. 'The Shadowmarket's no place to be wandering about without good reason. Specially not for young 'uns.'

Edgar turned his back on the man and whispered to Kate. 'SM! The Shadowmarket! I should have realised it before.'

'What's the Shadowmarket?'

'The City Below has four main places where people come to trade with each other,' said Edgar. 'The Shadowmarket is the biggest. If we can get in, no one will be able to find us in there.'

'But we don't have anything to trade,' said Kate.

'Maybe not,' said Edgar. 'Or nothing he can see anyway.' He turned back to the gatekeeper. 'Whisperers carry their stock in their memories,' he said proudly. 'We are here to trade secrets, and unless you are willing to pay for them, we will not be sharing any of our stock with you today.'

The gatekeeper grumbled and sank back into his little room. 'Whisperers,' he mumbled. 'Should've guessed.'

A shriek of metal sliding against metal sounded from the gate, and a narrow bar slid out of its locks and into the wall beneath the shutter.

'Thank you, sir,' said Edgar, giving the man a smart nod.

'Just keep to the left. And no wanderin'.'

With the way clear, Kate and Edgar stepped through the gate and rounded a short curl of steps, where the distant sound of people echoed from the walls.

'Do you really think this is a good idea?' said Kate.

'Not really,' admitted Edgar. 'But maybe we can find someone down here who knows the way back to the surface.'

'And how are we going to find someone like that?'

'I said it wasn't a good idea,' said Edgar. 'But right now it's the only one we've got.'

The steps took them into a wider tunnel that doubled back directly beneath the gatekeeper's room. A voice bellowed down from above them and the gatekeeper's face glared down through a hatch in the ceiling.

'Keep to the left,' he said. 'And watch out for wolves. A few of Creedy's beasts got out last night. Don't blame me if you lose a hand in there.' The man's laugh echoed around them.

'Wolves?' said Kate, as they walked on. 'Do you think he was being serious?'

Edgar took the lead, following a trail of candles laid down the middle of the floor. 'Let's hope we don't find out,' he said.

11

The Shadowmarket

The candles led Kate and Edgar into a fenced-off pathway that curled tightly beneath an archway of earth and opened out on to a covered bridge with a steep drop on either side plummeting into endless darkness. Edgar kept his eyes straight forward. He ran his hand along the side, shaking nervously as the wooden bridge sprang under their feet.

'This bridge has been here for years,' said Kate, sensing his nerves. 'It's not going to collapse now.'

'That's what the person standing on it when it *does* collapse will have said.'

It was the first time since leaving the Skilled cavern that Kate felt that she and Edgar were completely alone. She could not hear any shades. The air felt dank and empty. If the bridge did fall, no one would know. No one would find them.

Edgar walked tentatively across the bridge while Kate treated it like any other path, striding on past him towards a circular entrance cut into a wall of earth and rock. Edgar ran the last few steps and touched the solid wall with relief.

'We're here,' said Kate, pointing along the tunnel to an arched door just within reach of the lantern light. 'One Shadowmarket and not a wolf in sight.'

The door was huge, ancient and riddled with wood-worm. There was no handle that Kate could see, just two dangling lengths of rope where handles should have been. She and Edgar took hold of one each and pulled the great doors towards them.

The first thing that hit them was the noise. The doors opened out on to a mass of people shouting, talking and arguing with each other. Lanterns made from coloured glass were hung along the walls of a long, narrow cavern that looked like a jagged scar cut out of the earth. Long troughs of fire were slung beneath blackened chimney vents in the high ceiling and the air was thick with the smell of hot metal.

The Shadowmarket certainly earned its name. The moment Kate and Edgar stepped inside they joined a huge bustle of people carrying flickering lanterns, shuffling and chattering between clusters of market stalls that stood in groups like wooden islands across the cavern floor. Waxy candles oozed over the stall fronts, creating islands of light that captured the faces of everyone passing by in a dancing battle between light and dark.

Traders leaned across their counters, trying to attract the attention of potential customers. The busiest stalls were those selling food and clothes, but even from the doorway Kate could see traders selling more unusual goods. One woman was selling talismans cut from ancient bone, whilst another had tame rats for sale. Neither of them was attracting much business.

As Kate and Edgar walked forward, adding their hooded faces to the crowd, a hidden mechanism rattled to life within the walls and the huge doors creaked closed behind them. Kate had not realised just how many people lived in the City Below. There were hundreds in there, all moving between the stalls with bulging bags hanging from their shoulders.

Kate squeezed her way past a stall selling different kinds of clockworks, whose small counter was covered in clicking, whirring creations from children's toys to clocks that could tell perfect time or even predict the weather, though what use predicting the weather could be underground Kate did not know.

The next stall took up an entire circle all of its own with tables round the outside and a small furnace blazing in the centre. Its sign declared its owner a coinsmith, and a red-cheeked woman stood among the tables chatting to a customer while throwing pieces of metal into hot vats, sizzling them down and pouring them into presses to forge coins marked with a twisting letter S. Young children gathered round to watch steam billowing upwards as she plunged the presses into a sump of murky green water and anxious customers haggled with her over whether a metal jug was worth smelting into four coins or three.

'What now?' asked Kate, as she and Edgar were forced to stop.

'We try to blend in,' he said.

Neither of them had anything they could turn into new money, but the further they walked the more obvious it became that buying things with coin was not the preferred method of trade within the market. More often people leaned in, pointed to items they wanted and pressed random items of their own into the traders' hands as payment.

Two groups of stalls down from the coinsmith was a stitchery, where old clothes were snipped, measured, patched and resewn. Next to that was a carpenter whose stall was almost completely hidden beneath a shell of stacked chairs and stools of different heights. The next cluster included a soup seller whose recipes consisted mainly of mushrooms and roots; a bakery selling hot buns almost as fast as its tiny oven could bake them; and a cobbler who prided himself on the quality of his old leather, selling repaired boots decorated with patches of what looked horribly like mouse fur.

From the high ceiling to the wide floor everything about the Shadowmarket was big, and like most things in and beneath the ancient graveyard city, it had once been used as something else. Hundreds of small doors were sunk into its walls in rows that climbed at least twenty doors high. They might have been tombs, but they did not have name stones above them as Kate had seen in other burial caverns. Ladders linked the narrow ledges that ran beneath the doors, but many of them were broken, left without rungs or leaning precariously to one side. No one had any reason to use them any more.

'If we're quick, I bet I can grab us a couple of those buns,' said Edgar, breathing in deeply as the smell of warm bread overtook that of the coinsmith's fizzing metal.

'What do you think they are?' asked Kate.

'Apple, if we're lucky.'

'Not the buns. The doors in the walls.'

'Old tombs, probably,' said Edgar.

'And those?' Kate pointed up at the ceiling, where the flickering firetroughs were slung on pulleys, casting shaky light across the cavern.

'Cheaper than candles, I suppose,' said Edgar. 'Someone probably dug them up one day and thought they'd be useful.'

Kate was so busy looking upwards that she was not paying attention to where she was going, or to what was coming towards her. Edgar pulled her into a gap between two mushroom sellers, and together they looked out between the customers and spotted two dark-eyed people walking through the crowds.

Kate recognised Baltin at once, fully dressed, with eyes like thunder. The man walking with him was the one who had spoken up against her in the meeting hall, and they were both closely followed by at least six more Skilled, all looking warily at the people surrounding them.

Kate had assumed that the Skilled were well known, even liked, throughout the City Below, even though she had never seen them mix with ordinary people. Now she saw the truth. Most people who recognised them as Skilled turned away from them at once. Others whispered to one another or glared at them, and some even spat at their feet, cursing them under their breaths. Traders stood up behind their counters, their faces stern, making it clear that the Skilled could expect no service from them that day, and parents corralled their children close as if the Skilled might snatch them away.

'How did they find us so fast?' Edgar whispered, as the two men looked through the crowd.

'It must have been the spirit wheel,' said Kate. 'Baltin could have asked it where to find us.'

'All it had to do was send them the wrong way,' whispered Edgar. 'Is that too much to ask?'

Kate felt the veil shift a little as the Skilled drew closer. Frost pinched at her fingertips and she pulled them into her sleeves, turning away from the two men. 'I think we should move,' she whispered.

'Why?'

Kate could feel something building close by; a tiny vibration at the very edge of her senses. Then she heard the scream.

The crowd turned as one to look towards the source of the noise. A second scream followed the first and a woman standing next to a glove stall pointed up at the ceiling with terror in her eyes. Kate followed her gaze and saw what she was looking at for herself.

'She can see them,' she said.

'See what?'

A group of shades were moving across the ceiling, tumbling like spiders down into the people below. There were four of them, doing what they had done for many years: reliving the very last moments their tormented spirits could remember, the moment of their deaths. Those who could see them panicked, and those who couldn't tried to calm the others down. Some people tried to laugh it off, patting the frightened woman on the shoulder and looking at her with pity, and the stallholders were quick to assure their customers that there was nothing to worry about.

'It's the sickness,' someone whispered nearby. 'It's spreading again.'

Kate tried not to look at the shades. They might only have been shadows, but the sight of them plummeting to their deaths over and over again was still unsettling to watch. 'There are shades on the ceiling,' she explained to Edgar. 'How can they see them?'

Someone was already leading the woman who had screamed away, and one of the stallholders pointed accusingly at the Skilled.

'You did this,' he said. 'You brought the sickness here.'

Baltin looked down at the stallholder with clear dislike. 'We have done nothing,' he said.

'My customers are seeing creeps and ghouls and who knows what else, while you and your kind hole up safe somewhere, and you're tellin' me it's nothing to do with you?'

'That's right.'

'Why aren't you helping people like 'er? That's what you're supposed to do, isn't it?'

Someone laughed beside him. 'They won't do anything,' she said. 'They're cowards. Leeches. I won't be takin' their coin.'

'We did not offer you any coin,' said Baltin. 'We have no interest in any of you. We are looking for someone. Someone I am hoping you might have seen.'

'And why would we tell you if we had?'

'Because the girl we are looking for is dangerous, and if we do not find her you will have far more to worry about than a few "creeps and ghouls".'

'Is that a threat? He just threatened me!'

Baltin held his hands up in peace. 'I am sure you have all heard about what happened in the city square on the Night of Souls?'

A whisper of fear ran through the crowd. 'Those rich

types got what they deserved,' said one. 'A good scare never harmed anyone. We get worse than that down here every day.'

'What they saw was more than just a scare,' said Baltin. 'It was the beginning of something. Something that has to be stopped. We can prevent a great tragedy from happening within this city, but to do so we need to find this girl.'

The man with him held up a poster with a drawing of Kate's face and her name in black letters with smaller writing underneath. It was an official poster, stamped by the High Council, one that had to have been taken from the streets of Fume. Kate sank further back into the dark. She should have expected it, but seeing it for herself made it horribly real. She was wanted by the council. A price had been put on her head. Who knew how many people were watching for her in the streets above, and how many collectors were already prowling the tunnels of the City Below, hunting for her in the dark?

'The wardens are offerin' the freedom of the city to people who tell them where she is,' said the stallholder. 'What are you offerin'?'

'A promise,' said Baltin. 'If this girl escapes, the glimpses of the dead which you see as an inconvenience today will become a way of life before long. You all live and work in the sleeping place of the dead. This city was not meant for us, it was meant for them. The veil is weakening. If it continues to do so, life here will not only be difficult, it will be impossible. Not just here, but right across Albion as well.'

'And this girl of yours is a part of all that?'

'She does not know what damage she is doing,' said Baltin, 'but the veil is certainly weakening more quickly in her presence. None of you trust the High Council, and you all know that any "freedom" they offer you will be taken away as soon as the girl is in their hands. We have always helped ourselves here in the City Below. We may not like our neighbours, but we share these caverns and we have made them our home. Help us find this girl. Do not allow her to tear what we have built here apart.'

With one short speech Baltin's presence in the Shadowmarket had gone from being a threat to being an opportunity. Kate felt as if every eye was about to turn upon her, every hand point her out and deliver her to a man who wanted to kill her. But no one turned, no one looked. The poster was passed from hand to hand around the gathered crowd, and whispers spread back through the market, relaying what Baltin had said to those too far away to hear him speak. The marketgoers soon softened to his words, and as they whispered together Baltin struck the final blow to any hope Kate had of being left in peace.

'You should also know,' he said, 'that this girl has been convicted of murder.'

Silence fell across the nearest stalls.

'She is responsible for the death of the High Councilwoman, Da'ru Marr, upon the Night of Souls. She was an accomplice in an attack on two boatmen on the Thieves' Way that same day, in which one of them died, and I lost one of my own greatest friends at her hand. Three murders – perhaps more that we do not yet know of – and who knows how many more to come.'

The crowd spoke up loudly in answer to Baltin's words and he held his hands up for quiet.

'Kate Winters is a very devious young woman,' he said. 'She will lie to you, she may even attempt to bargain with you, but she is not to be trusted. Help me find her, and it will be best for everyone.'

Baltin did not wait for the crowd's reaction. He strode between them, his sharp eyes flashing from side to side as he walked, eager to snatch any sign of Kate he could find.

'What do you think?' asked Edgar.

'I think we're in trouble,' said Kate.

'The market should close soon, and I'll bet it gets locked up at night. I say we wait.'

'You think we should get ourselves locked in?'

'It would be safer, wouldn't it?' said Edgar. 'No one would be able to get in and find us.'

'Unless they decide to stay inside too,' said Kate. 'Once word gets back to the gatekeeper that there's a murderer in here somewhere, don't you think he'll let the Skilled look round once everyone's gone?'

'What do you think we should do, then?'

'Stay out of sight as long as we can, then move on.'

'Even if we do find someone who can point us in the right direction, we don't have anything to trade for the information,' said Edgar. 'And everyone will be looking for us now.'

'We can't just stay here, can we?' said Kate. 'I know what I'm doing. Follow me.'

The Shadowmarket thrummed with noise and chatter as Kate headed towards the walls where the stalls were much quieter and they could move more freely. Lanterns glowed dimly just above her head and people were sitting in pairs at small tables which had been set up against the wall, leaning over gaming boards, too engrossed in the movements of tiny playing pieces to notice her and Edgar walking by.

Kate kept her head down and walked with purpose, trying not to draw attention to herself, which worked well until a stack of used crates forced her to step aside and she found herself face to face with the woman who had been pointing up at the shades.

'You can see 'em,' she said, snapping her head round to look straight into Kate's eyes. 'You're a Skilled! You saw 'em too, didn't you? It can't be the sickness. Can't be. You tell 'em. Maybe they'll listen to you.'

Kate looked up at the ceiling. The shades were gone, but the woman was still staring upwards, waiting for them to emerge again.

'No one's going to listen to us, lady,' said Edgar. 'Just don't go shouting about whatever you're seeing and you'll be fine.'

'Fine? You call this fine?' The woman held up one of her wrists, which was shackled by a thin chain to a stall beside her. 'They're cartin' me off! Sick, they say. Don't want it spreadin'. If seein' things makes ya sick, why aren't they cartin' young lassie here off too?' She glared at Kate, and waggled a finger at her, suddenly recognising her face. 'You! You're her! The one Mr High-and-Mighty was talking about.'

Kate started walking away, more quickly this time.

'Sorry,' said Edgar. 'You must be thinking about someone else.'

'She's here!' the woman shouted. 'The girl you want. It's her!'

'Keep going,' said Edgar, as dozens of faces looked their way. 'Don't look back.'

'Kate?' Baltin's voice carried across the market. 'Seal the doors! Find her!'

'Don't worry,' said Edgar, taking hold of Kate's hand as they hurried along. 'No one's going to listen to him.'

But they did.

People chattered excitedly as word of the hunt spread through the market. There were people everywhere. Kate headed back to the cavern wall, but she could not see a way out. A few people climbed up on to stall roofs to act as lookouts, hoping to catch sight of a fleeing girl, but Kate was still walking, forcing her feet to stay calm even though she was desperate to run. So long as she kept her eyes low, few people gave her a second glance.

Ghostly shapes moved in the corners of her eyes and dim figures wandered along the walls ahead of her. At first she thought they were traders, but their faces were unclear and their bodies shone gently with faint energy. They were old spirits; shades of people who had died long ago. Their link to the living world was barely strong enough for any of them to appear to her for very long and they faded in and out of sight, oblivious of the clamouring throng of lives being lived around them. Every one of them was looking at the same place, focusing their attention on the same thing.

What looked like the broken stub of an old stone pillar stood out a few feet from the wall up ahead. It was waist high and ground to a flat surface at the top. Kate only looked at it for a second, but the book she was carrying became heavier as she drew closer to it. The veil had more influence there. Kate could feel it as she had in the skull room, like a window opening in her mind. She did not notice the prickle of frost on her fingertips, or the noise of the market fading around her. Soon her feet were slowing down, shortening the gap between her and the Skilled following behind.

'There's being inconspicuous, and there's stopping,' said Edgar, pulling her along. Kate could barely hear him through the pounding of blood in her ears. Her head felt as if it was being squeezed tight by two invisible hands. The veil was everywhere, and for a moment she saw the memories of everything that had happened in that cavern flashing through her mind.

The cavern's many doors flickered between being freshly hung and being decayed by centuries of neglect. Many of the shades around her disappeared. They had never walked here during their lifetimes, but the shades near the ceiling continued falling to their deaths one by one. Kate saw them clearly now: ordinary men and women who had lost their footing on a narrow walkway that once spanned the upper level of the cavern.

The veil carried her back further, until she saw bonemen carrying loosely wrapped bodies across the floor, each one coffinless and nameless, with no friends or family to miss them out in the world. And then there were the fiery braziers, set to burn beneath two separate openings in the ceiling. Their purpose was soon made clear as dead bodies were laid out upon them, set alight and left to burn down to the bone.

People buried in this cavern were not treated with the same care and ritual as those in the rest of Fume. Their charred bones were bundled together and pushed into the open mouths of the doorways in the walls, bundle after bundle, piled up on top of one another across the centuries. They were the bodies of wanderers, strangers, murderers and thieves, all loaded on to the Night Train and sent to their rest by towns who did not want anything to do with them or the responsibility of their remains.

This was a tormented place. Fear dripped from the walls, making it cold and uninviting. No matter how many traders and customers gathered in that market, the living could never outnumber the dead who still walked there. The tunnels around it were quiet: the only souls within its walls were those who were sealed there, trapped within that cavern, forced to walk its stones for eternity. The presence of so many living people acted as a buffer against the anguish of the lingering dead, but anyone who stayed in the market alone – Skilled or not – would soon sense the creeping pressure of thousands of souls still lurking within the dark.

Kate was just a few steps away from the broken stone when a group of people appeared around it. They were all shadowy and indistinct, each one dressed in the familiar grey robes, and they were talking to one another. Kate could not hear what they were saying, but one of them was clearly in charge, and when he looked up his image became as solid and real as a living person standing right in front of her. His eyes met hers and were instantly familiar, their surface glazed with a hint of silver, just like hers. The man turned away slowly, his mouth moving to silent words as something emerged on top of the stone. Kate stopped and stood beside it. A spiral was carved upon the stone's flat dusty face and the veil showed her something resting upon it. An open book, solid and real in the shades' time but just a shadow of its original self as its image bled into her own world. It was a book filled with words and warnings. A book that Kate knew very well.

*

'I think we should speed up a bit,' said Edgar, wheezing beside her. The sound of his voice broke Kate suddenly out of the memory. The spiral in the stone was still there, but the book and the people around it were gone. Edgar looked back towards Baltin's head, which was still cutting through the market crowd, gaining all the time.

'There were Walkers down here,' said Kate, her senses still caught within the veil. 'They were working with the bonemen. I think they were trying to use *Wintercraft* in this cavern.'

'Not really useful right now,' said Edgar. 'All we need is to get out of here. I think Baltin's got at least four more people with him. What are you looking at?'

'I'm not sure.'

Kate closed her eyes, trying to separate her mind from the veil, but when she opened them again the silver-eyed man was standing right beside her.

She refused to react. She had seen far worse things than a shade that wandered too close, but part of her knew that the man was more than just a memory and much more than a shade. She recognised him as the murdered man whose soul had been bound into one of the spirit wheels, and, despite the centuries that separated their two lives, he was watching her.

Wintercraft *trembled in Kate's pocket as the man picked his own veil-bound book from the stone and held it between his hands. He had been one of* Wintercraft's *protectors in his own time. He had guarded the very book Kate was carrying, just as she did. She had carried it back to a place where it had been used in the past and the veil was reacting to its presence.*

Any doubts Kate might have had that Wintercraft *was far more than an ordinary book dissipated in that moment. She wondered how many of its protectors' lives had ended brutally, and suddenly feared that her own life could be destined to end in the same way.*

'Whatever it is, it can wait,' said Edgar. 'We have to move.'

Kate turned away from the silver-eyed man and the veil pulled back from her. The sudden noise of the bustling Shadowmarket returned and she and Edgar ran together, following the cavern wall, searching for another way out.

Edgar was already out of breath. The further back they went, the quieter the market became. It was only a matter of time before someone realised what was happening and spotted the two of them. If they kept following the wall they would end up back where they started and Kate did not want to be captured by people who thought she was a murderer. She looked at the doors of the old tombs above her and made a decision.

'Blow out the lanterns,' she said, opening the glass door of the little light closest to her and extinguishing the flame. 'We have to climb.'

'What? You want us to go up there?'

'They're going to find us eventually if we stay down here,' said Kate. 'We can climb fast and hide behind one of those doors. If we're lucky, no one will see us.'

'And if we're not lucky?'

'We'll be no worse off than we are now,' said Kate. 'Baltin knows we can't go anywhere. We have to hide.'

The nearest ladder was half rotten, with rungs missing at least every third step. As Kate climbed higher she looked along the wall and saw Baltin reach the carved stone. The Skilled had split up and were fanning out across the market in pairs. She kept going and stepped out on to the first safe ledge she found. It was darker than she had expected up there and she followed the crumbling path, clinging to the cracks and bumps in the wall with icy cold fingers. 'In here,' she said, as Edgar climbed up behind her. She slid back the bolt on one of the doors in the wall. When she touched it the rusted metal gleamed fresh and new beneath her hand, as she looked into a memory of how the cavern used to be. A fiery torch flared into life beside her, but instead of firelight the flames looked silver, casting everything in a cold washed-out glow.

Edgar felt his way along the ledge as if the light did not exist and two shadowy men emerged from the veil behind him, carrying a large trunk of charred bones between them. Edgar felt nothing as the men stepped through him, opened the door Kate had chosen and tipped the bones inside.

'In here,' said Kate, trying to ignore what she was seeing. 'We'll be safe.'

Behind the door was an empty space with a sloping ceiling that dug deeply back into the earth and Kate was glad to see that there were no bones left inside. Someone must have scavenged from those tombs long ago, leaving nothing but dust behind. Edgar left the door open slightly once they had ducked inside, keeping a close eye on the people searching for them in the cavern below.

Kate was not interested in Baltin or the Skilled. The veil kept shifting between her world and a time when the little room had been filled with bones. It felt as if something was building in the air, desperate to be released.

She squeezed her eyes shut, but it did not stop. She could hear the screams of the falling shades, the crack of bone on bone, the voices of the men gathered around *Wintercraft*, and the sounds of the market still going on outside the door.

A man's shout echoed suddenly across the cavern.

'Did you hear that?' asked Edgar, peering out at what was going on. 'It's Baltin. I don't think he knows where we are, but he's not looking well. The rest of the Skilled don't look great either. I think something's wrong with them. Kate?' Edgar looked back, but Kate did not answer.

Edgar crawled across the dusty floor to Kate's side and found her slumped against the wall. He pulled out his matches and struck one, letting the light blaze upon her face. Her skin was icy to touch, but her eyes were open. Frost had caught upon the lashes and he couldn't tell if she was breathing or not.

Edgar was used to being around the Skilled when they were looking into the veil, but Kate was a Walker. Her spirit could walk freely into the space between life and death, often leaving her body behind. Kate usually warned him when she was going to do it, so he knew this time was different. He didn't know what to do for the best, so he knelt beside her, cupping her hand in his.

'Kate, come back,' he said quietly, as the match flickered out. 'Please come back.'

12

Fate Foreseen

Silas followed Dalliah into the house. She had refused to speak any further until they were inside, and she led him through into a large hall, past two wide staircases winding up to the floors above, and into a smaller room lit with firelight.

The heat in there was stifling after the freezing air outside. The room's walls were covered in framed paintings, and some were even sunk behind glass within the floor, every one of them depicting places that Silas knew very well. They were pictures of buildings, streets and landmarks that all stood within the walls of Fume. One was a full view of the city square with the lines of Fume's largest listening circle marked out across it in faint red light; another showed the sunken lake filled with floating bodies; a third showed the council chambers completely consumed by fire, the vast buildings reduced to skeletal remains of charred rubble and ash.

'I have witnessed every one of these events,' said Dalliah. 'The veil has shown me many things that are yet to be. I have hundreds more of these paintings around this house. Many of the events shown within them have already passed from prophecy into history, but none of the scenes in this room have happened yet. Except for one.'

She pointed to a small picture at Silas's eye level. At first glance it looked less detailed than the rest; a swirling mass of grey and black centred around a single point. Then he looked closer and saw that the mass was filled with shapes and forms. Shades: drawn within the mist of the half-life with a figure standing in the very centre looking up through them. It was a girl with silver eyes, her black hair caught upon the wind.

'I painted that picture many years ago,' said Dalliah. 'This year, on the Night of Souls, it finally came true.'

'You could interpret these pictures in any number of ways,' said Silas. 'If you wait long enough anything you see in them will come true.'

'Perhaps,' said Dalliah. 'But historic events are not as isolated as they appear to be. Each one only exists as a link in a far longer chain. When Kate Winters stood inside that listening circle she set in motion a cataclysmic chain of events that will allow everything you see here to come to pass. I have watched history unfold in similar ways many times before. I thought you might appreciate a glimpse into the future of our world.'

Silas looked further along the wall and saw a picture of Albion's monstrous Night Train – the train that had carried people into war and slavery for generations. The great engine lay on its side, its wheels broken and forced from its tracks. Its mismatched panels had been torn away by scavengers and its front grille was choked with creeping weeds. Another painting showed rows of dead bodies laid out in the streets of an Albion town and a third depicted the scene of a public execution. Scarred wardens watched over cages full of sickly people who were being released one by one and led into the hands of their executioner whose silver sword was raised ready to be plunged into the back of a prisoner kneeling at his feet.

'These pictures are not the future,' he said.

'The veil has shown me these events,' said Dalliah. 'The veil does not lie.'

'Even if it is true, how could one girl be responsible for any of this?'

'She has already caused the first stone to fall. The rest of our world will crumble soon enough.'

'Then perhaps it is better if Kate does die,' said Silas. 'She would not want to be part of this.'

'Are you sure of that? You do not know her, Silas. You cannot presume to know what she wants. She is a Winters, after all. Her family's priorities have often proved . . . unexpected, when placed under pressure.'

A door at the back of the room opened. Silas turned and Bandermain walked in, scraping the tip of Silas's blue-black sword along the floor.

'What the girl wants is no longer important,' said Bandermain.

'What is he doing here?' demanded Silas.

'*I* am protecting my investment. I am here to make sure that everything runs smoothly, including you. I remember you being more of a patient man, Silas. If you had waited, my men would have brought you here themselves. Lady Grey has had us watching for you for weeks. It is a shame they could not deliver you here as my prisoner, but you are here nonetheless. I call that a victory.'

'Your men could not even keep one prisoner under guard,' said Silas. 'They are slipping.'

'They do not know you as well as I do,' said Bandermain. 'I doubt any of them would have expected a man with your injuries to escape from that room. When I was told you were gone, I'll admit, I was impressed.'

Silas turned to Dalliah, keeping one eye upon Bandermain as he spoke. 'Do any of your pictures include an incompetent Blackwatch officer and his men?' he asked. 'I find it hard to believe the future has any use for him.'

'Officer Bandermain is here at my request,' said Dalliah, walking across the room and standing at Bandermain's side. 'He insisted upon testing you. He was understandably sceptical about the full extent of your capabilities and did not know if we could trust you.'

'I would say no,' said Silas. 'Men like us do not trust our enemies. We kill them.'

'Not in my house,' said Dalliah. 'Bandermain had to be sure the rumours about you were true before moving to the next stage of our plan.'

'*Your* plan?'

'Yes. Bandermain and I have an arrangement. One of which you would be wise to consider becoming a part.'

Bandermain cleared his throat and walked slowly towards Silas, barely concealing his hatred of him behind a grimacing smile. It was only when he drew closer that Silas noticed that something about him had changed since the last time they had met. His forehead gleamed with a thin haze of sweat, his lips were thin and bloodless, and his eyes were shot with red at the edges. His shoulders were hunched slightly, though he still kept his chin arrogantly high, and every breath made his chest quiver slightly, betraying a secret pain. He was hiding it well, but Silas could see that beneath his mask of strength Bandermain was a very ill man.

Bandermain swung the sword up smoothly and balanced the flat of the blade on his cut palm with the hilt laid upon the other. He glanced at Dalliah and Silas saw her nod slightly out of the corner of his eye. 'I believe this is yours,' he said.

Silas reclaimed his weapon, taking it from Bandermain and sliding it into its sheath as Bandermain stepped back. It was obvious he had not wanted to return the sword. Dalliah had ordered him to do it. The question was why.

'So the Blackwatch take their orders from you now,' he said to Dalliah. 'I see you have a new mistress, Celador. To return the weapon that killed your own men . . . I cannot say I would have done the same in your position.'

'My men died in battle,' said Bandermain, his voice cut with simmering anger. 'They were honourable deaths. That is all a soldier can ask.'

'There are more important matters at stake here than war and pride,' said Dalliah. 'Sometimes it takes more than one person to complete a task, Officer Dane. The Blackwatch have proved themselves very useful to me. You will come to appreciate their efforts once they deliver Kate Winters to us.'

'Why should that be of any interest to me?'

'The veil has shown me that the influence of her young life promises to be far-reaching. If you had known how

153

important she will be you would never have let her go. The girl's blood lives within your veins. You should not have left her behind.'

'She can take care of herself,' said Silas. 'She means nothing to me.'

Bandermain spoke up. 'You told me he would try to protect the girl,' he said, turning upon Dalliah. 'If he does not care if she lives or dies, there is no reason for him to call her here!'

Dalliah held up a hand to silence him. 'If he truly feels no responsibility towards her, his judgement will not be clouded by his conscience,' she said. 'He will not turn away from what must be done.'

'And what would that be?' asked Silas.

'I am not your enemy,' said Dalliah. 'We are the same. Equals.'

'If that is true, why send the Blackwatch to hunt me?'

'Because I can no longer afford to leave anything to chance. Do you know how many people are looking for you? Securing the Blackwatch was a necessity. If they had found you before I did, they would have delivered you straight to the Continental leadership. I knew you would be weakened here and they are very effective hunters. I could not risk them finding you first, so I made Bandermain an offer. I secured his services and those of his men for as long as it took us to find you. As you can see, their efforts were successful.'

'We knew where you were,' said Bandermain. 'My men have had eyes upon you from the moment you left Fume's walls, but we could not approach you within your own country. We had to lure you here, where you would be weakened enough to control. Fortunately, I have an asset posted within your capital that you and your council have overlooked for a very long time. One of my agents is stationed within your city walls. His orders are to gather information about your capital's weaknesses, its routines and the people in power. He has been very useful to me over the years.'

'Spies within Fume are nothing new,' said Silas. 'I have killed dozens of Blackwatch agents myself.'

'You hunt your enemies in the shadows,' said Bandermain. 'This one lives in clear sight. All I had to do was point him in your direction when the opportunity presented itself and I knew he would lead you to me. The right amount of gold placed in the right hands carries a great deal of influence in Albion society. At first he was just a spy, but the right opportunities taken at the right time allowed him to become much more. While you were gathering up your own people to send to war, he became a trusted friend of one of your High Councilmen. In time, every decision the old man made was discussed with my agent first. Through him, the Blackwatch were able to hear every secret the council had – secrets they never would have shared with someone like you. I know more about your country's leaders than you do, Silas. When the old man died, he had already named his successor. The indispensable friend who had been so helpful to him in his final years.'

'You have an agent on the High Council,' said Silas. 'Who?'

'Did you not find it suspicious that a High Council member would arrange a meeting with one of your known associates at a place you just happened to be?' said Bandermain. 'It was a gamble, sending him there, but when he talked to your friend about Dalliah Grey you took the bait perfectly. Who do you think has been coordinating the deliberately incompetent search for you? Do you really believe the wardens would not have found you by now unless someone was intentionally leading them away from your trail? My men have been inside Fume for years, watching your people eat themselves away from the inside. You and your wardens have done more damage to your country than we ever could. All we have to do is sit back and watch you destroy yourselves.'

'When I return to Albion, your man will be the first to die,' said Silas.

'I do not think so. You have already had a hand in the murder of one councilwoman. The wardens will not let you anywhere near the High Council again.'

The room flooded with Silas's rage. He was about to challenge Bandermain when Dalliah stepped calmly between them.

'We do not have time for your petty disagreements,' she said. 'We are all well aware of Silas's history, and we know the fate that befell his former mistress.'

'Da'ru is dead,' said Silas. 'As Bandermain and his men soon will be.'

'She and I communicated many times when she was alive,' said Dalliah. 'There was a time when I believed she might eventually be strong enough to help me complete my work. You cannot deny what she did was impressive. She did not have the abilities of a Walker, yet she mastered Wintercraft enough to bind a soul to her own.'

'I was there. I know what she did.'

'Da'ru's death was no surprise to me,' said Dalliah. 'I may not have foreseen it, but I knew it was inevitable. I followed her progress from childhood, and it was my research that first allowed her to locate the book hidden within a Winters grave. At that time, I believed all of the greatest Skilled families were long dead and that someone like Da'ru would be my only chance to regain what I had lost, but from the moment Kate Winters first entered the veil I knew I was wrong. Da'ru was a distraction. She was not ready for the world I planned to show her. Kate is different. She is the one we need.'

'I do not need anything,' said Silas.

'It has not been long since your spirit was broken. You may accept it now, but in fifty, eighty years, when everything you have known has changed, you will not be so amenable,' said Dalliah. 'Only the two of us know what it is like to be feared by the living and turned away by death. Our fates are the same. We will be left to walk this world together long after the last of our enemies and allies are dead and gone. But fate *can* be changed. We can reclaim our spirits and free them from the dark. This is your chance to make things right.'

'I am not interested.'

'You will be.' Dalliah reached out to touch Silas's face and he snatched her hand away.

'What are you doing?'

'Opening your eyes,' said Dalliah. 'The veil will answer us more easily upon my land. With my help, you can see what has become of Kate for yourself. If she dies before her time, our hopes will die with her.'

Silas felt the energy of the veil gathering around Dalliah and saw frost creeping across her fingernails and along her eyelashes as the veil closed in. He had no reason to trust her, but, suspicious as he was, a part of him was interested in what she had to say. She was the only person who knew what it was like to live his life, and how much he wanted to undo the damage done to his spirit. He wanted to trust her, so he allowed her hand to rest against his face and let his thoughts lift gently into the veil's cold mist.

The veil swept icily across the room, allowing Silas to see the energies of life carried deep within the people around him as if a filter had been placed across his eyes. Normally, the spirit carried in a person's body was visible as a bright all-encompassing glow that spread from the core of their body into a pale aura that misted around them. Dalliah's spirit was very different. She barely carried any light at all, only a tiny speck of white focused in the very centre of her chest, offering proof at least that she truly did possess a broken soul. But Bandermain's energy was the biggest surprise.

Instead of the soft light that normally surrounded the living, Bandermain's body was shrouded in a sickly glow. His spirit was there, but it was pulsing weakly, trying to pull away from a body that could no longer support it within the living world. Only Silas's veil-sight could reveal the truth. Bandermain's body was weakened to the point of collapse, his spirit eager and ready to pass into death. With energies like that, he should already have been dead, yet on the surface he still looked relatively well.

Bandermain was certainly a curiosity, but Silas turned his attention away from him and concentrated upon searching for Kate instead. He did not need to look very far.

The spirit of a living Walker who had not been trained to control her ability acted like a powerful magnet within the veil, attracting everything else towards it and shining brightly like a blazing light. The physical distance between them made no difference. The veil did not recognise distance or time; everything within it was connected. When Silas focused upon Kate, the veil revealed her to him.

Kate was barely alive, her body huddled limply inside an empty tomb of stone. Seeing her there, so close to death, sent a pang of guilt coursing through his soul. He had warned her to leave the city. When he left her behind he had trusted she would be protected. She was not supposed to be there. Not like that. She was supposed to be safe.

Aware of Dalliah's presence close by, Silas could not afford to reveal his fears for the girl. He focused all his concentration upon finding her instead. That tomb could have been anywhere within the maze of Fume's ancient underground caverns. There was no way to tell where.

Dalliah's spirit moved beside him, joining him in the veil.

'The Skilled turned against her, just as you warned her they would,' she said. 'They tried to kill her. She and the boy barely escaped. Now she is overwhelmed. The only knowledge she has of the veil is that which you gave her, and it was slim at best. She cannot control her connection to it, and if she does not gain control soon the veil will claim her, have no doubt of that. Even death will not find her spirit if it wanders too far, and if she survives the Skilled will still find her and finish her. You left Kate to the mercy of the wolves, Silas. This is the consequence of what you have done.'

There were many things in Silas's life that he had reason to regret, but at that moment he regretted nothing more than riding his stolen horse out of Fume knowing that Kate would be hunted. Knowing that there were precious few people she could trust. He had been alone for too long. He had let his own fears cloud his judgement. Kate had helped him when every other living soul feared him, and he had abandoned her.

'*Walkers have lived in Fume for centuries,*' *he said.* '*None of them were affected in this way.*'

'*That is because none of them lived in times like these,*' *said Dalliah.* '*Something has changed. The veil is weakening. The barrier between this world and the next is coming to an end.*'

'*That is impossible. The veil cannot fall.*'

'*Everything dies,*' *said Dalliah.* '*This world will die one day. Even we, eventually, will cease to live, though it may not be the form of death that we expect. All it takes is the right conditions. The correct sequence of events. Five hundred years ago, the bonemen made a mistake. They experimented with Wintercraft and changed the course of history. They were the ones who first tore the veil with their experiments upon the dead and the dying. They were ignorant. None of them knew what they were doing. History does not record the darker aspects of their work, but I was there. I saw the damage they caused with my own eyes. It took great sacrifices to repair what they had broken. They suffered for their mistakes and it was well deserved.*'

Silas caught the bitterness in Dalliah's voice when she spoke about the bonemen, and what was left of her spirit flared in anger at the memories her time with them had left behind. He was willing to assume that whatever 'sacrifice' the bonemen had made, she had been a part of it. She had been with them when they disappeared from history and it had left a mark upon her. He could not tell if it was rage or fear, but it was there.

'*What has that got to do with Kate?*' *he asked.*

'*When the bonemen tore the veil open, Walkers helped*

160

them to seal it again. The veil had threatened to overtake all of Albion, exposing the living to the half-life and blending the two realms into one. Albion was not ready for that, but our attempt to close the tear was only ever meant to be a temporary solution. As soon as the tear was brought back under control and the living world was separated from the veil once again, the seal we had created started to degrade. In those times, five hundred years was almost an eternity. The bonemen assumed that those left behind would have plenty of time to repair the breach fully before it ever became a threat to the living world again, but the bonemen do not exist any more – the High Council saw to that – and no one has risen to take their place. The Walkers are dead and the Skilled have ignored the threat of the veil for generations. They did not carry on the bonemen's work. Recently, one or two of them have dabbled with the remains of the dead, attempting to rediscover and understand the old ways, but it is too late. The Walkers knew that this was coming. They saw the threat from the very beginning, and now there are only two of us left. Me and the girl. The Winters family were always the best of us. It does not surprise me that their descendants were the only ones to survive.'

'If you are what you say you are, why do you need her?' asked Silas. 'What does she have that a Walker who has lived for five centuries does not?'

'She possesses something both you and I have lost,' said Dalliah. 'The power of a soul can be almost infinite when it is used the right way. We may have lost ours, but Kate Winters's spirit carries all the potential of her parents' family lines focused into one young life. The book of Wintercraft teaches the Skilled how to master their spirit; to use its energy as fuel to do what ordinary people cannot do. With the right *guidance, Kate could bring the restless dead down upon this world with the force of her will alone. You and I are echoes of the souls we used to be, Silas. We are revenants: neither truly dead nor truly living. We belong nowhere and trust no one. Only we know what it is like to suffer for the mistakes of the past. Kate has not suffered as we have. Her spirit is still intact. She is the only one who can influence a falling veil now.'*

Silas could see Kate's spirit struggling to reconnect with her physical body and knew there was nothing he could do. He could sense her fear, her confusion and an emptiness that was growing slowly inside her. She felt betrayed. When Silas had first met her, Kate's mind had been clear. Her life had been simple and happy. Now she was lost. The only thing keeping her connected to the living world was the presence of a second soul who he had not noticed before. Someone was right beside Kate; someone who had no connection to the veil at all, holding her hand as her spirit wound itself tightly around his, using him to anchor her to the world. It was a young soul, carrying with it the weight of a tormented past. It had to be Kate's stubborn friend, Edgar Rill. At the very least, she was not alone.

'If you need Kate's help to repair the veil, why didn't you just ask her?' said Silas, hoping to draw Dalliah's attention away from the girl. 'Why involve the Blackwatch at all? You will only drive her away if your men try to hunt her.'

Dalliah pulled her consciousness back from the veil. Silas let his mind return to the painted room and Bandermain stared at them both in surprise as Dalliah began to speak.

'There is a sickness spreading across Albion, allowing ordinary people to witness aspects of the half-life,' she said. 'People have begun to see phantoms and spirits. Many believe they are going mad and of all of them the Skilled will soon be affected the worst. I have seen this happen before. As the veil collapses and spreads, the assault of so many lost souls upon their senses will prove too much. Many Skilled died when the veil fell the first time, and more will die this time.'

'You did not answer my question,' said Silas.

'Because it is based upon an assumption,' said Dalliah. 'We were both cursed with this broken life. The veil is our prison, but when it falls everything will change. The protections the first Walkers put in place will collapse any day now, allowing the living world and the half-life to exist as one. Our spirits are both bound to the half-life, and when it falls they will return to us. We will be healed, and our lives will be our own. I do not want to *repair* the veil. I intend to help it on its way.'

'How? That cannot be possible.'

'If we release Kate Winters's spirit in the right place at the right time, we can control the tear within the veil. We can channel the veil through her, focusing everything upon one single point. We can be present at the exact epicentre of the event that will change the world. Every lost soul will be drawn to Kate before the veil spreads fully across the world. Our spirits will be there for us to claim!'

' "Release her spirit"?' Silas knew too well what that meant. 'You intend to kill her.'

'The veil will fall, regardless of anything you or I can do,' said Dalliah. 'It is too late to save it now. This way, we can use it to our advantage. We can take back what was stolen from us.'

163

Silas saw the spark of excitement in Dalliah's eyes and recognised her desperate need from dark times he had known in his own life. She was talking about changing the entire course of future history, allowing ordinary people to see into a world that most of them did not believe even existed. It would cause panic and chaos. Nothing would ever be the same if the veil came down. It would be the end of life as everyone knew it. The new age would not be one of science, peace or exploration. It would be one of fear, and Dalliah was ready to murder an innocent girl to make it happen.

Bandermain did not look at all surprised by what she was proposing. Perhaps he did not fully understand what could come of countless shades being free to sweep across the world, visible to every living eye, able to follow, influence and speak to the living. Dalliah was right. Everything would change.

The situation was worse than Silas could ever have imagined. He had travelled to the Continent for answers and had walked instead into the arms of a nightmare. The veil was falling, the High Council had a Continental spy in their midst, and the woman he had hoped might become an ally was intent upon changing the world for the worse, all for the sake of two broken souls.

Bandermain watched Silas closely, waiting for him to say something. Whatever arrangement Dalliah had made with him had to have something to do with his illness. There had to be a reason why he was still alive, and Dalliah was more than capable of extending a human life if it served her purpose. Until Silas knew more there was no way to guess how far Bandermain would go to honour their bargain.

Dalliah was staring at Silas, smiling as if he were her truest friend. She clearly expected him to see the world the way she did: as something expendable, something that could be crushed on their way to getting what they both wanted at last.

'I am talking about freedom,' she said quietly. 'Death will accept us when the time comes. We can regain our souls and we will be whole again. Surely that is worth the life of one young girl, Silas. Don't you agree?'

13

The World Beneath

Kate could see Edgar. She could hear him talking to her in the dark, but she could not answer him. He looked like a reflection of himself cast in a pool of water; ghostly, and not quite real. She could feel the touch of his hand on hers and she focused upon it, trying to break out of the veil and back into her life, but nothing she did made any difference.

Kate felt as if she was half awake, being pulled to the threshold of many different dreams. There was no order to it, and no reason for her to be connecting with the veil there at all. She concentrated upon her own world and felt the presence of the Skilled in the Shadowmarket, a group of them, each one looking into the veil, trying to find her. She closed her mind to them, but they were too close. Nothing could hide within the veil. They were coming.

Edgar's face moved back in front of her. He kept looking at the door. He knew they were coming too. 'Kate,' he whispered. 'I know this isn't a good time, but I have an idea.' He moved *away, letting go of her hand, and Kate felt her spirit's link to him break. It felt as if all the air had been pressed from her lungs at once and the shock of the separation jolted her spirit back into life.*

Kate felt a rush of blood returning to her fingertips. Her body breathed again and her fingers reached out for Edgar as he went to open the door, holding him back. 'What are you doing?' she asked.

'Welcome back,' said Edgar, a nervous grin spreading across his face. 'Do me a favour. Never do that again. I didn't know if I had to do something, or just leave you to it. We've got trouble outside.'

Kate did not wait for her body to settle again. She crawled to the door with Edgar and he opened it just enough for them both to see down on to the market floor below. She must have been inside the veil for a long time because the fires in the ceiling troughs had burned down to a faint glow and lanterns flickered across the cavern as people walked between the market stalls. There were fewer down there than there had been earlier and every one of them was busy carrying, lifting and moving about.

The clusters of stalls were being folded and packed until they looked more like piles of huge wooden boxes than counters and shelves, and the spaces in between the stalls were filled with people pushing small handbarrows or pulling wide carts, clearing the way ahead of them with shouts and whistles. Everyone seemed to have lost interest in Baltin and his men. Kate could not see any of them at first, until Edgar pointed to a group standing separately from the rest. They were the only ones who were standing still, and they had gathered in the light of a candle lantern held by the gatekeeper Kate and Edgar had met on their way in.

'They're packing up,' said Edgar. 'It looks as if everyone locks their stock away at night, but that old guy could mean trouble. I heard him make an announcement a few minutes ago. Everyone who leaves the market tonight has to give their names and be counted out. I think Baltin's told him about us. They'll be waiting for us at the exits, and if we don't leave they'll know we're still in here. The Skilled will have all night to find us if the gatekeeper stays here with them.'

'Baltin's not going to give up, is he?'

'Probably not. But I have an idea. Down there.' Edgar pointed to a large stall that sold well-made woollen rugs and shawls. The woman who owned it was loading her most valuable items into a handbarrow and padlocking large wooden panels into place around the sides, making sure the rest of her goods were locked up tight. 'We are going to stow away in one of those barrows,' he said.

Kate looked down at the woman, who was having enough trouble lifting a barrow full of rugs, never mind one with two people hiding in it. 'You're serious, aren't you?'

'We hide in one of the barrows and let the traders roll us out of here. Baltin and the Skilled will think we're still hiding in here somewhere and they'll waste a night searching an empty cavern, giving us a chance to get a head start. It's perfect. Tell me what possible flaw there could be in that plan.'

'Let's think . . . it's crazy, it will never work and it's going to get us both caught,' said Kate. 'We'll be seen before we're even down the ladder.'

'Not if we're careful,' said Edgar. 'That's what I was looking at. See? This ledge we're on leads right along the side of the cavern. Everyone's heading in that direction. There must be a way out over there. If we stay on the ledge in the dark, we can get closer to the exit, climb down and hide in a barrow. No one will see us. And even if they did, I don't think they'd say anything. They'll just think they're seeing shades again, and they won't want anyone to think they have the sickness after those others got carted off, will they?'

'What about the Skilled?' asked Kate. 'There are shades in here. What if they use the veil to find us?'

'I don't think the shades are being too helpful,' said Edgar. 'Otherwise they would have found us by now, wouldn't they? And if anyone sees us once we're down there, we can move swiftly on to my second brilliant plan. Head for the exit and leg it.'

'All right,' said Kate. 'Let's keep moving.'

Edgar felt his way out of the door and Kate followed him on to the narrow path where she quickly took the lead, picking her way carefully along the ledge towards the way out. The traders were too busy going about their business to care about anyone who might be walking above them. There were last-minute deals to be made and trading to be done with late customers who refused to stop bartering until the last item was packed away.

Just being there, looking out across all those people, reminded Kate of the life she used to have, when her days had been spent behind a bookshop counter, looking out through a window on to a market much like this one. She had never realised how safe she had felt back in her home town. Life had been easier then. Everything had changed so quickly she had barely had time to miss what she had lost. The bookshop had burned. Her home was gone and her only family had turned against her. She could never go back to that previous existence and she wished she had known just how precious it was.

She tested the sturdiness of each ladder she came to, hoping to find a safe way down, but did not trust any of them. Most were hung on rusted nails, and she had no intention of trusting her or Edgar's life to something that could give way beneath them. Edgar stayed unusually quiet as they walked, until at last her hand found a ladder that felt sturdy enough to use.

Kate made her way on to the rungs and then stopped, hearing people whispering beneath her. She edged down slowly, signalling for Edgar to stay where he was. They were not the only ones in that cavern trying not to be seen. She was just close enough to make out two old women clinging to the shadows, cupping tiny candle flames in their hands and arguing under their breath. They had large bags slung over their arms and looked around the cavern for several minutes before finally settling on a direction and scuttling off, taking whatever they were carrying with them. Kate waited until they had passed, then waved Edgar down and took the last few rungs to the floor.

The smell of dried tea leaves wafted from the nearest stall and Kate tugged up the hood of her coat. 'There are no barrows over here,' she whispered. 'The closest one's next to that vegetable seller. It's too exposed. We'll be seen.'

Edgar suddenly pulled Kate back into a hollow in the wall, hiding her from view as two people walked slowly by. Kate recognised one of them as Greta, the Skilled magistrate, and the determination on her face was chilling. Neither of them dared to move until Greta was well out of sight.

'That was close,' said Edgar. 'I think we can safely say they're not using the veil right now. They'd have sensed you in a second, wouldn't they?'

Kate nodded silently.

'At least they didn't see us,' said Edgar. 'One of the exits is right there. We should go unnoticed if we're quick. The Skilled can't be everywhere.'

Kate kept one hand on the cavern wall as she followed Edgar towards the larger of the two exits, where a long line of traders were waiting to push their barrows out and make their way home.

'Look,' she said, peering past a clothes stall that had already closed up. 'What about those two?' She pointed to two large carts that were both stuffed with rolled-up blankets. They each had two large wheels at the back, two wooden legs to stand on, and thin bars pointing out of the front, allowing them to be tilted back and pulled along. Each one was so big and heavy that it needed to be pulled by two men, making them an excellent place to hide.

Kate dared to move out among the closed stalls, where most of the lanterns had already been blown out. The line was moving slowly and the carts kept stopping and starting, giving plenty of time for stowaways to climb on board.

'That apple seller behind them might see us,' said Edgar.

'Not if we distract him.'

The floor around the closed-up stalls was littered with loose pieces of wood. Kate picked up a long thin stick and held it like a spear.

'Now I *know* you're crazy,' said Edgar.

'If we can get this in his wheel, he'll think it's jammed. What's your aim like?'

'Lousy,' said Edgar.

Kate brought her arm back, preparing to throw. 'Get ready to run as soon as he's looking the other way. Three . . . two . . . one.' She threw the stick hard through the air, aiming for the spokes in the apple cart's front wheel. The shot missed. The stick speared awkwardly between the side wheels and skidded beneath the cart. The apple seller kept walking, until the back wheel thumped against the fallen stick and the cart bounced, sending a sack of fruit toppling off the back and scattering apples out across the floor.

'Ha!' said Edgar. 'That'll do.'

It wasn't exactly what Kate had planned to happen, but it was good enough. Traders behind the seller helped him to rescue his fallen fruit while Kate and Edgar bolted for the blanket-filled carts.

'You go in that one,' Kate whispered. 'Split up. Less weight.'

Edgar did as he was told. The two of them climbed into separate carts and buried themselves between the blanket rolls. When the line started moving again, no one noticed the extra cargo nestled in among the rest. Kate tugged the end of one of the blankets over herself as the cart edged closer to the exit and she heard people arguing up ahead.

'You're not searching through anything of mine!' said one of the traders. 'I've got fine linens amongst this lot. You're not putting your filthy hands all over them . . . and you're *definitely* not doing anything with *that*.'

'Out of my way.' That was Baltin's voice. Kate felt the cart jolt as someone climbed up on to the side.

'You'll put filthy great holes in everything!'

'No one passes through this gate without being checked.'

Kate heard a dull thud as something stabbed into the fabric beside her. The blanket traders yelled in protest and Kate tucked her knees up, making herself as small as possible before Baltin slashed at the fabric with what sounded like a blade. She stayed deathly still, afraid to breathe in case he heard her. The traders shouted at him to stop, and he dragged two rolls down from the cart, threatening to send the rest of the stock toppling to the floor.

Kate heard sounds of a tussle as the two traders pulled Baltin off the cart, telling him that there was no one inside it and if he wanted to take his anger out on something he should go and find someone else's stock to destroy. The traders were tough, hefty types, and Baltin was wise enough to decide that he was satisfied with his search.

'Next!'

The traders threw the fallen rolls back on to the cart, and as they pulled away Kate caught a glimpse of Baltin behind her, stopping the apple seller and demanding to look inside his sacks. Her view was limited to objects directly behind the cart and she could not see Edgar's barrow anywhere; she could only hope that it had been checked and passed at the same time as hers by one of Baltin's men. She dared not risk raising her head out of her hiding place to look. Baltin had sounded desperate enough to do anything. If he had found her, Kate had no doubt that he would have used that sword on her there and then. She had been lucky, and now all she could do was lie still as the traders pulled the cart out of the Shadowmarket and into the tunnels of the City Below.

Once they were out of the market cavern most of the traders began heading different ways. Conversations were struck up between those who shared the same tunnels and the only things any of them really talked about were the sickness, Baltin's behaviour, and the sudden interest so many people had in the whereabouts of a missing girl.

Kate closed her eyes and tried to let the gentle movement of the cart relax her after the madness of the cavern, but all she saw when she closed them were the warnings given to her by the spirit wheel: the bird, the dagger and the mask. She wondered where Silas was and if the High Council was still hunting him.

She watched the ceiling go by as the traders carried her deep into tunnels she did not know, and was glad to see that they were heading upwards at last. The paths the traders chose curled gently uphill. They walked through old arched doors, past branching junctions and over a narrow bridge that rattled and creaked as they crossed it. Kate could feel that they were high up, at the top of a dizzyingly high drop, and the carts took it in turns to cross carefully one by one. She wrapped herself in one of the blankets and dared to look out over the side.

The first thing she saw was light. Thousands of bright firelights shining from spaces cut into the walls. The bridge hung perilously over a huge cavern sliced through by what looked like a river surging far below. The floor of the cavern was too dark to see, but the walls were alive with life. People were living there. Staircases had been built in zigzags between the many levels and there were at least twenty or thirty floors, reaching higher than the bridge and down beneath it. She could see rooms cut into the earth, with small fires burning within them for warmth, and there were families there; armies of children who ran up and down the staircases like excitable mice. As the cart neared the end of the crossing, Kate could hear music echoing gently from the cavern walls and the sounds of people talking carrying from the stones.

Kate had thought the tunnels and smaller caverns were all that made up what people knew as the City Below, but now she realised she was wrong. This was a true city. What she was looking at was a settlement all of its own. A place large enough to hold several thousand people and still not feel crowded. It was a world beneath the earth; an existence completely separate from the world outside.

The pathways were neat and clean. The air was clear and Kate heard the throbbing heartbeat of spinning fan blades high above her, drawing cool air down from vents cut into the ceiling. She half expected to see starlight twinkling through them when she looked up, but all she saw was the solidness of rock.

Kate had forgotten all about trying to hide. She could not help staring at the immensity of what was hidden beneath Fume's feet. People were not just surviving, they were happy down here. They were living.

Soon the cart left the bridge and began rolling gently down a winding slope, stopping and starting a few times. A quick glance up ahead showed Kate why. They were coming to a checkpoint. Three men and three women were talking to the traders pulling a metalworking barrow just ahead. Behind her, more traders were joining the line and at last she spotted Edgar's blanket-filled cart a short distance away. She hid beneath some loose blankets as the line moved and her cart came up to the barrier.

'Residents,' one of the blanket traders said brightly. 'Back from the market.'

'Make any good sales?' asked one of the women.

'Good enough. The rest of the stock got ripped up by some idiot at the door.'

'We heard something about that,' said the woman. 'You're not the only one who has complained. Make sure you salvage what you can.'

'Will do.'

The cart lurched and drove on without anyone looking into the back. Kate moved the blanket from one of her eyes and peered out again as it headed across a second small bridge and trundled right up to the front of the lowest houses. She had to get Edgar's attention somehow. They had to get out of the carts before they stopped or they would risk being found. Edgar did not look up. Kate waited as long as she dared, then – as they approached the middle point between a pair of lanterns hanging over the road – she crawled along the blankets, waited for her moment, and jumped.

14

Within the Walls

Kate ran for the shadows, staying out of sight as the second blanket cart rolled by. Edgar was still not moving, so she picked up a stone and lobbed it into the blankets. Edgar looked up, confused, and Kate waved to get his attention. As soon as he saw her he scrambled down from the cart and scuttled over to her hiding place.

'What are you doing out here?' he whispered.

Kate pointed to the ceiling. 'Do you see those vents?'

'Yes . . .' Edgar said slowly. 'If you're thinking of using them as a way out, I don't think either of us can climb well enough to even get up there.'

'I know we can't reach the vents,' said Kate. 'But what about chimneys?'

'Narrow dark things with fires burning away at the bottom? That's an even worse idea.'

'At least we know they go upwards.'

'And most of them are lit by the look of it.'

'Most of them. Not all,' said Kate.

She stared at the lantern lights of the carts still moving along the other side of the cavern. Something was happening on the bridge.

A few of the carts had stopped. Kate could hear traders shouting. They were pointing at something, trying to get the attention of the people manning the checkpoint, but no one was listening.

'What's going on?' asked Edgar.

It was hard to tell from so far away, but they did see a small baker's cart tilting precariously to one side at the far end of the bridge. The baker who was pushing it tried to stop it from falling but gravity took hold. The right wheel gave way and the cart plunged over the edge of the bridge, plummeting down into the distant river. At first it looked like an accident. The baker was shouting, other traders were holding her back from the edge, and then Kate saw a rope dangling from the ceiling with someone dressed in black clambering up it towards one of the vents.

'Look at that!' she said, pointing up at the disappearing man.

'Did he just pull that cart off the bridge?' said Edgar. 'Why would anyone . . . Look! There's another one!'

A second man was clinging to the wall on the opposite side of the cavern. He waited there for a short time, then let go, sliding down a long rope all the way to the ground. The more Kate and Edgar looked for them, the more men they could see taking up positions around the cavern.

'Blackwatch?' said Edgar.

'I hope not.'

'They're tricky enough for Blackwatch. And I've never

seen a warden do anything like that. What is that? Over there on the bridge.'

The traders were moving again, but instead of heading forward the carts were rolling carefully to one side to allow something else to pass through. Seven men dressed in long red coats strode across the wooden bridge. All of them were armed with bows, daggers or swords and they advanced right through the traders without being challenged. The guards at the checkpoint looked up. One of the women reached for her weapon, but before the others could react arrows cut through the air from the men on ropes and all six guards fell dead to the floor.

'Definitely Blackwatch,' said Edgar, already backing away. 'What were you saying about chimneys?'

'They can't know we're here,' said Kate.

'They must be stepping up the search,' said Edgar.

Kate's thoughts went immediately to Artemis and Tom. 'Do you think they've already been back to the Skilled's cavern?'

'No,' Edgar said quickly, already thinking the same thing. 'Tom and Artemis will be fine. They'll look after each other. Look out. They're coming this way.'

The seven men moved swiftly across the second bridge, and the few people who dared to stand in their way were taken down by the wall scouts, leaving the path clear for them to reach the main rock face. There was nowhere to go. Kate and Edgar hid in a darkened corner behind a stack of heavy crates as the Blackwatch made their way past. Then their boots stopped, and voices carried from somewhere nearby.

'You have had you chance,' said one of them. 'Enough warnings have been given. The girl was seen in the

Shadowmarket just a few hours ago. It would be unwise to hide her from us. Hand her over, or more of your people will die.'

A woman's voice answered. 'You have made a mistake by threatening my people,' she said. 'We have told you everything we know about the girl, yet you have returned to us and spilled blood simply to hear the same answer. Order your men to leave or we will be forced to defend ourselves. My people far outnumber yours. Your men cannot cling to our walls forever.'

'We will search this cavern,' said the Blackwatch officer. 'Your people will not stand in our way. My men have every door, sewer and rat hole under guard.'

'You will find nothing.'

'If you do not deliver the girl, you will no longer be of use to us. I find people become most co-operative once their leaders are dead.'

Kate heard the sound of a blade being unsheathed and the woman's voice became tinged with fear. 'Search all you want,' she said. 'She is not here.'

'Find her.'

Kate left the safety of the crates and crept into the first doorway she could see. She did not know where she was going. She did not care, so long as the Blackwatch did not see her. It took a few seconds for Edgar to realise she had gone and he hurried to catch up with her.

The room Kate found her way into was empty, but there was a fire burning in the hearth, making the chimney too hot and dangerous to climb even if she put the flames out. She moved through the house and climbed back out through a small window on to the cavern's main street. The children who had been playing on the staircases were gone, replaced instead by people who were curious to see what was going on down below. Many of them were armed with whatever they had to hand and looked ready for a fight.

'Where are you going?' asked Edgar. 'Do we have a plan?'

'Yes,' said Kate. 'We climb.'

She walked steadily, trying not to draw attention to herself, until she found a house in the wall that looked old and abandoned. Parts of its roof had fallen in, but she found what she was looking for inside. A fireplace, dead and cold.

'This cannot end well,' said Edgar.

'Your plan to hide in a barrow worked, so why shouldn't mine?' asked Kate, already knotting her hair back and leaning in to peer up the exposed chimney, which looked narrower than she had expected. 'It seems clear enough,' she said. 'You'll have to leave your backpack behind.'

Sharp orders were shouted outside. People were being told to open their doors and co-operate fully with the Blackwatch's search.

'Chimney it is then,' said Edgar, already wriggling out of the straps and hiding the bag behind an old armchair.

Kate ducked beneath the mantelpiece, slid her arms into the chimney and stood up inside it, feeling around for something to hold on to. Cool air sank down against her face and her fingers found the edge of a thin horizontal bar, the first of what looked like a full line of them that had been put there for sweeps to use. 'I think it widens further up,' she said. 'There's a ladder on the side.'

Kate reached up as high as she could and lifted her foot up on to the first rung. Climbing was easy enough once she got started. After she had passed the thin neck of the chimney shaft the wall sloped along to the right and opened out into a wider space where other chimneys linked with the main shaft. It was not as restrictive as she had first feared. The worst part was the soot. It coated everything and clung to her clothes and skin as she climbed, stirring up blackness in the filthy air. Edgar grumbled beneath her as her feet sent drifts of it scattering down on to his head.

The higher they went the more chimneys joined with the one they were in, and threads of smoke trickled out of some of the side shafts they passed. The fires at their bases must only have been smouldering but Kate tried not to breathe in case the smoke caught in her throat and her coughing gave them away. She concentrated on getting to the top. She couldn't wait to reach fresh air again and climb out into a city topped by a blanket of stars. The scratching sounds of fires being lit travelled along the side shafts, and half-caught conversations echoed from the walls. Two raised voices sounded close by, and when Kate heard them she stopped, trying not to make a noise.

Edgar looked up to see what was going on. Neither of them could see anything in the black, but the women's voices were clear enough.

'I'm telling ya, I heard somethin' in the walls!'

'Don't go sayin' things like that. Do you want the Blackwatch to come up here and start beatin' down my door?'

'What if it's her? What's her name . . . Winters. What if we're the ones who find her?'

'There's nothing there. Just leave it. I don't think we should— *Get your head out of the fireplace!*'

Kate and Edgar froze. Wherever the woman was, there

was no way she could see them. More smoke wisped up around them. Kate pressed her face to the arm of her coat to filter the air, but Edgar was not so quick. His nose burned, his eyes streamed. Kate heard him try to sniff quietly, but it only made things worse. Edgar heaved in a deep breath – tried to hold it back – but then the walls exploded with the sound of a loud, powerful sneeze.

'There is someone in there! Quick! Call someone!'

'Wait,' said the second woman. 'Think about this. If it is the girl, we can get a lot more by handing her over to the wardens. The Blackwatch aren't offering much, are they? We both know where the chimney goes. Maybe we can catch her ourselves.'

'All right. I'll light the fire. You head up a few levels. Maybe we can smoke her out!'

Kate did not care how much noise she made after that. She clambered up the rungs as fast as she dared and followed the shaft along two more steep slopes. Already-burning fires spewed heat into the chimney as she passed and the air filled with thick swathes of choking smoke. She had to stop, not daring to climb any further. Her eyes stung and her throat burned. There was no way they were going to make it to the surface through that. Edgar coughed somewhere beneath her, and more smoke billowed up from below.

'We have to get out,' said Kate. 'Go down again. We need to look for an empty shaft.'

Edgar held his breath and ducked down into the smoke. Kate heard a thud as she followed him back down a dozen rungs and she almost fell from the ladder in fright when Edgar's filthy hand reached out from a hole right beside her face.

'In here,' he said.

It was much harder climbing down a sloping ladder than it was climbing up. The air in Edgar's shaft was cleaner and cooler. No fire was burning at the end of it and the chimney was wide at the bottom, opening out on to a hearth far larger than the one they had climbed into a few floors below. Edgar hesitated just above the opening, and Kate looked down past him, seeing the glow of candle-light spreading in from the room beyond. She guessed what he was thinking. The room was not empty. She could not hear any voices, but that candle had been lit for a reason.

The walls echoed as a knock rattled the front door. Bootsteps scuffed over the floor, a lock clicked, and some-one charged inside.

'I need to use the fireplace!' It was the same woman they had heard a few chimneys away, except now she was out of breath from running up many flights of stairs.

'Use it?' said a man's voice. 'What for?'

'That girl everyone's looking for. I think she's up there. If I can climb into the chimney and take a look . . .'

'I can't let you do that.'

Smoke prickled Kate's nose as a plume of it curled in from the main shaft.

'Look, you can hand her over with us if you want,' said the woman. 'We'll take her to the wardens, not those foreigners downstairs. We can trade her in and finally get out of here. See some sun!'

'My mistress will return once she has dealt with the visitors. She will not appreciate returning home to the sight of your buttocks poking down out of her chimney, will she?'

The woman made an impatient noise, too distracted to be insulted. 'Then take a look for yourself. Tell me if you can hear someone moving around up there.'

Edgar tapped on Kate's ankle, warning her to move upwards, but the smoke was too thick. If they stayed where they were they would be seen and if they moved they would suffocate. Edgar's tapping became more insistent but Kate held on tight as something moved in the grate beneath them and a head came into sight.

'What can you see?' asked the woman.

The head turned and a man's face looked up at them in disbelief.

'Well?'

The man kept staring. 'Nothing,' he said carefully. 'Lots of muck.'

'Can you hear anything?'

'Er . . . no. There's no sign of anything up here.' The man's head disappeared and Edgar looked up at Kate, clearly as shocked as she was. 'I'm afraid you are hearing things, friend.'

'It'd be some find though, wouldn't it?' said the woman, sounding disappointed. 'A free ticket to the outside world at last.'

'That is what the wardens want you to believe. They'd have your head on a traitor's pole the moment you handed her over. Too risky, I'd say. It's better forgotten.'

The voices moved away. The door closed and Edgar whispered quietly. 'He saw us. What do we do now? Climb down?'

'We can't go anywhere else,' said Kate. 'Why didn't he give us away?'

Before Edgar could answer, the man's face reappeared

above the grate. They both heard the scratch of a match and he held the flame out beside him.

'You might as well come down,' he said, his voice darker than before. 'You have nowhere to go. The Blackwatch have made sure of that. They are lighting all the fires, and I can have this one hot and blazing in a few seconds, so I suggest you do as I say.'

The flame burned down to the man's fingertips as he watched them both. When they didn't move, he let the match fall. The flame fizzled and caught upon a knot of twisted bark.

'All right! We're coming!' said Edgar, dropping down into the grate and stamping out the flame. Kate was next, and when the two of them stood side by side within that room they both felt like scruffy servants who had wandered into a place they did not belong.

The fireplace that had appeared huge from above was perfectly in proportion to the room it served. Compared to other places Kate and Edgar had seen in the City Below, that one room was more luxurious than anything they had come to expect. It was a bedroom, with a four-poster bed carved beautifully from old wood and covered in layers of intricately embroidered blankets that must have taken months to make. There were coloured candles lit in glass holders all round the walls and large wardrobes locked with black keys, one of which had a beautiful red dress hanging on a hook beside it. There had been no hint of such splendour from what they had seen of the cavern outside, and Edgar was the first to ask what both of them were thinking.

'Who lives here?' he said.

'The leader of this community,' said the man. 'A

woman I have called my mistress for too long.' He was staring at Kate as if she was a work of art, not a soot-covered girl who was walking dirt all over the floor. 'But that does not matter now.'

'Why not?' asked Kate.

The man walked over to a small open window in the wall, unlooped a circular pendant from round his neck and held it out as far as he could, moving it so light flickered from its crystal face.

'What are you doing?' demanded Edgar.

'One of the many tasks I was sent here to perform. Please, make yourselves comfortable. We will not have to wait long.'

Kate did not like the expression on the man's face. It was a look of secret triumph and it made her uncomfortable.

'We're sorry about the mess on your floor,' she said, tugging Edgar's sleeve and leading him towards the door. 'We appreciate your not turning us in, but we're not who you think we are. We're just passing through, aren't we?' She nudged Edgar's arm.

'Yes. Er . . . thanks for that,' he said. 'Bye then.'

The man watched them all the way to the door. Kate half expected him to try to block their way, but there was no need. The door was locked.

'I find it is always best to be prepared,' he said, drawing a long blade from a sheath hidden within his clothes. 'For the past year I have acted as a servant to the lady of this cavern, but my true purpose here is far greater. I have seen your face, girl. I know who you are. You are not going anywhere.'

'Yes, we are,' said Edgar, rattling the door handle.

'You'd better come over here and unlock this door right now, before things turn nasty.'

'Do you think I am afraid of a worm like you?' said the man. 'If your face was not also known to me, you would be dead already.'

'Well, that's good to know,' said Edgar. 'Now, are you going to open this door?'

'In my own time. Once my countrymen arrive.'

'You're with them,' said Kate, suddenly realising how much danger she and Edgar were in. 'The Blackwatch. You're one of them, aren't you?'

'That is very true,' said the man. 'We have been looking for you.'

'Kate, head for the window,' said Edgar. 'I've got this.'

'No, there's no point. Who knows how many agents they have out there?'

'We still have to try.'

'No,' said the man. 'You don't. It is too late for that.'

Shadows moved along the pathway outside and the silhouettes of a group of men passed across the window. One of them already had the key. The door opened slowly, pushed open by the point of a long blade, and the Blackwatch's leader stepped inside. Kate backed towards the bed and Edgar stood between her and the advancing men. There was nothing either of them could do. The agent's eyes were vicious, his teeth bared in a wolfish smile.

'The hunt is over,' he said. 'Your lives are mine now.'

15

The Price

Dalliah waited for Silas's answer. There was no real choice to make, and he knew it. Even there on the Continent, Dalliah was clearly Skilled enough to work the veil in ways he had never seen. She could easily have used that ability against him to get what she wanted, so the only real question was why she had even asked him at all.

Even if the veil was falling, there was no telling what kind of damage interfering with it could do, and there was no guarantee that Dalliah's plan would even work. All she had was a theory, yet she seemed willing to gamble the entire balance of life and death upon a plan whose best outcome would only benefit two living souls. Silas could not deny the reward was tempting. To regain his spirit after so long was something he would do almost anything to achieve. Now was the moment for him to take a gamble. He had to buy himself more time.

'I will help you,' he said finally, all too aware of what

giving his word to Dalliah could mean. 'But *he* should have no part in this.'

'Bandermain's presence here is not open for negotiation,' said Dalliah. 'He will stay because I demand it.'

'Why? What use can he be to us?'

'The arrangement we have has not yet been fulfilled. He knows where his loyalties lie.'

Bandermain's eyes were heavy and a vein in his forehead pulsed noticeably beneath his skin. His eyebrows knitted together as he rolled his shoulders back, trying to make himself appear strong and healthy.

'Celador?' Silas said, as Bandermain's eyes met his with a feral look. 'How long have you been like this?'

'Not all of us are as blessed as you,' said Bandermain. There was venom in his voice, and he was about to say something else when the words were lost in a sudden flurry of racking coughs. Flecks of blood speckled his lips and he wiped them away with the back of his hand.

'The details are unimportant,' said Dalliah, turning away. 'Suffice to say, Officer Bandermain requires my assistance in order to maintain his health and in return he has pledged the services of himself and his men to our cause. The Continental leaders have given the Blackwatch orders to infiltrate Albion and cripple the High Council. I have no interest in getting in their way. They will continue to follow those orders. All I ask is that they follow a few of mine at the same time.'

'Whatever you have done for him does not seem to be working,' said Silas.

'His health is not your concern,' said Dalliah. 'He has done everything I have asked, and at the end of all this he shall receive his reward.'

Bandermain began to speak, but he coughed again, trying and failing to hold back the spasms that strained his lungs, forcing his fingers to claw at the cupboard beside him. As one of the Skilled, Dalliah could have taken his pain away in moments, but instead she just watched him impassively.

'This is how you treat your allies?' asked Silas.

'Bandermain knew what to expect,' said Dalliah. 'His sickness must sometimes be allowed to carry him close to death if he is to be of any use to me.'

'And he agreed to this?'

Bandermain had given up trying to look well and was concentrating solely upon breathing instead.

'He has proved himself strong enough for what I require,' said Dalliah. 'Every fifth day he must allow himself to move close to death. He has endured the experience many times. He will survive long enough to see this through.'

'He is certainly dying,' said Silas. 'Any fool could see that.'

'I'm not . . . dead . . . yet,' said Bandermain, looking up at him.

Silas smiled coldly. 'Entertaining as it would be to watch you dance with death, I could gladly save you the suffering and send you on your way.'

'You . . . would not . . . understand,' said Bandermain. 'I do . . . what is necessary.'

Dalliah placed a hand on Bandermain's shoulder. At first Silas thought she was going to heal him, or at least ease his suffering, but her touch was not a caring one. It was one of ownership. If anything, Bandermain looked worse the longer she stood with him, as if she were somehow actively taking his life away from him. Silas did not know how that could be possible. He had never heard of anyone who was capable of such a thing.

Bandermain noticeably weakened before Silas's eyes, but he faced the experience with a soldier's steadfast will. Silas was intrigued that he could allow his soul and his body to be abused in such a way. Whatever reward Dalliah had promised him, it was worth enduring near-death to possess.

'This affliction of yours. Is it contagious?' Silas asked. 'Have you been spreading your germ-ridden filth around your own streets?'

Bandermain coughed blood, leaving Dalliah to answer.

'He is infected with the creeping lung,' she said.

Silas instinctively took a step back. 'You let him walk out amongst people with the creeping lung? Either cure him or kill him. And burn the corpse before it is cold!'

'No,' said Dalliah.

'He is a walking plague!'

'He has only just entered the final stages. There is at least another day before he becomes severely contagious.'

'Then cure him and be done with it.'

'No. He has agreed to this.'

'No one *agrees* to suffer the creeping lung.'

'When we met, he was already ravaged by the disease,' said Dalliah. 'He owes me his life. What he is doing now could well allow the Continent to end this war. He is serving his country the best way he can.'

Silas felt something crackle on the air. The veil was settling across the room, attracted to the promise of Bandermain's imminent death. Frost sparkled upon Dalliah's fingertips and Silas realised what she was doing.

The creeping lung was a slow and painful death. Even the most capable among the Skilled had difficulty curing it, and the process of dying could drag on for days unless someone showed enough compassion to kill the infected. Dalliah was using Bandermain as a magnet, exploiting the veil's attraction to him in order to strengthen her own link to it. There was no telling how long he had been infected by the disease. Dalliah could have been keeping him alive for weeks, strengthening his body just enough to make sure death could not take him.

Dalliah stood listening to something within the veil. Silas felt it reaching out to him, but this time he did not enter it with her.

'You were right, Officer Bandermain,' she said. 'Your men have done well.'

Bandermain stood up as straight as his chest would allow. 'They . . . have her?'

Dalliah nodded once. 'They do.'

Bandermain smiled a bloodied grin of triumph. 'Then all of this . . . will be worthwhile.'

'Congratulations on a successful hunt,' said Silas.

'The prize shall benefit us all. If Dalliah is right . . . that girl's life . . . is worth more than rubies.'

'Her life is not important,' Silas corrected him. 'We intend to take her soul.'

Bandermain shrugged. 'They are one and the same.'

'No,' said Silas. 'They are not.'

'With the girl safe, we are ready to begin,' said Dalliah, withdrawing her consciousness from the veil. 'The boy she travels with. Do you know him well?'

'I know enough to never underestimate his ingenuity or his stupidity,' said Silas.

'The two of them have become closer than I had antici-pated,' said Dalliah. 'It appears Kate has claimed the boy, though neither of them appears to be aware of it yet.'

'Claimed?'

'It is an old technique. One that might have caused problems for us if I had not become aware of their bond weeks ago,' said Dalliah. 'When I first knew the Winters family, their Skill was already turning away from the healing and communicative arts to those involving spirit, blood and sacrifice. The warning at the front of *Wintercraft* was written by a Winters for all of the Winters who were yet to be born. *Those who wish to see the dark, be ready to pay your price*. Those are not just empty words. They were written because the family were already descending deeper into areas of veil study that not even other Walkers would dare to attempt. Kate is apparently no different. By not training her to control the veil, the Skilled have forced her to act upon instinct instead; a dangerous path for a Winters. Your bond with her was created through blood, but her link with the boy is equally important. He has become both her greatest distraction and her greatest strength. His presence grounds her to the world of the living, preventing her from realising her potential and protecting her from the more damaging abilities she does not yet know that she possesses. Her spirit has chosen him as its focus for now. She has become protective of him. He must be removed from her at the right time if she is to do what we require of her. If they are separated too soon, she will be more difficult to control.

'My men . . . know what to do,' said Bandermain.

'I do not doubt it,' said Dalliah. 'Silas, are you ready to do your part?'

'I am.'

'Then remain here while I prepare for the girl's arrival,' said Dalliah. 'I require nothing more from you at this time. Do not leave this room until I come for you. Will you obey?'

Silas nodded his agreement.

'You know what is at stake,' said Dalliah. 'We will do what must be done.'

Dalliah was a keen manipulator. She expected her orders to have some effect upon Silas, and he knew it. His refusal to react to her dominance over the situation would have told her as much about him as any other response, but he trusted her even less than she trusted him. She was too open with her information; too keen to insist that all three of them were equals when one of them was being held deliberately on the threshold of death and the other had all but been taken to that house as a prisoner. Silas kept his eyes upon her as she left the room. She was too calm. Too organised. Whatever she was planning, neither he nor Bandermain would truly be a part of it.

'You will get used to it,' said Bandermain, sinking down into an armchair the moment she was gone. 'That woman is a force of nature.'

'She has poisoned your mind,' said Silas.

'She has opened my eyes.'

'You are weak, Celador.'

'As weak as you? You came here of your own free will. I doubt she planned it any other way. The war is there ready to be won, Silas. Your country will lose. Forget about Albion. Your people have most definitely forgotten about you. Her offer sounds like a fine one to me.'

'I have pledged my help and I will give it,' said Silas.

Bandermain laughed, his voice dissolving into more racking coughs. 'Am I speaking to the man of honour, or to the strategist?' he asked. 'I know what you are thinking, because I would be thinking the same thing in your position, but whatever you have in mind, you will not win. I do not care what you think of this girl. All I care about is getting what I have earned. Dalliah says she can cure me and I believe her.'

'If she was going to cure you, she would have done it by now.'

'I *have* to believe her. The only other choice is death. Three of my men died from this disease before I even realised I had it. If running a few errands for a madwoman can rid me of it, I'll pay that price.'

'She is not a madwoman,' said Silas. 'I would feel better if she was.'

'Dalliah will not let you ruin this,' said Bandermain. 'That's why you are here. To be watched. This house is your cage as much as it is mine. You will not leave. Even if you did, she would bring you back.'

'I have no intention of going anywhere,' said Silas.

'Then that is one thing we have in common, at least.'

Bandermain sat back in the chair. Silas took a seat on the opposite side of the room and laid his sword across his lap.

'It would be a mercy to kill you,' he said, breaking the silence that had fallen between them. 'Unfortunately for you, I am feeling far from merciful today.'

'I appreciate that,' said Bandermain.

The two men sat, watching each other.

Silas could feel the veil still hanging within the room as Bandermain struggled for each breath. The creeping lung was a vicious disease: more of an infestation than an infection, caused by tiny insects that gradually ate away a sufferer's lungs from the inside out. Silas had seen people die from it before and he did not look forward to witnessing it again. It was a common threat out in the Continental wilds, and there was very little travellers could do to protect themselves against it.

Perhaps Bandermain had been suspicious of Dalliah's motives in the beginning, but now desperation had bought her his trust. Men upon the brink of death were willing to give an ear to anything that might earn them even a little more time in the living world. Bandermain's body had become his battlefield and, with Dalliah's help, this sickness was just another war that he fully expected to win.

Silas allowed the veil to creep steadily into his mind. If Dalliah was right and Kate had already been captured by the Blackwatch, there was nothing he could do for her. His crow would arrive too late to warn her about Bandermain's men, but he still had to confirm it for himself. His thoughts slipped gradually into the veil, but while a connection was possible it was weak at best.

All he caught were glimpses; flickers of images seen through the eyes of his crow as it flew across the walls of Fume. He saw the towers and streets soaked with pouring rain as the bird flew on, obeying his command. He let his thoughts fly with the crow, sinking back easily into the rhythms and energies of the veil that pulsed like a heartbeat all around him. The crow reacted to his presence, soaring faster upon the wind, speeding towards its destination as Silas reluctantly left it behind.

He focused solely upon Kate and the veil gave him flashes of what her eyes could see. Blackwatch agents were advancing towards her. He sensed her fear and felt her heart racing within his own chest. Then a different feeling crept across his senses. Something had changed. His body tensed, every muscle suddenly alert, and his consciousness returned quickly to Dalliah's room, where Bandermain was slowly walking across the floor towards him.

Silas's blade swept up to Bandermain's throat as he left the veil behind. Bandermain stopped walking. He had no weapon drawn and looked shaky on his feet, but Silas was not willing to take any chances.

'What are you doing?' he demanded.

'You can do what she does,' said Bandermain, wheezing painfully with each breath. 'You can see into the veil. You're one of them! She did not tell me that.'

'Perhaps because it is none of your business.'

Bandermain took a shaky step back and Silas carefully lowered his weapon.

'What did you see?'

'Only that Dalliah was telling the truth,' said Silas.

'Of course she was. She has no reason to lie.'

'She has many reasons. And most of them are on the other side of the sea, under *your* orders, collecting two young prisoners. The loyalty of your men is all Dalliah is interested in now. They have found what she wants.'

'You do not know everything.'

'What did she promise you, Celador? There are many ways to fight a war. Why are you so interested in helping Dalliah with hers?'

Bandermain turned his back on Silas and waved a

dismissive hand as he made his way back to his chair. 'Any victory . . . is still a victory,' he said, slumping down. 'She will give me . . . what no one else can. She can give me my life back.'

'She feeds you a handful of good days and forces you to endure the bad. That is not a life. It is torture.'

'That is what I was starting to believe as well . . . until you came.'

'Dalliah will never cure you,' said Silas. 'No one can.'

'I know that,' said Bandermain, coughing again. 'She told me there was another way. I did not believe her until I saw you . . . under that bridge, still alive. You are the proof. You have shown me what is possible.' Bandermain raised his hand and Silas saw the black stitches across his cut palm.

'Dalliah tried to bind your soul to hers,' said Silas. 'But she does not have *Wintercraft*. The binding cannot be performed without it.'

'She believed that it could,' said Bandermain. 'It is only a book, after all. Books can be copied, their contents remembered. It has no true power of its own.'

'It cannot be destroyed,' said Silas. 'And it always finds its way back into a Winters's hands. There is far more to *Wintercraft* than just ink and paper. I see the binding did not work.'

'There are some things even Dalliah cannot do,' said Bandermain, closing his palm. 'But the girl can. She will make sure of it. To live without fear of injury, sickness or death. *That* is life. You do not know how fortunate you are.'

'You would choose to live *my* life? Willingly?'

'I welcome it. I will see the end of this war. I will live to witness Albion's fall.'

'You have lost your mind, Celador.'

Bandermain laughed painfully. 'If I do nothing, I stand to lose far more than that,' he said. 'When my men bring Kate Winters to this house, she will give me the reward Dalliah has promised. She will be my salvation, Silas, just as she was yours.'

16
Waterways

'Edgar, don't do anything,' Kate whispered, as six more red-coated men poured into the room. All of them had scarred faces and fierce eyes. Their coats were old but neatly patched and their belts bristled with blades and black pouches. The leader was taller than the rest and the dagger he held was already stained with blood.

'You will both come with us,' he said. 'It would be best not to fight.'

Two agents stepped forward with ropes in their hands. One of them overpowered Edgar easily, pulled him away from Kate and tied his wrists together before pushing him towards the door. There was nothing either of them could do. They were outnumbered and outmatched. Kate held out her hands and let them be tied.

'That's right,' said the leader. 'We'll have no tricks from you, little witch.'

The Blackwatch searched Edgar for hidden weapons,

found nothing, and pushed him out of the door. Kate kept quiet. They did not search her and she was allowed to walk out into the cavern at her own speed. The people who lived in that place had gathered quickly to see her and her 'accomplice' brought out into the light. She heard shouts of anger and surprise as the Blackwatch walked them along the front of the houses and down endless flights of steps, but she kept her head high and her eyes down.

The Blackwatch took them down to the ground and walked them into a low tunnel that echoed with the rumbling sound of fast-moving water. There they divided into groups and Kate overheard the leader leaving orders with one of his men. She caught the words 'gathering point' and 'containment' but she could not hear enough to know what they were talking about. All but three of the Blackwatch agents remained in the cavern. Kate and Edgar were left with one guard each and, once he was satisfied his orders had been understood, the leader led the four of them deeper into the tunnel.

The darkness was broken by regular clutches of fire torches and it looked as if the path had been well used before the Blackwatch arrived. The rumbling sound grew louder the further they walked; shallow steps led gradually downwards and Kate could smell water in the air. The tunnel exit opened out into a tall vertical crack in the stone up ahead, just wide enough for two people to squeeze through side by side. Kate stepped through and found herself on the bank of a fast-flowing river, one that raced so quickly that it churned up ruffles of foam wherever it touched rocks jutting out from its cave-like banks.

A row of patched-together rowing boats were lashed to metal hooks sunk into the wall, pulled high up away from the water, and beside them a huge creaking waterwheel turned with the speeding flow.

The Blackwatch did not take Kate and Edgar towards the boats. The leader lifted a lantern from the wall and turned left instead, heading to where part of the tunnel had fallen in upon itself some time in the recent past. They picked their way over a pile of fallen earth and rocks towards a boat that was larger than the others, hidden from the view of anyone standing on their side of the river.

'Get in,' said the leader.

The boat was of an unusual design. It was much bigger than a rowing boat, its hull was thick and heavy and its rear half was completely covered by a curved roof that sealed the deck beneath it from every direction except the front. The prow curved in to a wide point lined with wooden guardrails that were hung all the way along with leather sacks. Two interlocked lengths of wood that could have been a short mast stood bare in the very centre and there were wooden chests nailed to the floor, each one locked with a thick padlock.

Kate climbed over the side of the boat and Edgar followed her in, then both turned quickly to face the men behind them.

'We have a long journey ahead of us,' said the leader. 'Sit down. Stay still, and you will see the end of this night in one piece.'

The boat jolted and scraped as the Blackwatch pushed and forced it down a cleared channel, grating it forward, shove by shove, towards the river. Water surged against the prow as the front half of the boat turned diagonally into it. Kate and Edgar sat down together on a bench that ran along the boat's exposed left side, clinging on to the guardrail with tied hands as water rushed over the deck. Kate heard a shouted order and the three men climbed aboard, letting the pull of the river do its work.

'Steady! Ready the poles!'

The river dragged the boat forward, pummelling the hull with its force, roaring against the wood until Kate felt sure it was about to burst through. Then the stern lifted clear of the bank and the river snatched the boat up in its watery claws, hurling it down the channel and forcing everyone on board to hold on. The boat bucked with the current, diving its prow deep into the water before being thrown back up again. The noise was deafening, water pounded hard against the hooded stern and the force propelled the boat wildly into a tunnel, where it began to shift and turn.

'Poles!' shouted the leader, his voice clear and calm.

The 'poles' were thick enough to be tree trunks, their flat ends already tattered and shredded from whatever use they were meant to be put to. Kate watched the wall on the right side of the tunnel speeding towards them in the lantern light. The dark-haired guard slid his piece of tree through a wide metal ring that pointed diagonally out of the boat – half hanging out over the water, half on board – and screwed metal bolts through the ring to hold it tightly in place.

When the wall came too close, the pole struck it first. Kate and Edgar screamed as the boat shook with the impact, throwing them across the deck and into the side of a wooden chest. Mud sprayed across the boat as the pole scored along the hard earth leaving deep clawmarks in its wake.

'Secure the cargo!' the leader ordered as the boat turned slowly away from the wall, pointing back into the centre of the river. 'Retract the pole!'

The dark-haired guard dealt with the pole, while the thinner man dragged Kate and Edgar back towards the guardrail. He lifted their arms and clipped their wrist ropes on to hooks meant for holding leather bags. 'Hold on this time,' he shouted at Kate. 'I don't want to have to come back looking for your corpse.'

Kate did as she was told, if only to save herself from the rocky water. The Blackwatch used the poles three more times to keep the boat safely on track, but the third time was definitely the worst. Instead of scraping through thick earth, the pole on the left side struck solid stone instead, splintering its head and smashing into the wall so hard that the guardrail buckled and cracked.

'What do they think they're—? *Arrgh!*' Edgar cried out. He and Kate twisted their hands out of reach of the grinding rocks and the boat scraped hard along the tunnel wall. Sparks flew from the metal hooks as the rocks chewed against them and they turned their faces away from the burning light.

The Blackwatch fought to bring the boat back under control but the river fought back. All Kate and Edgar could do was hang on, until the moment of relief when the boat left the wall behind and the tunnel opened into three separate paths, sending it careering down the central flow. The divided current slowed the river enough for the boat to gradually lose speed, and the Blackwatch leader stood at the very front, leaning out across the water as the vessel settled into the river's gentler flow. Kate dared to hope that the worst was over and the two guards used oars to steer the boat smoothly along the very centre of the current, eventually making them feel safe enough to let go of the guardrail.

'That is one way to travel,' said Edgar, as Kate pulled their ropes out of the bag hook.

'It is the only way,' said the leader, striding towards him. 'I see you have found your voice.'

'Hard not to with all that going on,' said Edgar. 'What are you trying to do? Kill us?'

'Not yet, boy.'

'Haven't you lot heard of ladders? It would've been much easier to just climb out of that cavern, you know.'

'We shall require the use of a boat where we are going,' said the leader. 'I suggest you keep any further opinions to yourself.' He turned to the dark-haired guard. 'Untie their hands and give them some food.'

'Yes, sir.' The guard walked across the boat and slipped a knife deftly through their wrist ropes.

'Where do you think this river goes?' asked Edgar, as the guard walked away.

The man stopped and looked back. 'We're taking you where all rivers go in the end,' he said. 'We're taking you to sea.'

Silas's crow liked being underground even less than it liked being out at sea. Its feathers were slick with rain and gritty with salt, and the close confines of Fume's streets already made it long for the freedom of the open sky. It hopped in between the bars that blocked the northern entrance to the Thieves' Way and fluttered in, flying gently above the surface of the underground river and following its sluggish course deep beneath Fume, into the lamplight of the smugglers' tunnels.

There were no humans to be seen. The crow blinked, searching for markers to follow. Silas's orders had been very clear. Find Kate. Deliver the message. It remembered the girl who had brought it back to life, but it did not like being away from its master for so long. It was aware of the girl's spirit on the river as the flowing water amplified the energies of the veil, letting it sense distant echoes of every soul within the river's sight. Kate was somewhere on the river, and if its master wanted the crow to find her, that is what it had to do.

The humans' lights lit the crow's way as it fluttered along the tunnels like a ghost. Wherever the river split it chose the path with the fastest water flow, taking it deeper and deeper underground. It dodged fishing nets that dropped from the tunnel roofs down to little anchors in the river bed, and was forced to glide close enough to the surface to feel the chill of the water on its chest feathers wherever the low roof dipped almost to the water. The vial the bird was carrying made its flight more awkward than usual, but it kept going, following a trail of river lights until at last the pounding roar of a second waterway thrummed through the earth.

The tunnel widened and bridges appeared across the water where the Thieves' Way drew in close to a stronger river. Their waters poured into the same tunnel, flowing just a few feet apart until the Thieves' Way turned to the left and curled gently away, leaving the second river to speed on. The crow checked the veil and changed rivers. The stronger river was older and followed an ancient path, carving its way through the earth and stone of Fume's deepest foundations on a course it had created over many thousands of years.

The humans who lived this far under the earth lived in clusters of tents in hollows cut into the walls, and the river's steep banks were filled with tiny one-man boats. The crow had travelled this far beneath Fume before, but only ever at Silas's side. It knew that it was a dangerous place to be, so when the first rock came speeding past its beak it was ready. The humans on the bank had not seen a living bird for many years, and their first instinct was to kill. The crow had a job to do, and it had no intention of ending up in a human's cooking pot. It swooped hard towards the rock-thrower, raking its claws through his hair, but the man's throwing arm was faster. A second rock streaked through the air. The crow swerved and felt a tug on its chest as the rock struck the little glass vial, smashing it and sending its neatly rolled note spinning down into the water below. The bird recovered quickly, flapped away from its attackers with an eerie screech and followed the river round a corner of jutting stone, leaving them and its precious cargo behind.

The crow flew on. It may not have its message any more, but it could still reach the girl. It was not long before buildings sprang up along the river; flat buildings that pressed into the walls as if they were being swallowed by the jaws of the earth. Waterwheels slapped the current, the river became straight and fast, and somewhere up ahead the girl was close by. The crow lowered its head and gathered speed. It streaked past a waterwheel next to a bank filled with rowing boats and let the veil lead the way, speeding round turns and on through a handful of branching tunnels until, finally, its target was in sight.

A boat pushed through the water up ahead, its bulbous stern looking like a half-sunk wooden bubble. The crow locked its sights upon it and with two strong beats of its wings settled into a spearing glide. The boat sloshed clumsily through the water as the crow matched its speed. Then it saw her.

The bird checked for enemies and spotted three men on the deck. The moment all three of them were looking the opposite way, it made its move, dropping down on to the hooded roof of the boat and scratching its claws gently into the wood. It opened its wings, stretched them out and let them settle back into place upon its back. The girl looked up and the crow sensed the presence of its master within the veil. Somewhere, Silas was listening.

Kate elbowed Edgar in the ribs and pointed to the bird perched on the boat's roof, its black wings shimmering in the lantern light.

'Is that what I think it is?' she whispered.

'It looks like Silas's crow!'

The crow ruffled its feathers, hopped along the roof and dropped smoothly through the air, landing proudly beside Kate. She reached out to touch it but it snapped at her fingers and lowered its head, eyeing her warily.

The Blackwatch leader crossed the deck to talk to his men and the crow hopped on to the battered guardrail behind Kate, staying out of sight.

'Do you think Silas is nearby?' asked Edgar.

'If he was, I think we would have seen him by now.'

Something sparkled on the bird's chest and Kate noticed what looked like broken glass looped into a string harness knotted round its back. 'There's something tied here,' she said quietly. The crow allowed her to unknot the damp string and the broken neck of a stoppered vial hung from it as she brought it down. 'I think it was carrying a bottle.'

'What? Like a message?'

'Maybe,' said Kate. 'Silas must have sent it here to tell us something.'

'Well, a lot of good that did us,' said Edgar. 'Do you think he might have—'

The Blackwatch leader glared across the boat at Edgar, silencing him at once. 'Who told you to speak?' he demanded, striding over to stand in front of him.

'Er . . . no one, sir,' said Edgar.

'Then I am telling you now. Be silent.'

The crow snapped its beak aggressively behind Kate, but the leader was already walking away.

'If the crow knew where to find us, Silas will,' Edgar whispered. 'Maybe he can help us.'

'Silas isn't here,' said Kate. 'No one is coming to help us.'

'Then what are we supposed to do? I suppose we could set the crow on them. It can be pretty vicious when it wants to be. Ow!' The crow had pecked Edgar's ear, and the Blackwatch leader turned again.

'Are you testing me, boy?'

Edgar was about to speak again but Kate grabbed his hand and spoke first. 'We just want to know why we are here,' she said. 'Where are we going?'

'That is not your business. You!' The leader turned to the dark-haired man. 'I told you to feed them.'

'Yes, sir.'

The man ducked into the back of the boat and soon re-emerged carrying a bowl of dried fish and soft bread. Kate took it from him before he could get close enough to spot the hidden crow and he spat at her feet before walking away.

'Nice,' said Edgar. 'I don't care how your men treat me, but they could at least treat Kate with some respect.'

The Blackwatch leader leaned over Edgar like a lion tormenting a rat. 'We respect her well enough,' he said. 'But some of us cannot forget what she is. My men do not trust the Skilled, but they will treat her well because she is worth something to them. You, on the other hand, need to learn your place.'

Edgar did not see the punch coming. The man's fist struck his nose sideways on, making it burst with pain, but Edgar did not make a sound.

'What did you do that for?' demanded Kate. 'Are you all right, Edgar?'

'Fine,' he said, grasping his nose and flinching a little as the leader patted him heavily on the top of his head.

'Now you will be quiet,' he said, 'or next time I will throw you over the side myself. Do you understand?'

Edgar said nothing, which the man took as agreement.

'Excellent,' he said. 'We will be out of the city very soon. Enjoy the peace while you can.'

Edgar would not allow Kate to check his nose, insisting that it did not feel broken, so they sat together, sharing the bread and fish with the crow and waiting for sunlight to appear in the never-ending maze of tunnels. But sunlight never came. The first glimpse Kate and Edgar had of the outside world was the glow of moonlight gleaming through an arch of metal bars. The underground entrances to the City Below had been sealed off, but the Blackwatch already knew about the bars and they were ready.

The dark-haired guard threw two anchoring lines over the sides of the boat, slowing it down and preventing the current from hurling it into the metal at speed. Chains creaked and the boat shuddered as the second guard jumped out on to the bank and worked at the padlocks holding the bars in place.

Kate and Edgar did not care what he was doing. They were too busy looking out at the beauty of a blue-black sky, feeling the cool touch of fresh air upon their faces and staring up at the silver moon when it peered out between the fast-moving clouds.

'I never thought I'd be so happy to see the moon,' said Kate.

The guard finished his work with the locks and the bars creaked open. The other waited for him to jump back on board and then the two anchor lines were unhitched. The current lifted the boat and sent it speeding out of the city's lower walls into clear air. The river left the city swiftly behind, carrying Kate and Edgar away from Fume, away from the Skilled and the wardens and the many nameless people who had been so happy to see them captured at last. There was nothing else for them to do but look up at the stars as the rain clouds cleared overhead and the river carried them between its darkened banks, away from the confines of the City Below and out into the open world.

17

Behind the Mask

Silas sat in silence, watching Bandermain's health deteriorating swiftly right in front of his eyes. The creeping lung was normally a slow, crippling disease, but without Dalliah's efforts to stem its course Bandermain's sickness was clearly making up for lost time. Soon he could do little more than sit and glare across the room, clenching his fists as he concentrated on his slow thin breaths. The sicker he became, the closer the veil drew in around the room, rejuvenating Silas's own body as Bandermain's gave way, and allowing him to connect with his crow far across the water once again.

Silas caught a glimpse of Kate and Edgar, both filthy and covered in black soot. He saw the Blackwatch's boat, the river and eventually the moon as the boat passed quietly beneath it. He could feel the gentle threads of the veil reaching down to Kate, curling around her but unable to fully connect, then he saw her hand resting within Edgar's and began to consider whether what Dalliah had said about the two of them could actually be possible.

The air felt different there in Albion, heavy and familiar, as if a blanket had been laid across the world. The Continent was bare and empty in comparison, but even though Silas recognised the feeling of home there was something not quite right about it. He allowed his concentration to lift and wander and then he sensed something else within the veil: a presence that hummed in his mind like a beetle caught within his ear.

It felt as if his mind was passing through clear air that was slowly being devoured by thick black smoke. The source of it came from somewhere in the east. The boundary between the veil and the living world was being worn away. The difference between the two was no longer so easy to sense. Silas could see gatherings of shades congregating at points where the veil was at its thinnest. He could feel their excitement, sense their anticipation as the living world moved nearer and nearer to their grasp.

Silas opened his eyes to the sound of the door opening as Dalliah walked into the room. Outside, the storm had passed, and the land beyond the uncurtained window was already shrouded in night. The veil had made him lose time. He had left himself vulnerable. He stood up at once, but Bandermain remained slumped in his chair.

'We are ready,' said Dalliah. 'Silas, please follow me. And help Bandermain to walk if he cannot manage alone.'

Silas did not want to help Bandermain and Bandermain had no intention of accepting any help. He heaved himself up off his chair and slung his heavy sword stubbornly across his back. Silas stood aside to let him hobble out of the room first and Bandermain was too ill to protest.

Curiosity carried Silas out of the house and back into Dalliah's overgrown land. High walls surrounded it on all sides, each one covered with the skeletal stems of climbing plants that spidered across the stones, and the ground was cobbled between patches of frozen grass.

Dalliah walked quickly towards a small building in the centre of the grounds, and Bandermain stopped twice to cough and compose himself, forcing Silas to stop too.

'Keep moving,' he said, drawing his sword and jabbing his back with the blade. 'You are wasting time.'

Bandermain looked up at Silas, clutching his shivering chest. 'Do not ruin this,' he said. 'I *need* this.'

Dalliah was too far away to hear Bandermain's words. Silas pulled him up and pushed him forward. He had no intention of letting an enemy walk behind him. 'Move,' he said.

'I know you don't want to be here,' said Bandermain. 'Do you think *I* chose this?'

'I know you think you're getting something out of it,' said Silas, forcing him on. 'But you're wrong. You are dying. Get used to it.'

Bandermain laughed quietly. 'You do not have to think about death,' he said. 'And soon, neither will I. I won't let you destroy this for me. Let it happen. We will both be better off.'

Silas kept walking.

'When I first found out what my leaders wanted from your country I thought they were insane,' said Bandermain, his words breaking with each breath. 'They think your High Council can communicate with the dead. They told

215

me they wanted to learn the secret for themselves, but I did not believe in the veil then. I was not interested in the Skilled. I thought they were witches, fools and liars. Then I met Dalliah and I knew that I had been wrong. When she told me about you . . . what had happened to you . . . I thought it was all just Albion propaganda. "The soldier who could not die." But you weren't a soldier any more. You were never sent into battle again. The High Council made you return to the ranks of the wardens. They were keeping you close by.'

'I was doing my duty,' said Silas.

'And now you are a traitor.' Bandermain laughed, forcing his lungs to spasm. His knees buckled. His hands grasped for Silas's arm but Silas stepped away and let Bandermain hit the ground. His body twitched, but Silas did nothing. Dalliah stopped and turned.

'Your new friend is dying,' said Silas. 'Now is as good a time as any to let him get on with it.'

Dalliah hurried back to Bandermain's side, crouched down beside him and laid her hand upon his throat. 'I cannot help him here,' she said. 'Carry him.'

'Why? Why is he so important?'

'He isn't. His orders are,' said Dalliah. 'Help him up.' Bandermain's eyes were wide and his mouth hung open as he gasped for breath. 'Pick him up.'

'No,' said Silas.

Dalliah glared at him in fury, but when she spoke she sounded calm, managing to keep her temper under control. 'This is very simple,' she said. 'Bandermain is no fool. If the Blackwatch return with the girl and find him dead, they have orders to kill her before she even sets foot within my walls.'

'If he passes the creeping lung to her she will be dead anyway,' said Silas.

'We need her alive, and we need him,' said Dalliah. 'Some of Bandermain's men are not as amenable as he has been. They will not hesitate to kill the girl and I will not be able to stop them before they do.'

'I will stop them,' said Silas. 'We do not need to appease the Blackwatch.'

'That is not your decision,' said Dalliah. 'You have spent barely twelve years without your spirit and already you believe you know everything. When you have lived a handful of centuries more perhaps you will understand that there are sacrifices to be made if you are to live any kind of meaningful life. Why do you think I am here and not in Albion? I lived on my home soil for two hundred years before they tried to hunt me. You lasted not much more than a decade. Do you not think the Blackwatch came looking for me when I arrived here just as they were sent looking for you? News travels swiftly over the water, Silas. Our presence terrifies those who are not like us and I too have been forced to make many sacrifices in my life. I have been forced to trade secrets, to find allies, to associate with people I would much rather see with their heads on sticks than sipping from a wine glass beside me. Bandermain is such an ally. If he dies now neither of us will get what we want.'

Silas looked down at Bandermain. His lips were tinged with blue, his wheezing had stopped and his body had fallen limp.

'I can slow his death but I cannot prevent it,' said Dalliah. 'Carry him.'

Silas grabbed Bandermain's arm and slung the dying man over his shoulder.

The walls of the building glinted as they walked towards it. Quartz-flecked cobblestones had been spread across the entire dome-shaped structure, making it look as if something was rising out of the courtyard, forcing up the cobbles like a whale breaking the surface of the ocean. Its door was made of swirls of iron and delicate panes of thin glass that shone blue in the rising moonlight. Dalliah unlocked it and stepped back, letting Silas carry Bandermain in first.

Inside the building was one single room; circular and small, but with the kind of atmosphere that set hairs prickling on the back of the neck. To Silas, the difference between that ominous room and the outside world was as clear as the difference between air and water.

'Put him down in the centre,' said Dalliah.

Silas walked forward slowly, carefully analysing his surroundings. The wall had no windows and its bare wooden frame was layered thickly with rows of yellowed bones. Some of the bones were decades old and others were boiled white and fresh. They were tied vertically to the wall, creating what looked like a gruesome fence, and hanging down from the ceiling in front of them were long cords holding thin candles and oil lamps, along with narrow-necked bottles and vials filled with what could only be blood.

'What is this?' demanded Silas. 'This is not true veil work.'

'It is the way I work,' said Dalliah. 'Lay him down.'

'Whose blood is this?'

'That is not important,' said Dalliah. 'Your blood is in here somewhere, if that is what you are asking. The Blackwatch had plenty of time to take it while you were in their hands.'

'Take them down,' said Silas. 'All of them.'

'Why? I thought you were a soldier. I expect you have spilled more than your share of blood in your time. This is no different.'

Silas dropped Bandermain unceremoniously to the floor. 'It is very different.'

'Why? Because you don't understand it? If everyone condemned everything they did not understand there would be very little else for them to do in this world.'

Dalliah knelt down beside Bandermain and once more pressed her hand against his throat. This time the veil answered her. Bandermain breathed in suddenly, rolled on to his side and spat blood across the floor.

'How many times have you done that to him?' asked Silas.

'More than I thought I would need to,' replied Dalliah. 'This time will be the last.'

Silas looked round at the hundreds of glass containers swinging gently with the movement of air in the room.

'Da'ru wore a necklace filled with blood when she worked the listening circles,' he said. 'Is this where she learned to do it?'

'I taught her a little of what time had taught me,' said Dalliah. 'She was my hand across the ocean. She could attempt techniques in Albion that I could never achieve here. She was a useful tool. I learned a lot from her mistakes . . . and from her successes.' Dalliah stood up and looked straight at Silas, daring him to say the words that were already on his lips.

'You told her how to use the circles,' he said. 'You told her where the book of Wintercraft was buried and you told her to experiment on the veil. On *me*.'

'As we can see, it worked very well,' said Dalliah. 'You should thank me. You have been able to see into a world that few people have ever known. You know the truth about the ways of the spirit. Perhaps you have suffered, but that is a small price to pay for what you have experienced. You have looked beyond the boundaries of our world. It has made you more powerful than your enemies and carried you beyond the limits of humankind.'

'Why would you do that?' asked Silas. 'What did you have to gain?'

'I needed someone I could trust,' said Dalliah. 'Someone who could see the world the way I see it. You were my first choice. The subjects who died before you were never meant to survive the procedure. Da'ru needed to perfect her skills. And she did so admirably. I only pointed her down the path the veil had already shown me. You were never meant to lead an ordinary life, Silas, any more than Kate Winters was meant to sell books in a dying town. With your skills, you could have changed Albion a thousand times over. You could have overthrown the High Council and taken their place if you had wished. I gave you a gift, Silas. And what did you do with it? You obeyed orders. You waited. You tried to ignore what had happened to you instead of exploring its possibilities. You wasted the greatest opportunity any man could be given, but how you spent your life was not important to me, so long as it led you to be in the right place at the right time. We are all following a path that was laid out for us long ago. Even him.' She nudged Bandermain's arm with the toe of her shoe. 'The veil did not show me the truth until much later, but you were meant to have your spirit torn.

You were meant to find Kate Winters and bind her blood to your own. Fate made sure you played your part in history, Silas. You are as much its pawn as any of us. That is why you are here.'

Silas looked round at the hanging bottles. There was no way to tell which one belonged to him, but if his blood was in there it meant traces of Kate's were too. Silas knew enough about the Skilled to see that something else was going on in that room, something that had nothing to do with Dalliah's plans for the veil. The place felt too strange. The air felt heavy. The longer he stayed within it the more effort it took to think. 'Those vials,' he said. 'How much of my blood did you take?'

'Enough,' said Dalliah, as Bandermain struggled to his feet. 'That was one of the reasons I chose you. You are an intelligent man, so it surprises me how stupid you can be sometimes. Wintercraft is not a warm and friendly discipline. Its strength comes from blood, suffering and pain. Kate Winters is already discovering that for herself. Even you recognised Wintercraft as the fastest way to free your spirit and find peace in death. You did not care what would happen to the girl when you were finished with her. You did not care what you were opening up inside her soul. There were reasons her family buried that book in the end and why the Skilled were so eager to keep it secret once it had resurfaced. But *Wintercraft* never remains buried for long. Walkers always find their way to its pages. The veil shows us everything. You believe that you have mastered the veil's secrets. You are wrong.'

Something sharp prickled inside Silas's chest, like tiny hairs stabbing the inside of his lungs.

'The creeping lung is a very interesting disease,' said

221

Dalliah. 'Tiny creatures that spread and pass between hosts, embedding themselves in human lungs and slowly eating away the tissue until there is nothing left. Did you think you would be immune to it here? Do you still think your body does not need to breathe?'

Silas tested his lungs, making them bristle more sharply with each deep breath.

'What the veil slows down, it can also speed up,' said Dalliah. 'Under the right conditions it can even transfer physical suffering from one body into another. We may not suffer the ravages of illness and disease, but we feel the shadow of them living within others and we can spread a sickness by influencing the soul. We can make a body believe it is suffering. We can turn it against itself and carry it right to the very point of death. How are you feeling, Silas?'

The first spasm gripped Silas's lungs like a fist. His chest heaved and he coughed speckles of warm blood.

'Our bodies do not degrade as quickly as those of others, but they are still quite fragile,' said Dalliah. 'We need to take care of them. You have been careless.'

'This is not possible,' said Silas.

'Why? Because Da'ru told you it couldn't happen?' said Dalliah. 'Where do you think she was getting her information? From *Wintercraft*? Don't be so stupid.'

Bandermain stared at Silas as if he was watching his entire world fall apart. 'You told me this wouldn't happen!' he said. 'You told me it couldn't affect him!'

'Silas is as healthy as he was the moment he walked in here,' said Dalliah. 'His body only *thinks* it is ill. He cannot fight it. His mind is not strong enough.'

Silas glared up at her.

'The girl is supposed to cure me,' said Bandermain. 'She is supposed to make me like him. But it makes no difference! Look at him!'

'Calm yourself, Celador.'

'He should not be able to die!'

'He cannot die. But that does not mean he cannot suffer.'

Silas gasped for breath. He felt as if he was drowning. His lungs were filling with blood. His body was not healing and the damage was spreading. He had become used to believing in his body's ability to repair itself and had spent many minutes underwater without any desperate need for air, but this was very different. His body was failing from the inside out. He had assumed, wrongly, that his lungs were no longer of any real use to him. Any energy his body needed was drawn directly from the veil. The veil had kept him alive, no matter what extent of abuse his body had suffered, and he had relied upon it to sustain him. He had not realised how precious his body still was to him until that moment.

'Pain is the only way to control you, Silas. Da'ru proved that. You are not as strong as you believe yourself to be. Not here. Not any more. I truly believed we could be allies, but now I know better.'

Silas did not feel his body when it hit the floor. His mind was focused fully upon his chest and the scratching pain, like needle-thin claws scraping inside it. He could hear Bandermain's voice close by and Dalliah speaking calmly in reply. He punched the floor, barely aware of the pain cracking across his knuckles as they crunched into the stones.

'You have done well, Celador,' Silas heard her say, as

darkness spread across his vision, leaving only a pinprick of light. 'Soon we will be free of our pain. Nothing has changed. The girl's death will save us both.'

Silas tried to move, but his limbs were heavy, his body as immovable as a tombstone knotted down by weeds. Then his sight gave out and all he had was the drifting emptiness of the dark. He reached for the veil, focusing hard upon the circle surrounding him. He could feel Dalliah's energy threading around the room in a gentle pulse, just enough to attract the veil. He should have noticed that. He should have sensed it, but it was too late for regrets. He felt the remnants of Kate's blood vibrating within him: Walker's blood. His cheek rested upon the stones, pressed within a tiny puddle of his own blood. Silas concentrated on that blood – willing it to connect with the circle and the veil. It took every ounce of energy he had left, but he felt the chill of the veil upon his face – the freezing touch of Wintercraft – as frost spread out across his cheek.

'What are you doing?' demanded Bandermain, but Silas was not listening.

Whatever Dalliah had done to him prevented the veil from healing his body, but she could not restrain what was left of his soul. Silas cast his mind out into the veil, fighting the pull of the pain as it struggled to draw him back. Bandermain and Dalliah stood over him, watching as his eyes glazed grey and his body fell still.

'What does this mean?' asked Bandermain.

Dalliah smiled and turned away, walking over to the building's iron door.

'Wait! What about our agreement?'

'You will have what you were promised,' said Dalliah.

Bandermain felt Silas's neck, searching for a pulse, but found none. The frost of the veil crept across to his fingers and he snatched them away. 'Witchery,' he whispered. 'What *is* this?'

But there was no one left to answer him.

18

Into the Dark

Kate looked back as the river curled swiftly away from the city and saw its huge torchlit walls stretching in a wide curve in both directions, further than the eye could see. If there had been any wardens posted at the river gate they were gone now. Edgar nudged her arm and pointed to something dark among some leafless bushes lining the riverbank. It looked like a black boot, and there was something glinting near it. A silver dagger held in a lifeless hand.

'So much for the wardens,' he said.

Kate watched the walls of Fume being swallowed by the night as the Blackwatch slid the split mast up to its full height and attached a large black sail that billowed powerfully in the wind. The leader took charge and soon the wind was powering them along faster than the river could flow, cutting through the wild counties of Albion and pushing them towards the distant eastern shore.

Once Fume's towers had fully disappeared over the dark horizon, Silas's crow suddenly became agitated. It clicked its beak sharply and shook its head as if something was trapped in its ear. Kate tried to calm it, but nothing she did made any difference. She grabbed hold of it to keep it still and the moment she touched its feathers she knew something was very wrong. Edgar was huddled beside her, glaring at the Blackwatch one by one, so he did not notice the look of shock on her face until she grabbed hold of his wrist, forcing him to look at her. Her eyes were fully black, she was breathing heavily and her skin was tinged with blue.

'It's Silas,' she said.

'Where?' Edgar looked out over the side of the boat, squinting at the banks.

Kate could not describe what she was seeing. She knew she was looking into the veil, but all she could see was darkness; the same kind of empty void she had seen around Silas when he entered the half-life with her on the Night of Souls. And then she felt it. Silas's presence, as near to her as Edgar was. 'He's here,' she said quietly. 'In the veil.'

'Maybe it's just a shade,' said Edgar. 'There's no reason to think—'

Kate gripped Edgar's hand tightly as images flashed suddenly through her mind. They felt like memories, but they did not belong to her. *She saw a town filled with white buildings and a circular room lined with bones. There was a Blackwatch officer standing beside her and candles and vials were hanging down from a domed ceiling.* 'It's Silas,' she said, as a heavy feeling clouded within her chest. 'He's ill.'

'What happened? Where is he?'

The two of them fell quiet as the thin officer walked beneath the sail and spoke quietly to the leader. He turned and pointed to Edgar, who shrank back against the guardrail.

'This doesn't look good,' he said.

Kate released the crow and let it hide in the space between them before the leader handed over control of the boat and walked over to them.

'Stand up,' he said.

'Why?'

The man heaved Edgar up by his wrist and the crow scuttled into hiding behind Kate. 'Where is it?' he demanded.

'Where's what?'

'There are feathers on this deck. Silas Dane's bird is here. Where is it?'

'I have no idea what you're talking about.'

The leader turned to his men. 'Find it. Kill it.'

Kate stood up before the officers could get close. She grabbed the crow and threw it as far as she could over the side of the boat. Its claws scraped the water as its wings beat hard into flight, and it fluttered in a wide circle around the lanterns in the sails, out of reach of the arrows that the dark-haired guard sent spearing towards it. The crow cackled up into the night sky, shadowing the boat while staying mockingly just out of bowshot.

The leader grabbed Kate by her coat collar. 'What did he tell you?' he demanded.

'Let her go!' Edgar pushed the man hard enough to make him pay attention and the stronger man struck him hard across the face.

'I have reconsidered the boy's position,' he said to his men. 'He is no longer welcome on this boat. Kill him.'

'You can't do that!' Kate cried.

'Do not tell me what I cannot do.'

'You could have left him behind. Why bring him all the way out here if you were just going to kill him?'

'My orders were to keep him alive until he became an inconvenience,' said the leader. 'That moment has passed.'

'Don't you think whoever sent you here should make that decision for themselves?'

'You have said enough, girl. I suggest you remain silent.'

The dark-haired guard had pinned Edgar against the guardrail and was pressing a dagger blade up against his throat. Edgar tried to hold him back, but he was not strong enough to do anything to help himself. Kate tried to pull the guard away, the blade drew a thin bead of blood and one of Silas's memories forced its way suddenly to the front of her panicked thoughts. *He was standing in front of a dark house, looking at a hooded woman. Kate knew that face. She had seen it twice before: in the memory captured in the skull and in the vision shared by the spirit wheel. That woman had been there when the bonemen died centuries ago, and now Silas was with her, greeting her by name.*

'Dalliah Grey!' she shouted, repeating Silas's words without even thinking about it. The atmosphere on the boat changed at once. 'You're working with her. Aren't you?'

All three of the Blackwatch looked surprised by the mention of the woman's name. The dark-haired guard's eyes flickered back to his leader and Kate saw something else within them. He was not just surprised to hear the name – he feared it. The leader's expression, however, gave nothing away

'What do you know about Dalliah Grey?' he demanded.

'I know enough,' she lied.

The dark-haired guard looked back at the leader, still pinning Edgar against the guardrail. 'This is witchery,' he said quietly.

The leader glared down at Kate with suspicion. 'Or she overheard one of you two mention the name,' he said. 'She knows nothing.'

Kate glanced at Edgar, making sure he was all right. 'I know that Dalliah has met Silas Dane,' she said quickly, piecing together what she had seen within the veil. 'Dalliah is one of the Skilled. You don't trust her, but you listen to her. You wouldn't have brought both of us on board unless someone ordered you to do it. She sent you here, didn't she?' Kate knew she was taking a risk, but there was nothing else she could do.

The dark-haired guard spoke first. 'No one said they knew each other,' he said. 'She was supposed to come quietly. No trouble. Dalliah lied to us.'

The leader raised a hand to silence him, never taking his eyes from Kate's face. 'Bandermain trusts Dalliah,' he said. 'This changes nothing.'

'What about the boy?'

Everyone stood in silence, waiting for the leader to make his decision. 'We will spare his life,' he said. 'For now.'

The dark-haired guard stepped back, and Edgar's hand immediately went to his neck.

'I don't know how you know Dalliah Grey, but one

more word out of your friend here and orders or not I will kill him myself,' said the leader. 'You have earned him a few more hours of life at most. I suggest he spends it in silence.' He walked away and Edgar stared at Kate as if she had just achieved the impossible.

'What was all that about?' he whispered as loudly as he dared. 'Dalliah Grey? Where did that come from?'

Kate leaned in to check his neck. The guard's blade had left a tiny cut and when she touched the skin it sealed at once. 'I think it was Silas,' she said. 'I saw a memory in the veil. He told me her name.'

'Well, I think you've just made those guards afraid of you.'

'It's Dalliah they're afraid of, not me.'

'That's not what I saw,' said Edgar. 'You stood up to them and it saved my life. Thank you.'

The crow continued circling high overhead as the boat made its way through the wide river channels towards the coast and the Blackwatch took shots at it whenever they thought it was straying too close. When they began to reach the large settlements that were scattered across the eastern wilds Kate and Edgar were sent into the covered section of the boat while the Blackwatch posed as traders, talked their way through the river gates and sailed on.

Slowly, the night lightened into dawn. Kate managed to sleep for a short while, resting her head on Edgar's shoulder, and Edgar was leaning back against the guardrail snoring loudly when a sudden explosion jolted them both awake. Edgar grunted and blinked, bleary-eyed. 'What's happening?' he said. The two of them blinked in the brightness of the rising sun and a streak of red flame burst into the sky above the boat.

'A fireflare,' said Kate. 'They're signalling someone.'

The land on either side of the river was covered in frosted green trees that glimmered in the sun light, and where the river wound between them Kate noticed something strange about the horizon. There were no hills in the distance, not even a single smoky plume from a fire marking an outlaw settlement or the beginning of another village. The horizon was dark, bleak and completely flat.

'Edgar,' she whispered, pointing through the trees. 'Edgar, look. I think I can see the ocean.' She stared out to the east, half afraid and half amazed by what she was seeing. 'I've never seen the sea before.'

The morning sun glittered upon the water, illuminating the cresting tops of distant waves and making them sparkle with light. It looked as if the sea was higher than the land, its waves rearing up ready to swallow the wilds in one mighty flood, but the waters were still and calm, and in that eerie place between the land and the sky a greater danger sat like a black scar upon the water. The silhouette of a ship was anchored out to sea. It looked to Kate like a wreck that had been dragged up from the ocean floor, skeletal and sinister. Green glass lanterns hung along its side and its empty masts loomed tall and ghostly in the sunlight.

The boat bounced gently as it passed through the shallow river mouth and out on to the open sea. The thin guard stood on the roof of the boat and flickered a second signal to the ship, using a circle of glass pressed against his palm to reflect the light of the sun. One of the ship's green lights winked in reply and the boat cut swiftly out towards it.

Kate and Edgar held on tightly to the guardrail as dark water surrounded them, fathomless and deep, and the closer they got to the ship the clearer it became. There were people on board, moving around on the deck, and the skeletal shapes Kate had noticed were damaged sections that had been singed by fire arrows or cracked by catapults. Most of them were badly patched, leaving scars on the ship that made it look battleworn and barely seaworthy.

'So . . . do we have a plan?' asked Edgar.

'We see what they want,' said Kate.

'And then what?'

The men on the ship slung ropes down to the boat as it bumped gently against its hull. Once it was secure, rope ladders followed.

'Prisoners first,' said the leader.

Edgar was first to climb the ladder and he turned to help Kate step up on to the deck behind him. They were met by unsheathed blades, letting them know exactly who was in charge on that ship.

'Prepare to set sail,' said the leader, stepping expertly up from the boat. 'We have what we came for.'

Two officers bundled Kate and Edgar quickly through a trapdoor in the deck, pushed them down a flight of steps and forced them into a small room that was split in half by a wall of bars. The dark-haired guard shoved them through a gate set into the bars and stood blocking the doorway.

'Won't be long now,' he said. 'I'll be glad to leave this rat-bitten rock of a country behind.'

'I'm sure it'll be glad to see the back of you too,' said Edgar.

The guard grinned. 'For now,' he said. 'Not for long.'

'What does that mean?' asked Kate. 'You're going back?'

'That depends on how good a little witch you are, doesn't it?' The guard stepped back, slammed the gate and locked it tight. 'You'll stay quiet in there,' he said. 'If you know what's good for you.'

The ship raised anchor, the sails were unfurled and Kate felt the great vessel lean and pitch as it began to gather speed, heading east towards the Continent, out into the unknown. Kate and Edgar could not talk freely with a guard nearby, so they spent the journey in nervous silence, neither of them knowing what to expect on the other side.

The further the ship sailed from Albion, the more distant the veil became until Kate had difficulty sensing it at all. It was as if a deep noise that had been reverberating in her mind for weeks had suddenly stopped, making her realise how quiet the world was without its relentless hum. The air grew colder, drawing steam from her breath, and she knew they were entering cooler waters when scratches of ice began scraping along the length of the hull.

Kate curled up on a narrow bedroll and tried to sleep away the journey. Hours passed slowly. When she did sleep she dreamed of Silas and the dark creeping edges of the half-life, and when she woke it was to the sound of the door lock scraping back and a dull bell tolling somewhere in the distance, chiming out the hour. The dark-haired guard entered the room and Kate reached over to a sleeping Edgar, shaking him awake.

'Rest's over,' said the guard. 'We've arrived.'

19

Blood Work

Silas couldn't see. The veil was not answering him and every one of his senses had failed. He was sealed in. Trapped in darkness. Powerless to do anything except hold on to his thoughts, let go of everything else, and drift. If he had been an ordinary man, death would have been waiting for him in that emptiness; instead there was nothing but the dark.

Memories flickered over one another . . . erratic and out of his control. The strange pressure of the veil stripped him of his sense of time, dampening every part of his being until he was not even certain that he was still thinking. He felt lost, empty, and forgotten. Perhaps this was what Dalliah had been talking about – his form of death. An ending with no end. Nothingness. Unable to move or speak with only smothering darkness around him, separating him from the world, sealing him within his own corner of the veil, silent and alone.

A flurry of light burst into his thoughts and for a moment he glimpsed the living world through his crow's eyes. Then the link was broken, the image lost. His crow was there, the world was still there, and that moment had given him a thread of hope. He still had a connection to the living world. It might be weak, but it was his.

Silas focused upon his crow, trying to regain that connection, but part of him held back, part of him did not want to fight to escape that place. The veil was already claiming what was left of his spirit, binding him tightly within its web, and already he was starting to forget. Fragments of his life were breaking away, stripping back his memory beyond his days as a warden and a soldier, spreading back into the few distant memories he had of his family: his mother, father and sister. He saw their faces and remembered the sparkle of silver as a warden counted a handful of coins into his father's hand.

That was a memory he could not forget, when, at ten years old, he had been sold to the wardens for less than the price of a carriage wheel. Twelve coins had been all his life was worth then. Twelve coins that would be spent feeding his sister; the sister he had loved enough to not complain when his parents had walked him to the meeting place and sold him into a life of order, discipline and death. He concentrated upon the last time he had seen his family, the promises they had made that they would see each other again, and the haunted look in his mother's eyes when the warden led him out of sight.

The veil could not strip that memory away and he held on to it, using it to focus his resistance. He had spent years crushing that memory into the back of his mind, seeing it as a weakness. Now it had become his strength.

The veil could not draw any closer. Its hold upon him faltered and in the midst of the emptiness he heard the crow screech out a short call. Heaviness pressed down around him.

Pressure sealed him in, constricting him. He saw flat stones laid out at an awkward angle in front of his eyes and felt the chill of the solid ground as he became aware of his body and his chest tried to heave in a single choking, spluttering breath. The veil fell away, his eyes opened, and he saw Bandermain standing over him, sword drawn, circled by candlelight.

'I saw you die!' said Bandermain, looking at him as if he had just crawled out of a grave. 'You were dead for hours! Your skin was cold!'

Silas's hand closed secretly around the hilt of the stolen dagger in his belt. His body felt alien to him, his fingers clumsy and unfamiliar. The confines of flesh and bones clung around him like a metal cage and it was an effort to move at all, but even that feeling was better than the draining emptiness of the half-life. He got to his feet, making Bandermain step back. His chest still prickled. The veil had healed the damage that had been done to his lungs but it was only a matter of time before the disease took his body to the brink of death again. He had bought himself some time; now he had to use it.

Silas struck before Bandermain had time to react, stabbing the dagger blade deep into his thigh and drawing his sword, ready to fight. Bandermain roared with pain and dragged out the bloodied blade. Silas watched him, waiting for him to react, until Bandermain's confusion bled into rage and his sword swung, metal striking metal as Silas parried the blow.

Strike after strike scraped and slammed along the edges of their blades, the sounds of battle clanging from the walls as Silas shifted from defence to attack. His sword was lighter, quicker, and found Bandermain's skin enough times to draw blood and grunts of anger from his enemy, but the battle was more equal than Silas had expected. Bandermain's blood-fury willed him on, pouring every ounce of frustration into his sword blows, fuelling them with adrenalin and fierce desperation as his illness weakened him. Silas's strength and skill thrived upon facing an equal opponent. Every hit was hard earned, every block powerful enough to shudder his bones. Decades of hate between the Continent and Albion welled up between the two men. It did not matter why they were fighting, only that they should.

Silas could feel the energy of the circle weakening him as he fought, draining him slowly, sapping his strength as the battle waged on. The blood-filled vials shone upon their cords all around him as Bandermain launched another attack, wheezing and wavering as blood returned to his lips. Silas knew then that he was fighting the wrong enemy. Those vials were used in blood work. He had seen Da'ru attempt similar experiments during her work for the High Council, using the energy in a person's blood to weaken their body, trap their spirit within the veil or bind them to a certain place. Bandermain and Silas were as helpless as each other under Dalliah's influence. She had sprung her trap and she was using them both.

Bandermain roared with rage as his sword swung back for a mighty strike. Silas anticipated it, but instead of blocking the blade he dodged to one side, landing a hard kick to the back of Bandermain's injured leg. The momentum of his swing threw Bandermain off balance as his knee buckled, the sword crashed from his hands and he fell to the floor. Silas stood over him, blade pointed down at his throat, and Bandermain looked up.

'You won't do it,' he said, whistling in each difficult breath. 'You won't risk angering her. You need Dalliah as much as I do.'

'You are a leech,' said Silas. 'You feed from her skill with the veil, while she feeds from your connection to it. Without her, you will die. She has given me nothing.'

'You came here for answers, exactly as she said you would,' said Bandermain. 'You will not throw the opportunity away.'

'You are beaten,' said Silas, pressing the blade closer to Bandermain's skin. 'Your life is mine to claim.'

'No,' said Dalliah. 'It is mine.' The door to the courtyard had opened and she was already walking inside. 'You are stronger than I anticipated, Silas,' she said. 'The veil should still have you, but it will claim you again soon enough.'

Silas could already feel his blood thinning and his muscles beginning to ache. He kicked Bandermain's sword away and swung his own weapon up through the air, slicing through the cords holding the vials closest to him and smashing them to the floor. Blood crept out of the shattered glass and spread eerily towards the centre of the room.

'Smash them. Crush them. It makes no difference,' said Dalliah. 'I can still use them.'

Silas sliced through more of the strings, raining glass and blood around the room as long as his strength remained.

'You want to feel you are doing something. I understand that,' said Dalliah. 'You do not want to admit that you are no longer in control. But I am not your enemy, Silas. This blood the Blackwatch took from you is not truly yours. It is as good as Winters blood now. Kate's essence lives within every drop. You did well to find her, but you cannot protect her from me. She is as much a slave to the forces of Wintercraft as you are. The veil has shown me her future. You cannot stop fate.'

'You will not subdue her with tricks like this,' said Silas, snatching a vial in his hand and throwing it to the floor. 'She will resist it.'

'She has not resisted me so far,' said Dalliah. 'The right thought, the right memory presented to her at exactly the right time . . . she is already mine. You gave her to me, Silas. The blood link between you and Kate allowed me to influence her mind. She had no defence against me. Even if she had tried to resist, it would never have been enough. She is not like the rest of her family. She trusts too easily, and her greatest mistake was in ever trusting you.'

Silas took a step back as the blood pooled around his feet, spreading into shallow grooves on the floor and tracing the faint outline of a skull cut into the stone. It was so faint that he had not even noticed the carving until the blood filled its curves like poured ink. He looked closer at the floor around it and saw the faint ghosts of more carvings: a skull, a bird, a wolf and a flame, and beneath his feet was a snowflake, the ancient mark of the Winters family. They were exactly the same symbols as those found on spirit wheels within Fume, and the more he looked, the more he found, spread in a spiral around the room.

'Kate has protected *Wintercraft* well,' said Dalliah. 'She has kept it close to her and she has studied it. You walked into the veil together and her blood lives within you. Experiences as powerful as that create bonds as inescapable as family and kinship. I recognised your loyalty to the girl long before you did. You let her live for a reason. You knew her life meant something, and you know that what I am doing is right. You just refuse to accept it.'

The energy of the veil vibrated in the air. Silas could sense Kate close by.

'Your work is over,' said Dalliah. 'Now you will stay silent. This room will help you to do what is right. It is here to help you, as it will help Kate.'

'I know what this room is,' said Silas. 'It is a prison.'

Dalliah smiled. 'You should have used your mind more often than your blade. Perhaps then you would not have found yourself in this situation. You might still have been free.'

'You cannot hold me here. My blood is not bound to yours. Only Kate can work a circle in that way.'

'And she *is* working it,' said Dalliah, touching one of the remaining vials of blood and making it swing upon its string. 'Kate has barely begun to understand what Wintercraft truly is. I manipulate her connection to the veil in any way I see fit. Having your blood to work with allows me to open her eyes to the heart of the veil. Have you looked into the darkness, Silas? Have you seen the place where your spirit lies?'

Dalliah snapped the vial from its cord and trickled a line of blood over her fingertips. The last time he had seen someone attempt blood work was the day his spirit had been broken, but this was something very different. Silas's eyes clouded white and a high-pitched screech pierced his mind. Bandermain got to his feet, watching with interest as Silas struggled to block out a sound that only he could hear. It was the screech of lost shades; a cry of torment and desperation.

Silas knew that sound. He had spent the first two years of his new life hearing those voices every day, drowning out every other sound and haunting him in his sleep. It had taken him a long time to ignore them, until eventually he had learned to block them out almost completely. Souls bound so deep within the veil were beyond the reach of all but the most skilled Walkers. They were the truly lost. Every one of them abandoned, forgotten and sealed away with no hope of release into life or death.

Echoes of his soul's prison still bled into Silas's life every day. Now Dalliah had used his blood to break down the barriers he had built between himself and the truth, throwing the door within his mind open once again. His knowledge of that place gave him some defence against it. He was ready for the wave of anguish, pain and desperation, but his was not the only blood Dalliah was working with, and somewhere inside the veil he heard Kate scream.

The dark-haired guard pressed his hand over Kate's mouth, muffling the scream that began the moment their carriage rattled through the last of Grale's back streets. They were travelling through a dark frosted forest, following a trail so narrow that branches snapped and scratched against the windows as the carriage rattled past.

Edgar was sitting in the seat opposite Kate, watching as her eyes blackened and changed to white, swirling with the clouded energies of the veil. 'What's happening to her?' he demanded.

Kate grabbed the carriage door handle but the guard held her still. Edgar had never seen her act that way before.

'We were warned this could happen,' said the leader. 'It will pass.'

'What do you mean, "it will pass"? It shouldn't be happening in the first place,' said Edgar. 'Look at her!'

'It will pass,' the leader said again. 'We will be there soon.'

'Kate!'

Kate opened her eyes, shivering, and saw Edgar crouching in front of her, clasping her icy hands. The two Blackwatch officers were watching him, the atmosphere in the carriage was heavy with threat, and for a moment it was hard for her to tell whether she was still inside the veil or not.

'You're all right,' said Edgar. 'You're back. You're safe.'

No words came anywhere close to the terrifying void Kate's mind had just been shown. Emptiness. Lifelessness. Nothingness. She had walked into the half-life before, but even that was nothing compared to the empty terror of what she had just seen. It was the worst kind of prison; a prison of the mind and soul, and she never wanted to see anything like it again.

Silas was the only person who had ever been able to draw Kate's mind into the veil against her will, but this time she knew that he was not the one responsible. She could feel the shadow of a woman close by, watching her within the veil.

The trees parted outside the carriage windows, giving way to a high stone wall broken by a pair of open gates. The land within those walls was filled with death; thick with the memories of many lives that had been ended too soon.

Kate glanced out of the carriage window as the wheels rattled slowly across the cobbles and caught sight of a large house on the other side of a wide courtyard. She recognised its twin spires, its boarded black windows with candlelight flickering behind them, and the sense of cold isolation, as if nothing existed outside its walls.

The driver pulled the horses to a halt outside a small circular building, beside a door made from glass and iron. He opened the carriage door and stepped down first, holding out a hand to help Kate to the ground. Kate jumped down without his help and a woman stepped out of the shadows beside the door. If she had not come forward to greet them, Kate would have believed she was a statue, she looked so lifeless and still. She felt the same sensation she experienced whenever she stood near to Silas: a feeling of emptiness and a sense of threat that could only come from people with broken souls. The woman pressed a bloodstained hand to her chest and bowed slowly.

'Welcome, Kate,' she said coldly. 'My name is Dalliah. I have been waiting to meet you for a very long time.'

20
Blade & Claw

Now that Kate could see the woman for herself, she had no doubt of who she was. She was the person she had seen in her vision through the spirit wheel. She might be older, but for someone who had to have lived for centuries she did not look very different from the young woman Kate had seen in her vision of the past; the woman who had condemned so many of the bonemen to death. She had the same sharp eyes, the same aura of dominance, and a sense of secrecy that made Kate think she was missing something that had been put out in the open for her to see. 'You knew the bonemen,' she said, not caring how impossible her words seemed. 'You ordered them to kill each other and bound their souls into the spirit wheels.'

'Very good,' said Dalliah. 'Few people possess a mind open enough to accept the truth of my existence during our first meeting. Even Silas was uncertain, and he and I are very much alike.'

'You're not like him,' said Kate.

'In certain ways, of course, you are right. Silas was blind to the truth of this world before his eyes were opened, whereas I saw the truth from the very beginning. The veil has shown me everything. All that has been, and all that will be. You may see the same, in time.' Dalliah reached her bloodied hand out to Kate, who did not take it.

'Why are we here?' asked Edgar.

Dalliah looked at him as if a dog had just opened its mouth and spoken. 'We are standing upon the brink of everything,' she said. 'We are about to bear witness to the birth of a new world. Everything that has happened was preordained, the future is the same, and even you will have your part to play.' She stepped aside and gestured to the door. 'Please,' she said. 'Silas is waiting for us inside.'

Kate stepped forward, but the Blackwatch leader held her back.

'Our work is done,' he said. 'What news do you have of Bandermain? Is he alive?'

'He is close to death,' said Dalliah. 'Had you taken much longer it is doubtful he would have survived. This girl will give him the help he needs.'

'Where is he?'

A man's strained voice carried from inside the building. 'Let her in!' it said. 'The girl. Now!'

The Blackwatch leader handed Kate over at once. 'Take her,' he said. 'We have done as ordered. I trust it will be enough.'

'As do I,' said Dalliah. 'Wait here with your men. You two, come with me.'

With three of the Blackwatch and Dalliah Grey

246

surrounding them, Kate and Edgar had no choice but to walk through that door and face whatever was on the other side. Kate went first, determined to lead the way. She could sense Silas close by. The veil, which had seemed faint and erratic since she set foot upon Continental soil, thrummed against her senses, her connection with it strengthening with every step. Kate knew how to recognise a listening circle when she sensed one, but what had been created inside that room was something else. Something older, more primitive and infinitely more powerful.

She stood still just a few steps inside the door and saw the bones lining the walls, the hanging vials, and the dimly glowing carvings on the bloodstained floor that her sensitive eyes could see clearly in the candlelight. The air was thick with energy but there was no listening circle there, no half-life and no shades. This was something she had not read about in *Wintercraft*.

Edgar was beside her. 'Now that is something I never thought I would see,' he whispered.

When Kate saw what he was looking at it took a few seconds for her mind to take it in. Silas was lying on the floor on the other side of the room, with a red-coated man standing over him holding the blade of his own blue-black sword to his neck. Silas was conscious, but only just. His eyes were shot with blood as they turned slowly to meet hers and his body was still.

'Silas,' she said; her nervous voice was barely more than a breath. She tried to cross the room to reach him, but Edgar held her back.

'Don't, Kate,' he said, looking round the bone-covered walls. 'There's something wrong in here. Don't . . . move.'

Kate caught the flicker of a warning in Silas's eyes and

stayed still, clenching her fingers into fists as Dalliah stepped between her and Edgar.

'Bandermain, what are you doing?' demanded Dalliah.

The red-coated man looked almost as ill as Silas. He was clutching his chest with his free hand, his voice thready and breathless. 'I have to know,' he said. 'I have to be sure.'

'He is no longer here to satisfy your curiosity,' said Dalliah. 'Your men have delivered the girl. You have earned my trust. It is time for you to receive your reward.'

'No.' Bandermain held the weapon steady against Silas's throat. 'If you can do this to him, what is to stop you doing it to me once I am changed? Look at him. You caused this. His life may be endless, but *that* is no way to live.'

'My treatment of Silas is only a precaution,' said Dalliah. 'He is a danger to me. You are not.'

'But I *will* be.' Bandermain's voice was growing louder and the strain of talking made him cough hard. 'No one should have that much power over another life.'

'What's wrong with him?' asked Edgar, taking a few steps back.

Bandermain snapped his head round to glare at him, and then turned his spit-soaked lips towards Kate. 'I knew Silas Dane long before you and your kind got your hands on him,' he said. 'His life was his own. He fought and bled for his country and it was an honour to stand against him. Now all it takes is one witch to set him on his back. One witch to poison his life!'

Dalliah stepped forward, pulling Kate with her. 'This is what you wanted,' she said. 'The girl is here. Do not turn your back on what we have achieved together. Leave Silas and accept your reward.'

'I will find no pleasure in taking the life of an unarmed enemy,' said Bandermain. 'But if what you say about Silas is true, he will survive. If not . . . I must know how far your witchery goes. A swift slice to neck and I will hold Silas's head in my hands. Let us see if he is still breathing after that. Let us see if this suffering is worthwhile.'

Bandermain leaned forward and pulled Silas off the floor by his bloodied shirt. 'I will give you an honourable end,' he said, raising the dark blade high over his shoulder. 'Death by the sword. If you survive, I will accept the path I have been offered. I will take this gift and start my life again. To face death – the ultimate enemy – and live . . . let us see if that truly is a battle Silas Dane can win.'

Dalliah stood watching as the sword reached its height, but instead of saying something to stop Bandermain she looked interested in what he was about to do. She wanted to see what was going to happen next.

'No!' Kate and Edgar shouted together as the sword flashed down towards Silas's neck. Edgar looked away and Dalliah stared wide-eyed as it streaked towards his skin. What came next all happened in a single moment.

Silas's sickly eyes looked up at the sweeping blade. He snatched hold of the hand holding his shirt and twisted it hard, snapping Bandermain's wrist and forcing him to let go. Silas fell back, out of reach of the sword, and Bandermain struggled to recover his balance as the glass in the door exploded in a burst of black feathers and splintering shards. Silas's crow slammed through it and flopped on to the floor, dazed and unsteady on its glass-dusted wings. Its claws scratched the stones and it launched itself, screeching and fluttering over Edgar's ducked head, towards the man attacking its master.

Bandermain did not see the bird coming until it was too late. He brought the sword down again, desperate to deliver a mortal blow, but Silas dodged and struck him hard in the throat, making him buckle and fall. The crow took its chance and flew at Bandermain's face in a feathered frenzy of beak and claws. The sword slid from his hand as he tried to break his fall and Silas reclaimed his weapon, sweeping it up as he got to his feet. Bandermain yelled in fury as the crow scratched at his face, barely managing to keep its snapping beak away from his eyes.

'Crow.' Silas said the word quietly, but the bird still heard him. It ceased its attack at once and fluttered awkwardly on to Silas's shoulder, out of reach of Bandermain's grasping hands.

Bandermain glared at the bird with a crazed look of fury. 'Keep that filthy thing away from me,' he said, drawing a dagger from his belt with his good hand and spinning it in his fingers.

'Get used to that feeling,' said Silas, glaring at Bandermain from beneath his eyebrows as his own neck twitched with pain. 'You want to know what it is like to live my life? Well, now you are living it. For weeks you have allowed this woman to take you to the edge of death and claw you back from it. You fear death. I see that. But what she has done to you is a far greater cruelty than simply watching you die. You are a tortured man and you do not even see it. You believe that my life is a reward to be handed out for a job well done, but you do not yet know what it truly means to fear something, Celador. No one should live as I do. No one should be denied the death that is rightfully theirs. That is cruelty. *That* is pain.'

'I could have killed you,' said Bandermain. 'No one can

survive a blade to the neck. Not even you.'

'Perhaps one day someone will put that theory to the test,' said Silas. 'But not you, and not today. You wanted life. I am proof that you can have it, but it does not come without its price. Do you still want what I have? Do you want to look into the current of death and turn away from it forever?'

Bandermain looked at the people around him and pointed his dagger shakily at Kate. 'You,' he said. 'You can heal me. You can take this sickness away.'

'She cannot heal this disease,' said Silas. 'No one can.'

'She *will*,' said Bandermain.

Dalliah pulled Kate closer to the sick man, so close that she could smell the scent of blood upon his breath. 'She may not be able to heal you,' said Dalliah, 'but she can *save* you. You are a worthy man, Celador. I will have need of you when the veil falls. Do not allow death to claim you now.'

Bandermain looked frailer every moment, until he barely had the strength to hold the dagger, and as he weakened Kate felt the energy in the room change. Silas had noticed it too and, whatever it was, it was having a direct effect upon Bandermain. Kate did not know what to do. Silas had had his chance to take his life, but he'd held back. She did not know if Bandermain was truly an enemy or not, but she could not stand by and watch a man die without doing something.

'Let me try,' she said.

'No,' Silas said suddenly. 'Stay away from him.'

'The only thing Kate will do here is what *I* tell her to do,' said Dalliah. 'You cannot afford to waste your time on foolish men, Kate. The veil is falling. If he will not accept the binding there is nothing your Skill can do for him. It will be a shame to see him die like this. I expected more from him. But if he wishes it . . .'

'No!' Bandermain grabbed Kate's arm in a feeble grip. 'Do it,' he said quietly. 'Let me have what Silas has. Let me live. They said you could do this for me. I do not want to die like this.'

Bandermain's face was wild and terrified. Kate tried not to look directly at him and she looked over at Silas instead, who was trying not to show how ill he was. Just moments ago Bandermain had attacked him, but it was hard to separate who was an enemy and who was a friend in that room.

'You have the book with you,' said Dalliah. 'I know *Wintercraft* is here. It will tell you what you need to do. All you need is a blade.'

'Take mine.' Bandermain handed Kate his dagger, hilt first, and when she took hold of it she deliberately clasped his uninjured hand in hers. She could feel the muscles quivering beneath his skin and could sense the veil hanging like a silvery aura around him, waiting for death to carry him into its current. He did not have long. As soon as she touched him Bandermain began to breathe more freely and the bird-claw scratches faded upon his skin. Kate heard the crack as his broken wrist snapped back into place and Bandermain stared at it as if it was the most amazing thing he had ever seen.

Kate could see Silas questioning her with his eyes, unsure of her plan. But Kate did not have a plan. The building they were standing in did not hold a listening circle, but that did not matter. Listening circles were created to channel the veil at places where the barrier between it and the living world was at its weakest. There on the Continent the veil was so far away that it needed to be attracted towards a circle, not pierced by one. With all the bodies buried beneath her land, Dalliah had recreated her own miniature version of Fume: a grave-yard inhabited by the restless souls of the dead. Kate could sense hundreds of those souls gathering around her, their presence tingling like eyes on the back of her neck. Every one of them was bound to that place; to the blood that had seeped into the soil, and to the memory of their deaths still hanging over them. Those souls carried the veil with them as Bandermain's spirit reached out for death.

Kate reached deeper into the veil, letting it flood across her senses in a way that was very different from what she had felt within an ordinary listening circle. The power of what was happening within that building just outside the reach of normal sight overwhelmed her. The candlelight that had glowed gently when Kate first walked in now revealed itself to be a carefully crafted lie, a veneer created by Dalliah to hide the raging maelstrom of destructive energy brewing underneath. Kate did not know how she had not sensed it before, and she was certain that if Silas had known what he was walking in to he never would have entered that room.

Opening her mind to the veil there was like lifting her head out of a gently flowing river and being dragged under by the pounding force of a raging waterfall. The full extent of the veil's attracted energy plummeted down around her; raw and disorganised, primal and wild. Listening circles were built to harness those energies; they tamed the veil and allowed it to be manipulated safely, but this circle simply called it forth and let it slam into its stones, fierce and uncontrolled. Kate braced her mind against it, defending herself against the awesome power of something far greater than any single life. The veil was one of the world's greatest secrets, one of the unseen threads that held the world together. Standing there, staring right into the heart of it, she could see that it was falling apart.

Memories flickered in the misted glaze that hung across her eyes, belonging to the living people standing within the room as well as the Blackwatch waiting patiently outside its doors. Kate glimpsed the minds of everyone there; everyone except Dalliah herself. Then she saw Edgar, just standing there, calmly ignorant of the invisible forces thundering down around him. To his eyes this room was just like any other room with bone-clad walls and bloodstained carvings on the floor and for a moment she envied him. He did not have to see what she could see. He did not have to struggle with the veil every day and be persecuted for something he could not control. Even Silas could not see the truth about this place and its influence was affecting him and Bandermain the most.

The racing energy scrubbed through the air, making it impossible for anyone except a Walker to connect with the veil. It was moving too fast, leaching into the earth, rejecting the lost souls that were not yet free to pass into death and then retreating back towards Albion. As it moved, its absence left a vacuum in its place, preventing Silas and Dalliah from being able to heal and speeding up the progression of Bandermain's illness. Kate could not even begin to understand how Dalliah had created that place, or how she was able to stand within it so calmly, conducting conversations as if nothing was happening when it felt as if the ground was about to open up and tear everything apart.

'Bandermain's spirit shall be bound to me,' said Dalliah, reaching out to her. 'The blade. Give it to me.' Kate handed her the dagger and watched her draw the silver twice across her palm, leaving two deep cuts behind.

Bandermain walked awkwardly towards Kate, his strength failing. 'Now mine,' he said as Dalliah handed the blade back to Kate, and he held out his own already scarred hand.

'This can't be undone,' said Kate. 'If I do this, you will never go back to the way you were. You will never get your spirit back.'

'Yes, yes. I know all that,' said Bandermain, impatience cutting through his words. 'Get on with it.'

Kate hesitated then, allowing the memory of how Bandermain had received those scars to bleed into her mind. Dalliah had already tried to bind his soul to hers twice before, and she had failed. The silver in the blade hummed gently as Kate's energy ran through it, ready to do something that she knew she might instantly regret.

'*Do it!*' said Bandermain.

Kate lowered the dagger just enough for Bandermain to sense that she was having serious doubts.

'You said she would do it!' he said to Dalliah.

'She will honour our agreement,' said Dalliah.

Silas dug the point of his sword into the floor, helping himself to stand. 'Things are not as simple as they first seemed, are they, Celador?' he said.

'Quiet!' Bandermain's eyes flickered briefly to Edgar, who was trying, and failing, to get Silas's attention. He lunged for him, grabbed his neck and locked it beneath his arm, holding him off balance so he could not squirm away. Edgar flailed his arms, trying to wriggle free, but stopped the moment another of Bandermain's daggers pressed against his back.

'It is a simple enough task,' said Bandermain, panting to catch his breath. 'Do it now, girl. Or I will show you how blood spilling should be done!'

21

Lost

Bandermain's anger flooded into the veil and Kate started to lose control. Everything she was seeing and feeling started to blend together; the veil, the memories, everything that was happening in the room throughout its past, present and future, until she was no longer sure what was happening and what was not. The vision the spirit wheel had shown her dominated her thoughts. Nothing made sense. Her head was splitting with pain, and then Dalliah was beside her, a calm face within the growing darkness as her mind began shutting down, desperate to escape the confusion.

'You are a true Winters,' said Dalliah. 'Your connection to the veil is so strong you are more like a shade than one of the living. But like so many of your ancestors, you lack the tenacity to get things done.'

'She is not one of your experiments,' said Silas's voice.

'But I will use her, exactly as you did,' said Dalliah.

'We have both learned that to achieve anything we must take what we want. Do not pretend that what I am doing is beneath you. You have done far worse.'

'I showed her what she was,' said Silas. 'That is all. Nothing like this.'

'And I am showing her what she will become. There is no difference.'

Kate saw Silas walking towards her; a black shadow against the veil's silvery light.

'Do not interfere,' said Dalliah. 'You knew what was going to happen. You cannot stop it now.'

Kate could hear Dalliah's words, but she could also hear something else underneath them; a whisper creeping through the veil. It was Dalliah's voice, but it sounded different – more distant.

'*Bandermain can help us repair what has been broken,*' she said. '*Save his life. We need his strength.*'

Kate looked over at Edgar, standing completely at Bandermain's mercy, and all she wanted was for everything to stop and give her time and space to think. She wanted her mind to be clear again, but even in the midst of all the confusion there was one thing of which she was perfectly sure. Even if she could bind someone's soul she knew that she could never bring herself to do it, and that certainty was more than she had had to hold on to for a long time.

'No.' She said the word out loud. 'I can't do it. I won't do it.'

Bandermain's sickly face turned as red as it could manage, twisting with rage and disappointment. And even though Edgar was scared, he smiled proudly at Kate, letting her know that she had done the right thing.

But Dalliah was unfazed by Kate's refusal. 'How will

you learn how capable you are if you do not test yourself?' she asked. 'This is your chance to become more than just the girl who made the Night of Souls real again. I will show you how to complete the work your ancestors began centuries before you were born. They knew this time would come. The veil has been weak from the very beginning. They knew it would fall one day, and they knew there would be Walkers here to help it along its way. The bonemen of Albion had a chance to show everyone the truth about our world. They had an opportunity and they turned away from it. You have already revealed the veil to many closed minds. Soon you will be able to show everyone a side of life that they could never have imagined. You are the only Walker I have been able to find. There should have been many more of us here at the end, but the last part of the plan must fall to us alone. We need Bandermain and his men to carry out that plan.'

'I don't care about your plan,' said Kate.

'The Skilled should have let you enter the veil from the beginning,' said Dalliah. 'They should have helped you instead of holding you back. Do you want to continue denying what you are? Or do you want to accept it?'

'What . . . is *happening*?' demanded Bandermain, struggling for breath. Death was close. Kate could not see it, but she could feel it, and so could he. It was coming for him.

'Quiet!' Dalliah glared at Bandermain, but this time he refused to be silenced.

'If no one here . . . is willing to help me,' he said, 'I will not . . . enter death alone.'

Somewhere inside her, Kate knew what was coming. The spirit wheel had warned her of it, Bandermain had already threatened to do it, but when the moment finally arrived she could not quite accept that it was real. The confusion of the veil pulled back from her eyes as she focused completely upon Edgar, whose brave smile melted into shock and pain as Bandermain's dagger sank deep into his back.

Kate stared as Bandermain pulled out the bloodied blade and she stood in horrified silence, unable to react, as he pushed Edgar to the floor. Silas shouted something and stepped towards Bandermain, but it was too late. The dagger fell from Bandermain's hand and he crumpled to his knees, unable to speak, unable to breathe, as the creeping lung finally claimed what was left of his life.

'Kate!' Silas turned to her as Bandermain slumped wide-eyed to the floor. 'Get out of here!'

But Kate could not move. She was staring at Edgar lying still upon the floor. His blood trailed into a carving of a bird cut into the stone and her eyes stung with tears.

Something moved across the floor. It looked as if the stones were rippling outwards from Bandermain's lifeless hand, moving towards Edgar. Kate could tell it was not a trick of the veil, but it had to be impossible. Silas snatched a candle from a cord hanging from the ceiling and threw it between Edgar and the creeping stones. The flame crackled and spat, and the moving floor changed direction, spreading around the source of burning heat. Only then did Kate really know what she was looking at. The tiny insects that had eaten Bandermain's lungs away were seeping out of his body and spreading across the floor in search of a new host. The floor was crawling with them, their tiny forms barely visible to the eye, moving across the ground like a cloud of dust.

Kate reached up, grabbed three ceiling candles and dropped them in front of her. Then she grabbed two more and clasped them in her hands, ready to protect herself as the creatures spread.

'The physical body is so frail and weak,' said Dalliah, standing beside her. 'You should know by now that the mind is where true strength lies.'

'Shut up!' Kate shouted, dropping another candle as the bugs spread her way. She had to get to Edgar.

Silas saw what she was doing, unhooked one of the few oil lamps and threw it into the centre of the creeping mass. Glass smashed, oil spread and flames burst into life, searing the tiny creatures before they could advance any further. Silas threw another lamp towards Edgar, setting fire to the sleeve of Bandermain's red coat, and a third smashed at Kate's feet, forcing her back, away from the growing flames.

'Stop!' Kate screamed, as Silas smashed a fourth lamp dangerously close to Edgar's head, sending glass shards sprinkling across his wild dark hair. 'He's not dead! He can't be dead!'

Silas's skin was slick with sweat. Between the creeping lung and Dalliah's manipulation of the veil, he was not thinking clearly. The crow flapped its wings restlessly as Silas grew weaker, but Bandermain's body had to be burned. Nothing else mattered but making sure every last one of those creatures was dead.

Dalliah pulled Kate towards the door. 'Listen to me,' she said, her voice pouring into Kate's ear like poison. 'As long as you are alive the people around you will always be in danger. You do not want that. I can see that your friend's pain disturbs you, but you are not strong enough to help him now. Leave him, come with me, and I will help you bring an end to this. You do not belong with him any more. You belong with me. I will show you the way. Let me help you. Let us do what needs to be done.'

Kate struggled to keep her eyes open as Dalliah's words washed over her, and her cheeks were damp with tears. 'I have to help him,' she said. 'I have to bring him back. Edgar!' She could hear Dalliah's veil-voice whispering quietly beneath her spoken words. She saw Edgar's chest rise and fall as he breathed in painful breaths, choking on the smoke that had begun to spread around the circular room.

Silas fell to his knees, willing himself to stand but no longer possessing the strength. Whatever Dalliah was doing, Kate knew she held all their lives in her hands. She was the only one who could stop this. Kate could give Dalliah everything she wanted; all she had to do was say yes.

'I couldn't bind that man's soul,' she said. 'It wasn't right. I couldn't do it.'

'Everything can be overcome,' Dalliah said carefully. 'No plan rests on the shoulders of one person alone. We will not suffer too badly for his loss.'

Kate turned to face her. 'I'll come with you,' she said, firmly wiping her tears away. 'I will. Whatever's wrong with the veil, I want to help you put it right.'

'No,' said Silas, his voice rasping, but still strong. 'She is lying to you, Kate. Do not listen to her.'

'Your ancestors wrote *Wintercraft* for you,' said Dalliah. 'But you have not seen everything it has to teach you. There are secrets within its pages that you will never discover without me. I will teach you, and soon you will know everything your family knew; everything I already know. I will hide nothing from you, Kate. Silas has had his time. He is the one who destroyed your life. He stole everything from you. Do not allow him to steal your future as well.'

As Dalliah held Kate's hand, her mind began to clear again. She began to feel comfortable and safe, and Dalliah's presence gave her a feeling of belonging that she had not felt for a very long time.

'Come with me.'

Kate allowed Dalliah to lead her towards the door, away from Silas, away from Edgar.

'It is too late for them, but their spirits will not be lost. They will remain bound to this place, just like all the other souls I have collected. This is the way it is meant to be. You can trust me, Kate.' The veil-voice echoed Dalliah's words. *'Trust me.'*

Kate found herself nodding slowly in agreement. Dalliah stepped carefully across the symbol-etched floor, crossed the carvings that glowed in the firelight and pulled Kate out into the open night.

The Blackwatch and their carriage were waiting outside. Dalliah forced Kate into the lead officer's hands and he held her tightly, preventing her from going back inside.

'Where is Bandermain?' he asked. 'Did the girl succeed?'

'Your commander is dead,' said Dalliah. 'The girl is not to blame. His disease was too far advanced. If you had found her sooner he would have stood a better chance.'

The officer signalled for his men to investigate. One of them entered the smoke-filled building, holding his sleeve over his mouth and nose, and emerged moments later.

'Three bodies,' he said. 'Blood everywhere.'

'Bodies?' Kate's voice was a whisper. He was wrong. He had to be wrong.

'Your commander fought with his last breath,' said Dalliah. 'He lost one battle, but he will carry a greater victory into his grave. He claimed the life of Silas Dane. Celador Bandermain is a hero.'

The Blackwatch officer considered Dalliah's words and bowed his head with respect. 'Then I must thank you for your efforts,' he said. 'Your attempts to save his life will not be forgotten. Bandermain's name will live on.'

'I'm sure it will,' Dalliah said quickly. 'He was willing to do what had to be done for the good of his country. Will you continue the work we planned together in honour of his name?'

The officer stood to attention. 'Of course.'

'Good. Then order your men to burn this place down. Burn the house. Burn everything. Our plan remains unchanged.'

'You can't do that! Edgar is in there!' Kate struggled to free herself but the two Blackwatch guards were already lighting torches and crossing the courtyard to set fire to the main house. 'No. Wait!' she cried. 'You have to get them out! *Silas!*' No one was listening to her. A thousand thoughts were battling for her attention at once, but all Kate saw were the flames licking higher and smoke pouring out of the domed building's door as Dalliah turned her back upon it.

'I require your carriage and your ship,' she said.

'Yes, my lady. My men will assist you in any way they can.'

'I shall require horses and a messenger bird once

we reach Albion's shores. Do you still have your men positioned within Fume?'

'Yes, my lady. Everything is ready.'

'Then let us begin.'

The Blackwatch leader forced Kate up into the carriage and he and Dalliah climbed in on either side of her as the great black house glowed with inner firelight.

'We can't just leave them!'

Dalliah rested her hand on Kate's wrist, the veil-voice crept through her mind and she felt herself giving in, watching the house's windows bursting in the heat of the growing flames and listening to the crackle of the circular building as its wooden frame split and burned.

'Edgar,' Kate whispered, but Dalliah's touch slowed her thoughts until she was no longer sure why she had said his name. She did not know why she was crying, or why the rising flames made her stomach knot with fear.

She watched through the carriage window as the two Blackwatch guards returned, walking straight through the pouring smoke like ghosts and climbing up into two seats at the front of the carriage.

'We shall reach our homeland soon,' said Dalliah, her voice gentle and eerily reassuring. 'It has been many years since I set foot upon Albion soil. This time I intend to stay.'

Once the two guards were back on board, the reins snapped and the horses sped swiftly to a trot, pulling the carriage away from the rising fires. They stopped just once to let the dark-haired guard open the gates and climb back on board, and then they were off, heading out deep into the forest. Kate watched the icicle-laden trees flash by in the evening light, their transparent fingers sparking like crystal as the carriage disturbed them, knocking them loose to smash upon the frozen ground.

The moment Dalliah passed out of the gate her connection with the energy in the circular building was broken. The energies fell, and Kate looked back as fire engulfed everything in the distance until all she could see was the glow of the flames.

'Do not worry about the past,' said Dalliah. 'We carry everything we need with us wherever we go. We need nothing else. Don't you agree?'

'Yes,' said Kate, but the word felt alien to her. She felt as if she was forgetting something, but she no longer knew what.

'Work the horses harder,' Dalliah ordered. The Blackwatch leader relayed the message to the driver and Dalliah smiled at Kate when the forest swallowed the burning buildings and she turned away from the window at last. 'I want to be at sea within the day.'

22
Fate

As soon as Dalliah's link to the circle was broken, Silas's broken spirit plunged back into his body and he forced his eyes open. He was on his side, lying beneath a thick layer of darkening smoke, and something was pecking at his nose. Firelight flickered gently across his crow's black feathers as it tried to wake him and flames were devouring the wooden walls, leaving bones scattered and singed on the floor as the cords holding them burned and snapped. Close by, Bandermain's clothes smouldered upon his lifeless body. His red coat was fully ablaze, his face turned towards a dark shape sprawled across the floor.

Silas got slowly to his feet, his body recovering slowly as it came back under his control. He tested his injured lungs and found the pain had lessened considerably. His chest was clear. Whatever influence that room had over him had been broken by Dalliah's absence. She had used the power of his own blood against him and he could no longer feel a single scratch or bite as he breathed in the hot black smoke. The injuries that had driven him into the darkness of the half-life were only impressions . . . manifestations, but they had felt real enough. If Silas had any doubt about the extent of Dalliah's Skill it faded at that moment. She was a formidable woman. She had defeated him easily and she expected his body to burn, leaving his broken spirit lost within the veil for eternity.

There was enough of the veil's influence left within the room to repel the ill effects of the smoke and Silas walked straight through it, making his way over to the dark shape lying beside Bandermain. He walked round his enemy's burning body and crouched down beside Edgar. The boy was not moving. Silas lifted one of his arms up, hoisted him over his shoulder and carried him to the door. One hard kick was enough to send it splaying out on its hinges, feeding more air to the fire inside.

Silas carried Edgar out into the courtyard and saw Dalliah's black house being torn apart by flames as he laid Edgar on the ground.

'Owwww . . .' Edgar groaned and his eyelids flickered. Silas pulled his eyes open with his thumbs.

'How many of your nine lives do you have left now, Mr Rill?'

Edgar coughed weakly.

'Keep still,' said Silas, carefully inspecting the dagger wound. 'You have lost a lot of blood. I can stop the bleeding but I cannot heal you here. It looks as if you hit your head when you fell. I thought you were dead.'

'Where's . . . Kate?'

'Gone,' said Silas, opening Edgar's bloodstained coat and tearing strips of fabric from the jumpers underneath.

'Dalliah took her?'

Silas pressed the fabric strips against the dagger wound. 'The wound is a clean one,' he said. 'If the blood clots quickly enough you should survive.'

'*Should?*'

'We have more important concerns.'

'I'd say this was pretty important! Ow!'

'*I* will find Kate. You will stay here.'

'I'm all right!' lied Edgar, trying to stand. 'I can walk.'

'Goodbye, Mr Rill.'

'What? Wait!'

Silas left Edgar on the ground and strode through the smoke towards the open gate.

'Silas?'

Edgar's shouts carried across Dalliah's land. Silas ignored him. The boy was unimportant. All that mattered was reaching Kate before Dalliah took her out to sea.

His boots thumped into the gravel, carrying him out through the gates, where he stopped and searched for something he hoped would still be there. Movement to his right made him turn and a large eye blinked at him from the darkness. The horse he had stolen from the stables in Grale was standing calmly in the trees. His crow took flight, flapping up into the branches overhead while Silas stepped towards the animal and rubbed its wide nose. 'A beast without fear,' he said. 'I was right.' Silas's touch calmed the horse and he leapt smoothly up on to its back. 'So much for fate,' he said, guiding the horse swiftly back out on to the path.

The pair of dead trees loomed over him as he rode towards the crossroads leading back towards Grale. The town lay to the north, Dalliah's house to the east. He still had time. All he had to do was ride . . . but then his thoughts turned to Edgar: an injured man, left bleeding and alone on enemy land. The horse gave him an advantage. It gave him speed. No matter what else was at stake, his conscience would not let him leave a fallen man behind.

Edgar heard the echo of hooves pounding across the ground and blinked into the darkness, half expecting the Blackwatch to have sent someone back to finish him off. A great beast thundered towards him. He managed to stand, but the dagger wound blazed and his head swam. He had done his best. He had tried to help Kate, and if he was going to die there he would at least die on his feet knowing he could have done no more. Then the rider slowed the horse to a walk and circled round him, holding an arm out for him to take.

'You may not be able to run, Mr Rill,' said Silas, 'but you can ride.'

Edgar could not believe what he was seeing. He reached up and grabbed Silas's hand, and let him heave him up on to the back of the horse.

'Hold on,' said Silas, and Edgar clutched the belt of his leather coat, clinging on tight.

The horse turned back towards the forest and raced into a gallop, speeding towards the trail through the trees. The path to Grale ran downhill most of the way, and at the few points where the trees were thinnest and the trail ran due west, Silas caught brief glimpses of moonlight sparkling upon the surface of the sea. Dalliah's carriage had a head start, but his horse was well rested and its hooves thumped into the dirt at a thundering pace. The track wound tightly between the trees and the horse raced on, finding extra speed as he guided it down the path.

The sky lightened into a mist-filled morning. The horse slowed to a steady pace, but by the time they reached the edge of Grale Dalliah's carriage was still nowhere in sight. Silas knew the Blackwatch would be watching the main routes into the town so he took a sharp turn off the forest road, sending the horse plunging through the trees and out into Grale's back streets.

Edgar's grip grew weaker as they rode over a river bridge, heading for the dock, until his fingers slipped completely at a tight corner and Silas had to grab hold of his arm to stop him from sliding off. He could not afford to slow the horse, but Edgar was unconscious. His condition was far worse than Silas had thought. The dock wasn't far. He could hold Edgar until then, but if he died before they reached it the delay he had caused by helping him would have been for nothing.

Behind Silas, in the distance, plumes of smoke and flame reached towards the sky from Dalliah's burning house. He looked for his crow and spotted it flying high above him, matching the horse's speed. It circled down, close enough to hear Silas speak. 'Follow the girl,' he said. 'Do not leave her side.'

Edgar was slipping further from the horse and Silas had to make a choice. Stop and help him, or let him fall. The crow flew over the rooftops, heading for the ship, whose sails were already being unfurled. The carriage must have reached the dock, but the ship would not set sail immediately. There was still time.

He slowed the horse to a stop, lowered Edgar to the ground and slid down beside him. His breathing was shallow and his back was wet with blood. 'This is not the best time for you to die.' Silas glanced up at the ship as he rolled Edgar on to his side, and his fingers tingled with cold as the veil gathered around them, preparing to take Edgar into death. He pressed his hand to Edgar's neck, trying to channel what little energy he could reach to help the wound heal. Nothing happened. The veil was too weak, his connection to it thin and fading.

Silas tried to concentrate, but he was too distracted. He could leave the boy and make it on to the ship before it sailed. He was all but dead anyway. Nothing would be lost. Letting him go would be the sensible thing to do, all he had to do was walk away, yet he still kept his hand against Edgar's neck, cursing the boy's weakness under his breath, his impatience building with every second his body remained still. Then at last, the veil answered. The blood within Edgar's wound began to clot and the flesh knitted slowly. Edgar's body trembled, his chest began to move and his pulse quickened to a steady pace.

Silas grabbed hold of Edgar's shoulders. 'Can you hear me?' he asked. 'Can you move?'

Edgar opened his eyes, his strength returning, as a clear bell rang from the dock and the Blackwatch ship began moving out into open sea. Silas stared out towards the ocean. He was too late.

'Where's the ship?' asked Edgar.

'Where *is* it?' Silas struggled to contain his anger as the boat turned out to the west. 'It's out there!' he said, pointing to the moving sails. 'Where we should be!'

'It's gone?'

'I should have left you to die. You were all but gone anyway. I should never have gone back for you!'

'Don't hold anything back,' said Edgar. 'Just say what

you feel.' The bloodied rags had fallen from his back, the blood had stopped and the wound was healing. 'I didn't ask you to come back for me. I wanted you to go and find Kate.'

'I could have reached the ship,' said Silas. 'I could have stopped her. If you were not so weak this could have been over.'

'Don't blame me for this,' Edgar shouted. 'I was quite happily dying on the back of that horse before you decided to help.' He lowered his voice a little. 'Thanks for that.'

Silas glared at him. 'I should kill you myself,' he said. 'Do you have any idea what Dalliah is going to do with Kate? Do you know what will happen if they succeed in making the veil fall?'

'That won't happen. Kate wouldn't do anything like that.'

'Kate does not know her own mind! Not any more.'

'If you stopped shouting and thought about this for a second . . .'

The Blackwatch ship's lanterns illuminated one by one as it sailed deeper into the night, with the black speck that was Silas's crow trailing dutifully behind. Silas's hands tensed into fists and Edgar spoke quietly.

'I'm just saying, how far can they get?' he said, pointing out to sea. 'They're right there. If you wanted to do something to the veil, where would you go?'

'Fume,' Silas said at once.

'And are you saying that in this whole town there is not one person who will rent us a boat? This can't be over. I've been stabbed, threatened, chased, and I pretty much died right over there. Now I'm stuck here with you and the Continent are planning to invade Albion. You might want to stand here and beat yourself up about all this, but I am not going to let an ocean stop me from helping Kate. If I have to swim across the bloody thing myself I will!'

Silas smiled wryly. 'But a boat would be easier,' he said.

'So let's find one and get out there!'

Silas looked down at Edgar. 'The wardens would have liked you. You would have made a fine recruit.'

'Thanks . . . I think.'

'If you insist on staying alive, you can at least make yourself useful,' said Silas. 'Sell the horse, quickly. We have an ocean to cross.'

Kate stood on the deck of the Blackwatch ship, looking back towards the Continent as the land slowly slipped away. Dalliah was busy giving her final orders to the crew and the great sails heaved above them, carrying them back through the freezing sea towards Albion's shores.

'You will be back home soon.' Dalliah had walked up beside her. 'You will feel better as we draw closer to Albion. The veil will welcome you back again and any confusion you are feeling will pass.'

Kate said nothing.

'Fume is not what you believe it to be,' said Dalliah. 'It was never meant to be a city, nor was it ever a simple resting place for flesh and bones. Its purpose is far greater than that. *Wintercraft* will open your eyes. It will reveal to you the truth that lies beneath the stones, exactly as it was meant to do. The circle you opened on the Night of Souls was only the first key in a far greater lock. It is up to us to open the others. Do you understand me, Kate?'

Kate looked at Dalliah, her silver-tinged eyes reflecting the light of the moon.

'Good.' Dalliah turned her away from the ocean and led her towards a cabin at the back of the ship. 'You may rest now. And try not to think about anything that has happened before today. None of it will matter soon.'

Kate walked into the cabin alone and Dalliah locked the door behind her. *Wintercraft* felt heavy inside her coat. She took the book out, sat down on the narrow bed and placed it beside her. Just touching its cover made her head feel a little clearer, but the clouded feelings did not completely pass. She carried it over to the tiny cabin window and opened the glass, bracing herself against a blast of icy wind as she looked back towards the Continent, unable to shake off the feeling that she was leaving something important behind.

Something outside the window caught her attention: a black shape gliding just above the waves. Kate looked closer. There was a bird out there. A crow, shadowing the ship, with motes of frost speckling across its beak. The crow looked up at her and called out once, before lowering its head and settling back into its steady flight.

'Silas,' she said quietly, but she could not remember why the name mattered. Whenever she tried to concentrate upon it, the memories slipped away.

She watched the crow for a while as the ship cut swiftly through the icy waves, but something about its presence made her feel empty inside. Eventually, she closed the glass against it and lay down beside her book, trying to fall asleep.

The world outside the cabin was cold, the sea dark and empty, as ghosts of ice drifted secretly by the window in the night. Kate dreamed of fire, of daggers and blood, her spirit caught in a dark place created by Dalliah to keep her thoughts locked in. The dreams were not enough to help her free the memories that were sealed within her mind. She was too tired, and she no longer trusted her own thoughts. All she knew for certain was what Dalliah had told her. The ship was carrying her towards a fate laid down for her by her ancestors long ago. She had a responsibility to uphold. She knew she had important work to do, and she would not turn her back upon it. She would not let her family down.

That thought kept Kate company upon the long journey, and she hugged the book close as the sun began to rise across the sea. She did not see the crow settle upon her window ledge, or hear it tapping on the glass. Dalliah had set her mind adrift upon the veil, and out there on the ocean all Kate felt was completely and powerlessly alone.